HOLY FAMILY

HOLY FAMILY

a mystery by
JOHN L. MYERS

Boston ♦ Alyson Publications, Inc.

Typeset and printed in the United States of America.

This is a paperback original from Alyson Publications, Inc.,
40 Plympton St., Boston, Mass. 02118.
Distributed in England by GMP Publishers,
P.O. Box 247, London N17 9QR, England.

This book is printed on acid-free, recycled paper.

First edition, first printing: October 1992

5   4   3   2   1

ISBN 1-55583-200-8

To Diana J. Gabaldon, who showed me the rock
under which this book was buried.

And to Derek, who, as always, lifted the heavy end.

Special thanks to

- My fearless "Beta Readers" Margaret J. Campbell, Diana J. Gabaldon, Janet McConnaughey, and Robert Riffle, who are always full of ebullient encouragement and ruthless criticism. This story never would have been told without your tireless aid.

- Jim Bennett and Deacon Maccubbin of Lambda Rising bookstores, who, years ago, introduced me to a world of books in which all the gay characters don't have to die or go to prison.

- Judith McNaught, who taught me the difference between innate talent and hard work at a time when I needed to know the difference.

- My mentors in the Creative Writing Program at the University of North Carolina: Louis Rubin, Lee Smith, and especially Max Steele, who took a bungling redneck boy from the mountains and, through various forms of encouragement and threats of bodily harm, worked their writers' magic on his soul.

- But, first and foremost, Sasha Alyson, who has the patience of a saint and who cuts me no slack.

I am humbly grateful to one and all.

—J.L.M.

If there is no enemy within,
the enemy outside cannot harm us.
—AFRICAN PROVERB

Winter, 1936

The towering statue of Mother Seton spread her arms across a colorless afternoon landscape, shadowing trees and barns with her benediction of peace. Her head came up over the tops of whispering trees and smiled down at the small campus below. The ever-loving hands stretched out, holding the secrets of the place. The quiet rush of the falling snow filled her cupped hands, covering the marble palms as it covered all evidence of human life, erasing man-made scars on the land, hiding and sheltering, drawing everything it coated down toward sleep.

Snow blew up against the roof dormers of Carter Hall, at the Franciscan seminary of St. Aloysius, a cloister of buildings isolated on the edge of Mary Redeemer College, hidden away in the mountains of western Maryland. But even such a remote and holy place could not hide the presence of evil, as death again walked the snowy campus that night.

In a room on the third floor, three young seminarians huddled wide-eyed in the open doorway, whispering among themselves.

The headmaster pushed his way past them, seeming not even to see them. The heavy wooden door slammed in their faces, cutting off their view of the monsignor from the bishop's office in Baltimore, purple stola dragged hastily around his neck, as he knelt and hurriedly crossed himself.

As the headmaster set to work, the monsignor's lips moved slowly in a useless prayer for the dead. It was a waste of the monsignor's breath: death had come by the boy's own hands. "Eternal rest grant unto him, O Lord, and let perpetual light shine upon him..."

On the wall near the window, the shadow of the boy, the second one to die in the room, swung to itself, suspended from a rope tied to an iron hook in the ceiling. A sheath of black cassock waved a funereal banner in the currents of warm air that passed around the room as the priests paced among themselves and prayed. Beyond the lower hem of the garment, two bare feet pointed toward the floor.

They once were white, but now were mottled, black with death. Purple from the unearthly cold that permeated the room despite the hissing steam radiator. And they were blue with the shadow of the patiently waiting grave.

Gently, the two men lowered the body to the floor, loosening the rope from around the neck, and then relaxing as their pent-up breaths again moved in and out of their bodies. They touched the cold skin of the boy with gentle respect, as if he were but sleeping. The headmaster put his hand over the eyes and pulled them closed as he mopped the dead lips with his handkerchief, taking away a trace of blood from the chin.

The monsignor continued his murmuring as the headmaster then pulled the heavy curtains over the window facing outside. In the dim light of the room, the student's desk chair on the other side of the room slid away from the desk and just as quickly returned. Both men froze, unable to move or speak as the feet of the empty chair barked across the bare wood floor. In another room, it would have been a familiar, almost unnoticed sound. But here, with no one standing by, the sound of the chair screamed at them, making them jump with fright.

Both men heard the single lilt of a laugh and then the sound of an unseen pencil scraping against paper. The monsignor stammered, unable to remember where he had been in his prayer, and the headmaster crossed himself with trembling fingers. And as he brought his fingers back to his lips, another sound came to them. An unearthly, evil laughter rang around them and brought them back to their knees.

"Again," the voice sang out to them from the sounds of the laughter of legions of tormented souls. "Again, he is mine, and we are strong." The monsignor from Baltimore fell with a slap, hitting his face hard enough on the floor to bring blood. The headmaster twisted at his collar, as if unseen hands were toying with his throat.

Outside, the bell for the evening Mass was muffled by the snow that hooded the nearby chapel, blotting out the voices of the choir singing:

Kyrie eleison. Criste eleison. Kyrie eleison.

Lord, have mercy.
Christ, have mercy.
Lord, have mercy.

✝

Winter, 1991

There were worse times to go dragging through a bar looking for new faces and adventures. At the moment, though, David Harriman couldn't think of any of them. All around him, as he trudged his way down P Street away from Dupont Circle, large flecks of white dry snow fell from the night sky and stuck to his hair and jacket. A large frozen-over fountain stood in the middle of the circle; beyond that, a perimeter of huddled bodies – little more than crumpled gray spots that delineated the white of snow falling on the cold stone benches. The little park around the fountain was quiet, and there was a hush to the night, as if everyone else in the world had the common sense to stay inside that night. No one had ever accused David Harriman of using common sense.

One of the bad things about being on the prowl during a January blizzard in Washington, D.C., is that one has to make a decision between looking good and freezing to death. Sharp blasts of wind blew up the tiny canyon of buildings on Connecticut Avenue. The icy cold air hit the back of his jeans and stung the tender skin on the backs of his legs. David muttered to himself as he tried to push his hands down farther into the pockets of the thin Perry Ellis coat that was doing nothing to keep the cold off him. It was time he graduated up to a size 34 Levi's, as these 33s, besides becoming unnaturally worn at the knees, were beginning to bind around his waist.

Just before he got to 21st Street, he made an abrupt turn around the side of the Chinese all-night bagel store and stomped across a half-empty parking lot. He tried to brush away the bits of snow that had begun to freeze in the wild curls of his long auburn hair. That's another thing he had learned about bad weather: you can't wear a hat while on the prowl.

In the middle of the lot stood another building, dark and unlit from the inside – or at least the false windows gave that impression. He stopped at the door, not noticing the "Be Nice To Our Neighbors" sign that warned against screaming out in the throes of passion in the parking lot for the enjoyment of the diplomatic residents of the embassy next door. David stamped the last of the snow off the bottoms of his boots, and went inside. As the door swung open, a blast of hot music blew away what was left of the snow and ice in David's hair.

At the front door, a bored, lonely-looking black man chatted up a regular in the vestibule leading to the main bar and dance room. This was the Lodge – one of the better after-hours dance clubs in town. David nodded a greeting to the men and mounted the stairs, climbing to the top – to the video room and the "back bar."

He saw something just then – in the back of his mind, playing against a fine screen that divided what his mind was seeing from reality. Over the years, he had come to call them his "twinkles." It was a talent that he had inherited from his mother – the ability to see things that weren't there, but that would be soon. The stairs kept moving away from David as he walked up, the way they would in one of those bad dreams you have as a kid. It was as if something in his mind stopped him from going up there. David rarely listened to *anything* his mind told him.

The doors leading into the upstairs bar were the double-swinging kind with frosted glass in the top half. "Saloon" was etched into the glass. As David's fingers touched the panes, they were unusually cold for the entry to a room that was filled with overheated men. He pushed the doors away, and they opened with a whoosh of air. As they closed behind him, all the sound from below was gone.

He looked around the crowded room. Every stool at the bar was occupied; all the walls were lined with people, all standing in a configuration he had seen countless times before. The bar was crushed with men loitering at the rail or trying to flag down the harried bartender. And behind them, David knew the order of the Greek letters inscribed into the front of the bar – Lambda Chi, Sigma Nu, Delta Upsilon, Zeta Beta Tau. Downstairs, the first floor was made up to look like the living room of a Tudor mansion, complete with a working fireplace and a giant hat rack carved to look like bear cubs climbing a tree. This room on the second floor was supposed to be the "party room." David moved past the bar toward a back corner.

In the back room, the walls were painted black and the customers leaned precariously around dark railings and circular chest-high tables. Everyone's attention was drawn to one end of the room, where a video screen lit the wall. In the living room below, there were film clips mixed to go with the dance music. Over the upstairs bar, those scenes played on five Trinitron monitors bolted to the ceiling. In the back room, six men, projected larger-than-life on the wall, had sex together by a pool in a nondescript rented California house. David leaned against the wall and instead watched the men in the room.

"I've seen you before." The voice came to him from the side. He had not expected it. This wasn't the type of room where David generally expected to be making conversation.

"It's possible," David said, not taking his eyes away from the men on the rail. He stood with his back to the video sex. "I get around."

"Not that much, I don't guess. I've never seen you out at night."

"Work nights," David said. He tried to make himself look casual as he leaned against a table that teetered, one leg shorter than the others. Even though he hadn't had time for his first beer, his head felt light. "Don't get out a whole lot."

"I've seen you in the daylight, actually." The boy stepped around in front of him, blocking his view. "You work at Hudson's. I saw you there over Christmas."

"I waited on a lot of people over Christmas," David said, examining the young man who stood before him. The kid had long, stringy, mousy brown hair that crept over the collar of the button-down shirt he was wearing. Farther down, he had those jeans that had lots of little frayed holes sliced into them around the thighs. The skin that peeked out was a strange color – not exactly white, and not exactly tan. Sort of gray.

"I didn't buy anything from you," the young man said, drawing a Budweiser can to his lips and sipping. "I don't need any of that expensive shit myself. I was there with my brother."

David was feeling a tinge of ennui with the conversation. He wasn't in the mood to talk shopping habits with this pretty young man who had interrupted his evening's entertainment by standing in his line of sight. "And who is your brother, pray tell?"

"Granville Hudson." He said it in a matter-of-fact way as he extended his hand to David. "My name is Michael Hudson." Instead of going for a handshake, he planted his right palm firmly on David's chest and began fidgeting with the top button of his shirt. "I came back three times that week." He stepped in closer, until David could feel the heat radiating from the kid's body, and the second hand joining the first at working the buttons. "You were always busy, or not there."

"I'm just part-time," David said, putting his hands over the ones working to undress him. He stopped their movement as the third button was about to work free. "That job's just to tide me over until I find something else." He gazed down into the dark eyes that were boring into him with all their strength. The kid had a pretty good hard sell. "Something full-time."

Michael Hudson took one more step and stood so close that their thighs rubbed together. He shifted his weight from one foot to another until he stood with both his legs straddling one of David's, his warm crotch rubbing against the thin fabric of David's worn jeans. David glanced around the room and noticed that a few of the pairs of eyes on the back wall had moved from the depictions of sex on the wall to implications of the real thing on the floor. Michael Hudson glanced behind himself to see what snatched David's attention.

"We could go some place more..." Michael Hudson put the cool tips of his fingers under the placket of David's shirt, not touching the skin, but tickling the triangle of hair that stood up, just behind the fabric. "...more private."

The movement ran a chill down David's back that caused him to reflexively step closer. He could say one thing for Michael Hudson. The guy sure knew how to get what he wanted.

"How about a dance first?" David stepped back a pace so that he could catch his breath. "You *do* dance, don't you?"

"All kinds." Michael Hudson took David's right hand and pulled him toward the saloon doors and down the stairs toward the lower bar.

✝

Within an hour, they were standing outside David's apartment, Michael burrowing his cold hands up beneath David's jacket as David tried to wrench the house keys out of his jeans pocket.

"You don't move too bad." Michael pulled away as David fiddled with his keys in the door. "For an old guy." His hands spread flat across David's bum and gave a gentle squeeze as David turned the deadbolt and pushed the door open into his dark apartment.

"Thanks." David swatted the wall for the light switch. "I think."

Then David was sitting on the sofa. The lights were gone, except for one lamp above, by the bed, that cast a dim yellow glow and left the lower half of the apartment in near darkness. Two sweaty drink glasses sat on the table by the sofa, and Michael Hudson stood over him, peeling the jeans down over his hips, adroitly leaning over to pull the pants legs over his ankles. Underneath, a red ciré thong made a small basket in the front. In the back the straps went high around his waist and met in a tiny one-inch triangle of fabric over his tailbone. The rest was bare. On the left cheek was a tattoo: a grayish white skull with glowing yellow eyes, and below that, two daggers crossed above a single drop of red blood.

Michael pulled the white undershirt over his head and turned to David, shaking his hair free as he dropped the shirt into the pile of clothes on the floor. David tried to hide his gasp as Michael started toward him.

David's eyes moved down the length of him until he reached the hipbones, where the string of red fabric stretched at Michael Hudson's drawing fingers.

"Like what you see?" Michael stepped up onto the sofa and, straddling David, lowered himself slowly into David's lap. As they passed by his face, David noticed that Michael's thighs smelled of soap and a fresh shower.

Michael settled into David's lap. The nylon straps made little prickling noises as the fabric snagged against the rough denim of David's jeans. Without saying another word, Michael grabbed two handsful of David's hair, and yanked so hard that David grunted in pain as Michael pulled David's face into his.

He latched his thighs around David's waist. David, locking his arms around the boy's back, stood, supporting Michael's weight with his hands cupped around the boy's ass. Michael held on, supporting his weight with David's hair. The pain of the pulling at his head stoked David's excitement and he stepped toward the stairs up to the loft. Their faces crushed together again as David took the first step up.

✝

David lay pressed into the tousled sheets of his bed, sweaty and exhausted. He moved all his fingers at once, checking to make sure he still had use of them. In the background, he heard the water running in the bathroom as he fought not to fall asleep. He knew he had to get up and drive, and, unlike the previous two hours, that meant driving the car. He rolled over, put his feet on the floor, and kicked the four blue foil condom wrappers away as he stood, feeling his way toward the closet. He tried to remember how many of the four each of them had used as he dug across the back shelf for a sweatshirt and a fresh pair of jeans. The dull ache in his groin as he reached above his head to pull down his clothes made him wish that he had stopped maybe one condom earlier.

Thirty minutes later, David stopped the car in the block circling above P Street Beach, back behind the bar where the evening had begun. Beside them, people probably still lurked around below in the bushes, not bothering with introductions and pleasantries as they went about their anonymous business of hasty, soundless sex. In front, the windows were still lit all the way up the side of the *U.S. News and World Report* building. A rat scurried across the street in front of the car as the brakes whined them to a stop.

"You sure I can't drive you home?" David said as he turned to Michael, who was working at the seatbelt clasp.

"Positive." He beamed back at David, giving him an affectionate pinch on the cheek. "You've been great." He rubbed his hands along the openings on the sides of his jeans, which brought up ridges of gooseflesh. "Really great."

"We're glad you approve." David clicked off the headlights. "How about same time again next week?"

"I'll be back up at school," Michael said, frowning for a second. "I could sneak you into the dorm, though, if you want to. I have a private room. It would be really hot."

David considered the offer for a few seconds, remembering back, too many years ago, to his own adventures with young men in dorm rooms at Carolina. "It might be fun at that," he said. "Will you call me?"

"Got your number right here." Michael patted the breast of his coat, on the spot where he'd stashed the matchbook with David's name and number written on the inside.

"I'll be home again next weekend, then." Michael leaned over the seat and took David's face with both hands, pulling David to him in one last kiss. "Now that I've got something to do besides sitting around watching TV and hanging out in the bars."

"Can't imagine what you mean by that." David gave him a good-bye pat on the butt as Michael stepped out of the car and pushed the door closed.

Around the other side, Michael leaned back in the window and said, "You better get some rest." He traced one gloved finger around David's tired-looking eyes. "'Cause you sure as hell aren't going to get any when I get back into town next Friday night."

David waved to him as Michael started off down the street toward his car, one of three left parked on the block. It was a new Honda – the great-grandchild of his own rusting Urban Guerrilla – parked between a muddy pickup and a new silver Saab.

Halfway down, Michael turned and waved, giving David a welcoming smile that almost made him jump out of the car to run to Michael and kiss him again. But he did not.

✝

A key scraped in the silence of the deserted hallway. On both sides, vacant rooms sat silent, unused. Dust settled on the floors and walls like a sentinel, waiting forever for the return of young men to the halls that had once boarded hundreds of eager minds waiting to be taught. The rooms had been sealed years before, and now housed only ghosts and the memories that made them.

The gloved hand of a late-night visitor reached into the room and turned the switch, lighting the single lamp on the ceiling.

Inside the room, all the dust was gone. Against the opposite wall, video cameras, seismographs, and computers sat, quiet and dark. They waited patiently for the ghost-watchers to return: those who came and watched the room, waiting for it to move again. But in the stillness of this January night, a real body occupied the room, not one of vapor and dreams.

Posed quietly on the floor, as if in sleep, the body was placed in the center of the room, naked except for a tightly coiled rope around its neck. Once, the body had belonged to a young man eager to learn. Now, it was only a part of the room.

Against the opposite wall, a shadow, unseen to the visitor, appeared across the faded paint. A black shrouded figure of a boy, hanging from a hook in the ceiling. The visitor in the room was too busy to notice the shadow that was gone as quickly as it had appeared, sucked back into the folds of the heavy curtains that had long since faded to brown.

The visitor was also too busy to see the crucifix on the opposite wall. It tilted from side to side, rotating until the head of Christ pointed toward the floor. The faint sound of laughter was no more than wind in the trees as the gloved hands placed the body and the rope across the floor, just so.

Then, with a turn of the switch, the light was gone, and the body and the shadow were alone.

✝

Saturday, 9:00 a.m.

David Harriman sat on his sofa looking out onto the mangled traffic of Pennsylvania Avenue, Southeast, watching white flakes falling from a gray and sunless sky. He sipped a warm mug of tomato soup that tasted of the can, and sighed in disgust as maintenance workers slowly pushed salt spreaders up and down the sidewalks in front of his building. At least they were busy. Being unemployed was a bitch and a half.

His cat, Andy Frank, didn't care. He sat on the ledge of the giant stained glass window above, in the blood red light from the pane closest to him, sleeping, waiting for feeding time. The window, once the south transept of Holy Family Catholic Church, was now part of David Harriman's bedroom in 850 Pennsylvania Avenue, Southeast – the Holy Family Condominiums. David's small one-bedroom unit was a two-level studio with his sitting room and kitchen on the ground floor and the bedroom directly above. The stained glass window filled the entire south wall of his bedroom with a presentation of the martyrdom of Saint Lawrence by fire on a gridiron. David's friends called it the McWindow.

"I thought bartenders were supposed to be like accountants. Those guys can always find jobs." He spoke to the landscape in front of him. "You get bounced out of one job and another comes along right behind it." He had repeated the words so many times, he didn't even notice when he said them any more.

Early in December, Bob Reid, the owner of Tyrone's Conglomerate, the Capitol Hill in-crowd bar where David had worked, decided that he was on to better opportunities in New York and announced to the staff on a Wednesday that the bar would close for good the following Sunday.

Now, David was reduced to being a temporary counter jumper. He took a job with the Hudson Stores as Christmas help, a job that he did not like. He had to dress up in a suit every day and go downtown. All that trouble to sell shoes and handbags on Dupont Circle. The only fun he'd had so far was from the woman who was going to surprise her husband, an attorney with Riggs Bank, with a monogrammed leather riding crop for Christmas.

Now the holidays were past the horizon. He knew because his case of waiter's foot was clearing up, now that he could go back to lounging on the sofas in the store rather than working the gift box and tag counter. Also, the calls from his mother, Madge Harriman of Granite Falls, North Carolina, and Hollywood, Florida, became daily occurrences of the same ritual of "When will you come again to visit," followed by "Soon, Madge, soon." He did not refer to Madge as Mother; never had.

He sipped the tepid paste in the mug, winced, and sat it down on a stack of house and home magazines piled on the floor. They weren't his. William had left them there in his haste to pack his bags and run off to the Embassy of Luxembourg in New York, where the grand duchess had personally requested his services.

David noticed the red ring the cup made on the cover of the top edition from the residue of tomato puree that had dripped down the side. As he picked up the magazine, a boarding pass fell out and drifted out of his reach to the floor. It was for the Concorde to Paris, their farewell tour of William's homeland before the grand duchess told him to get a *real* life or another job. So much for William.

The snow was not letting up, and the bundled maintenance workers outside grumbled softly to each other as they passed with their salt-spreading machines. Cars skidded through the intersection at Pennsylvania and Ninth, not stopping for the lights: no one in Washington knew how to drive on ice and snow. He once again felt the urge to go back to bed and sleep away the rest of the day.

The phone rang upstairs, causing the cat to stir. After the first ring, he heard Andy Frank jump from the window ledge and land softly on the carpet. David watched the black form dashing down the stairs toward him as he started up toward the telephone beside the bed.

"Guess who's home today?" The voice on the other end, not bothering with introductions and pleasantries, sounded like Donna Reed on steroids. Years of friendship and late-night drunks had killed the need for preambles. Andy Williamson, the computer nerd's computer nerd, and former star of the drag queen stage as Miss Betty Benoit (Elizabeth on formal occasions), was David's closest friend in Washington.

"Let me guess. You're snowed in."

"Right-o. Saved me a trip to the hinterlands today. Had a job in Reston."

"Want to come over and watch it snow?" David sounded even more glum than he felt. "I can loan you a pair of fuzzy bedroom slippers and we can bake brownies."

"Oh boy. A sleep-over party," Andy said. "Who else'll be there?"

"Just us boys, Miss Hard Drive. And bring some Jiffy Pop."

"Microwave?" Computer keys clicked in the background. David wondered if Andy even knew what pencil and paper were used for these days, other than an exhibit at the Museum of American History. "No. Original please."

Andy's voice shrilled at the invitation to go out into a raging snowstorm to travel halfway across town from his well-heated apartment in the former J.B. Hurst store downtown. He would probably wear snowshoes and one of those awful rabbit fur hats like Washington men assume they wear in Russia.

"How about booze-ola?"

"My pantry's full," David said, trying to cough up some excitement. The cat had passed out in his favorite roost-of-the-month, and all David could see, peering down from the bedroom, were two hind paws sticking up out of the kitchen sink.

"Well, it sounds like you need to run out and build a snowman or something. You've got to get into this winter wonderland scene!" Andy was more perky than usual that day. He must have braved the pre-snowstorm lines at Safeway to stock up on Jolt Cola before the flakes started to fall. "You got any good Brenda Lee albums, or do you want I should bring some?"

"Yeah. A snowman. Actually, *any* kind of man will do right now."

"Oh, I see." Andy pronounced the sentence as if it were all one word. "It's one of *those* moods. What was it the blind guy with one leg said to you last week at Tracks? 'Sometimes, the old right hand just isn't enough.'" When Andy giggled, he sounded like a chirping mechanical bird.

"Andy, please."

"Okay, okay. I won't say, 'I told you so,' even though the words fairly jump off the lips. But *no*. We won't mention the poor child up there in New York City, in that cold, nasty old embassy. Wonder if he's found a suitable wife yet? It's been all of four weeks."

"Andrew."

"Yes?"

"Bring the Chippendales playing cards. I feel like a round of honeymoon bridge."

"Sure. As long as you don't steal the Jack of Hearts again, you're on. It took me *forever* to get those lipstick smudges off his..."

"Andy."

"Yes, darling?"

"No more caffeine for you, okay?"

As he hung up the phone, he rolled over on the bed, glancing again at the cover of that morning's *Washington Post*. "Cave Dwellers' Son Found Dead in 'Haunted' Dorm Room" was the headline. The hapless victim in the photograph was the young man who had smoked David's bed two nights before. Michael Hudson was the son of one of the wealthiest families in Washington – one of the Cave Dwellers. He was also the brother of David's boss at the shoe store.

✝

Saturday, 1:00 p.m.

"Oh, my goodness." Andy Williamson took the news more quietly than David had expected. "Murder, eh?"

"Is that all you've got to say? 'Murder, eh?'"

Andy studied the singed foil pan of Jiffy Pop between him and David. He pulled back at the dome that had expanded around the previously exploding kernels. "What else do you want me to say, hon? Did you off the kid?"

David did not respond at once, but instead studied the salt shaker shaped like Betty Boop sitting in a bathtub, and he wondered if the entire thing would fit up inside Andy's nose. "He was alive the last time I saw him." David gave Betty another couple of shakes into the mixture. *"Real* alive, if you know what I mean."

"Oh, please." Andy's eyes never left the popcorn as he dug to the bottom for the half-popped pieces to chew on. "I really don't want to know about your love life with the New Coke generation."

"They don't make that any more, you know. They went back to the good old stuff."

"And maybe you shouldn't 'make it' any more, if your dates end up dead the next morning. Have you ever thought about changing your deodorant or perhaps thought of investing in a more industrial strength mouthwash?"

"Andy, darling, this is *serious.* Have you ever seen the inside of a prison?"

"Only once." The popcorn kernels muffled his voice as he spoke with newfound excitement. "I took the guided tour at Alcatraz. You know, the Rock. And I ain't talking about the guards either, honey." His eyebrows arched as the fond remembrance of spending time behind bars on the deserted island came back to him through the haze of caffeine and salted corn.

"I mean, there I was, on that lonely island in the middle of San Francisco Bay. No fresh water except what came over on the boat with us. No dirt or trees except what had been brought over when the place was built. For God's sake, no phone lines. Anywhere."

David curled up with half the Chippendales cards fanned out in front of him, making his wish list for what he wanted next Christmas.

"It was the scariest feeling of my life," Andy said, digging the last handful out of the popcorn pan. "Once that boat leaves you behind out there, you are alone. There's no way off the island, except to take a ride out on the back of a shark.

David sat and stared at him with a blank, emotionless look, trying to gain Andy's attention.

"What?" Andy said. For a second, his eyes sharpened and his head tilted as he looked deep into David's expression of blank remorse. "My God," he said. "You're serious."

David turned away from his friend to the snowy landscape outside and watched a lone Metro bus skitter across the lanes of the street outside. Pedestrians standing on the sidewalks at the intersections jumped back up onto the cement, moving clear of the wide path the bus cut in the slush and snow. David imagined, inside the bus, the panicked look on the faces of the riders, and of one or two in the back who laughed, braced themselves to their seats, and thought it was a giggle.

"Yes," David said. "Very serious. Deadly serious."

David told what had happened to him two nights before, of standing alone in the bar, and of the youngest member of the Hudson family coming up to him, inviting him to dance first in the vertical position, and then in the horizontal. David told him of leaving the young man standing, happy, on a dark street behind the bars off Dupont Circle, the circling drive of 23rd Street that separated the line of buildings from Rock Creek Park, and the dangerous, shadowed bushes of what, in the summer, the gay men of Washington referred to as P Street Beach.

"Not a good place to put a guy out and leave him in the middle of the night," Andy said. The skin on the top of his head shone out from under his Auschwitz victim haircut a bright, embarrassed red.

"His car was fifty feet away from where I stopped," David said, trying to replay the scene in his mind, to see if he had forgotten anything. "The road was deserted, and he waved me on and walked to his car as I drove away. I assumed he was going to jump in his car and head on home. What if there was someone waiting for him?"

"What if it was a random crime?" Andy added. "There's a lot of trouble down there at night with the skinheads, you know. A lot of men who should have been someplace other than standing in those bushes with their jeans around their knees have gotten really fucked up down there. It's a bad place, David, and you know it."

Andy put one cool hand on David's and did an impatient pat as he said, "You know it."

"But what about the police?" David crumpled up the wasted Jiffy Pop pan. "I figure it's just a matter of time before they find that matchbook that I..."

"Matchbook?" Andy's forehead disappeared for a second as his eyes grew to take over the top half of his head.

"I left him my name and number, you know." David's voice faded away as he said, "For next week."

Andy Williamson said nothing for a while, other than silently patting David's hand with his. The only thing David could think about just then was how very cold Andy's hands were, and he wondered if they were always that way. The comforting thought of something so pedestrian as Andy's hands helped him avoid thinking of someone he had slept with so recently now being dead.

David wanted anything, just then, that would blot out the words he had heard. A segment of his love life was suddenly the lead story on the morning news.

✞

Saturday, 8:00 p.m.

The plane coming into Washington was almost empty that day. No one in their right mind wanted to fly into National Airport during the heavy snowstorm that had been raging for the better part of a week. Alexander Tucker already missed the sunny, calm days of his home in California. And he hadn't yet left the plane.

As the jet started its descent into what looked like the Potomac River, he shuddered once and felt inside his breast pocket for his rosary. His fingers numbly made a circuit around the beads before he realized what he was holding in his hands. Father Michael-Lee, his housemate back in Hermosa Beach, had stuffed it into his pocket as he boarded the plane at LAX and he had paid little attention to it until then. As he looked down, he saw that he was saying his prayers with a string of glow-in-the-dark beads that snapped together. He laughed silently to himself as he thought of Father Michael-Lee, who spent his life bidding for the whoopee cushion concession in heaven.

As the plane slammed to the ground and coasted home, Alexander said, "*SWEET* Holy Mother of God..." Once the plane was easing into the jetway, the grandmother sitting in the row ahead peeked over the top of the seat, her eyes widening as they moved from the coppery sheen of Alexander's sun-bleached blond hair and ruddy face to the pale white collar that encircled his throat, leading down to his black vestments. She uttered a short "Oooo" as she caught sight of his naked ankles sticking out from his black suit trousers, and his careworn penny loafers with shiny Abe Lincolns in them. She climbed out of her seat and made down the aisle toward the exit, nodding a simple "Father" as she left the plane.

"Don't much like to fly," Alexander said, making the sign of the cross in the air toward her retreating figure.

Outside, in the boarding room, a priest even younger than he was waiting with a woman Alexander took to be a nun: a very large, muscle-bound woman in orthopedic shoes, a very literal soldier of the Cross.

"Father Alexander." The young priest extended his hand quite cordially as he stepped forward. "My name is Father Julius and I am here on behalf of His Excellency..." Just as their hands were about to touch, Julius looked as if he thought better and pulled his hand away. "And this is Sister Mark, your bodyguard."

"I really don't think it's necessary that I have a..." Alexander was knocked off his balance by the woman making a dive for his bags.

Sister Mark directed them toward the exits as she said, "The car is waiting at the curb, Father. They're expecting you. We have to go now, or we're going to get stuck in traffic." The last words faded into the din of the building as the woman picked up Alexander's two bags and started dancing her way through the crowd as quickly as she could manage, dragging along two large suitcases and two bewildered priests as she went.

The car was waiting, just as promised, at the curb directly in front of the door, blocking the taxi lane. As Sister Mark cleared the electric double doors of the terminal, banging the suitcases against both sills, a uniformed driver jumped around the front of the car and opened the back door, standing at attention. Father Julius waved Alexander into the backseat, and Sister Mark popped open the trunk and threw in the luggage as if they were laundry bags. Then she joined the driver in the front and the car sped away from the terminal, almost taking out three pedestrians, a taxi, and a Hertz shuttle bus.

"Are we in some kind of a hurry here?" Alexander settled back into the deep crimson upholstery of the car's interior, laying his palms flat against the tops of his legs. Julius had taken one of the jump seats and was scooting as far away from Alexander as he could.

Julius's eyes darted about the car, and finally settled on a neutral spot on the floor between the two men's feet.

"You said, 'His Excellency,' in there. Does that mean that we're meeting with the archbishop tonight? I really do need some more time to..."

"While you are in Washington," the voice of Sister Mark came through the speakers at either side of Julius's head, "you will be under the direct supervision of the staff of the

Apostolic Pronuncio. You will not, however, stay at the embassy. We have lodgings for you close by, in the city. You will have full use of the delegate's staff and this car as long as you need them. But you may not wander out on your own, and you may not discuss your project here with anyone outside Vatican staff. Are we quite clear on that point, Father?"

"Yes, ma'am." Alexander leaned back into the soft seats and gave a small Nazi salute, as he drew one finger across his upper lip, mimicking a moustache.

Father Julius looked away quickly, outside the car, and covered his mouth with his twitching fingers, fighting hard to keep the giggle inside.

Alexander sighed and resigned himself to his corporate captivity as the car sped back into the city, the occupants holding onto any available door handle or strap as the driver took them around two-wheeled curves and stood the car on its nose at stop signs.

"Since this may very well turn out to be the last ride of our lives," Alexander grabbed for the door handle to hold onto and missed, "maybe we should have a drink." He opened the bar and looked inside. Anything he wanted, as long as that was sherry. He clicked the bar shut. "Then again, maybe not."

The terror in Father Julius's eyes was assuaged as the car slid to a stop in front of a rawboned old house, sooty black and topped with pointed towers and leering gargoyles. The maw of a garage door opened and the limousine disappeared into a cave of absolute darkness. Behind him, Alexander watched as the door slowly rolled shut and the dim light from the street outside disappeared with the singing of the car's brakes.

A second later, the door opened and Sister Mark's friendly but demanding face peeked in, bringing a muffled squeak out of Father Julius.

"This is it, Father," she said. "Let's not keep the man waiting, shall we?"

✝

Saturday, 9:00 p.m.

Monsignor Liam Odell was not in the mood for trifling – especially when he received long-distance calls from Vatican City about young priests from out west who were already branded as troublemakers. Odell wasn't sure why the archbishop had pawned off the young Father Alexander on him, but knew better from his fifty years of service to the Church than to ask questions of his ecclesiastical betters.

Monsignor Odell slid his chair – a recycled bishop's throne from a long-demolished parish – up closer to his desk, hopping up in the seat and jumping the carved mahogany legs across the carpet. The crisp satin of his vestments crinkled as his buttocks slid on the crackled leather of the chair's cushion. Again, he looked at the telegram from His Holiness, announcing the addition of Father Alexander to the project at St. Aloysius. The research was a complete bust, and now there was a death to contend with. Father Alexander was to be given one last chance – as one of the world's experts at exorcism – before he was defrocked for collusion with the Devil. And before the *Post* had a chance to run any more "haunted room at the seminary" stories.

"Can ya believe this, now?" he muttered to himself and to whichever saints were listening to him in the large empty room. It was probably no one but Jesus, who the monsignor often thought must have better things to do than listen to the late-afternoon utterances of an old parson. "The boy's not even thirty years old yet." The yellow paper of the message fluttered in the grasp of his long pink fingers. "How can you be a world's expert at anything at that age?"

Odell pushed the telegram onto a sharp spindle of messages and notes that stood off to one side of his desk. He leaned back into the unyielding chair, sighing, trying to work a stray finger underneath his collar, which was beginning to chafe. The new batch from London was not working out to his liking – too much starch.

Cherished boy or whipping boy, Odell thought to himself. What a choice for a young priest. His Holiness had left Alexander no clear middle ground between. If the young father could not clear up the problems at St. Aloysius (even though no one had yet been able to send the spirit to its rest for fifty years), Alexander would be out on his ear. A stranger, never to be spoken of again. A discarded failure to the Faith. But, if Father Alexander could rid the seminary of its spectral visitor, he would be welcome in the fold, a hero of his order.

"Farty old man." Odell spoke to the photograph of the bishop that grinned back at him from a small brass frame at the opposite edge of his desk. "Why in Hell do you always leave the hard ones to me?"

He stopped, thought of an old rumor about the bishop as a young classmate, when they were at seminary together. Something about the future bishop and a visiting Franciscan lecturer on Hebrew mythology.

He chuckled to himself and pushed away from the table. "Almost *always* leave me the *hard* ones, Jimmy." He picked up the photograph of the bishop and dropped it into his open desk drawer, locked it, and put the tiny gold key into the deep pocket of his robe.

Three soft knocks at the library door followed. He took them at once to be his assigned problem from Los Angeles. "Enter," he muttered just loudly enough to be heard. As soon as the words were out, he wished he had given himself enough time to get out of the reds he wore to Benediction and back into blacks. It had been the celebration of the Conversion of St. Paul, and Odell had been kept late in the church by an eager postulant who digressed on the travails of being stricken blind in order to see the way of God.

The double library doors swung open and his assistant, Father Julius, a young man one year out of seminary, waved Father Alexander into the study. Father Julius studiously pulled the doors shut as Alexander stepped into the room. The assistant paused, unsuccessfully trying to read the reaction on Monsignor's face.

"Sit down, boy." Monsignor lazily waved one loose hand toward the closest chair. He called it the alms chair, because it was where he seated meddling parishioners with money, to milk the donations out of them: the front legs were two inches shorter than the back. The awkward position often brought unfound generosity from those anxious to leave the powerful spell of the old man. "We have a lot to talk about."

"Thank you, Father." Alexander stepped mildly around the room, as if afraid to touch any of the furnishings for fear of breaking them. Actually, it was the warning he'd brought with him from the archbishop of Los Angeles, that this was his last chance before he would be doomed forever to life outside the ecumenical gate. Alexander had made a serious judgment error in his last job that almost cost him his life and, to hear Bishop Mehs tell it, his soul.

The young priest lowered himself into the alms chair as Monsignor Odell floated toward him, a white-topped pink head glaring at him from a cone of flaming red satin.

"You already know why Bishop Mehs has sent you to us," Monsignor began. "It is because of that house in Beverly Hills."

Even if the sudden assault was expected, Father Alexander still blushed with rage at the mention of the scandal. "I was doing my job." An earnest fire rose in Alexander's eyes. Odell could see the hunger in them – the quest to do the right work, and to make no compromises along the way.

As Alexander nervously stroked the rack of blond hair away from his eyes, Odell wondered if the young priest knew how to surf. Even beneath his loose-fitting traveling clothes, Odell could see that Alexander was ... athletic.

"I'm afraid, Father..." Odell crossed over to the window that looked out over the front of the house. Below, traffic crawled along Massachusetts Avenue, away from the circle where he lived. "...the Church doesn't want to hear your explanations of the episode." Above, he thought he heard the sound of his second housemate, young Father Milos, the expatriated Rumanian, running water in the shower. "We all have God's work to do." Water gurgled through pipes in the walls behind the paneling.

"I cleaned that house." Father Alexander gripped the arms of the alms chair tightly and spoke to his shoes. "There hasn't been another fire in that house. Or another ... attack."

"I won't hear of it." The backward wave of Monsignor's hand wiped away the rest of the thought before Alexander had time to regale him with the deeds of the Evil One. Odell spun quickly around, heading toward the decanter of sherry he kept waiting on a console by the door.

"We won't speak of such..." He thought of the stories Bishop Mehs had told him of the sexual attacks on the male inhabitants of the house by vaporous satyrs. "...of such vile things." The decanter clattered loudly against the rims of the glasses as he poured two short drinks and placed them on a tray.

As Father Alexander took his glass from the tray, he said, "This one has been walking the halls of that dormitory for fifty years. What makes you think that I can get him out?" He saluted Odell in the air with his glass.

"Because you are the last hope." Odell returned the greeting. He leaned over the desk and pulled the skewered message from the pile and handed it to Alexander. "Read this." He shook the paper under Alexander's nose. "The Holy Father is putting a lot of faith in your talents, but if I may be frank, son..." He took a long sip from his glass and set it down, empty, on the desk. "You had better not screw *this* one up."

Odell thought of running across the room for another blessing of the wine before continuing the story, but decided against it. "Everybody and his brother, including..." He pointed toward the ceiling, indicating the head office. "...will be watching you this time."

Father Alexander sat, steel-eyed, not reacting. He had probably heard the threats already, and Bishop Mehs was world renowned for his nickname of "God's Attack Dog."

Monsignor Odell sat in his chair, jumping it up under the desk again. "Of course, you know the consequences." He picked up a pen and pretended to be signing an important paper. He could feel the tiny line of perspiration breaking out around his forehead. "You will be sent down, if you fail."

"Not even sent away for 'treatment,' eh?"

Odell knew what the boy meant. He couldn't bring himself to visualize it — a reformed sodomite as a minister of God. Sent here to drive away the forces of Satan himself. He shook his head and said, "They won't even let you be an altar boy, if you fail."

"And if I refuse?" Father Alexander slid forward on his chair, supporting his weight with his legs. Broad golden hands gripped onto the chair, turning as red as his face as he waited for Monsignor to answer.

Maybe it was the stories of Alexander and his earlier fornications playing on his mind, but Odell thought the young priest had the look of a man who was about to die the little death. It made him momentarily jealous — to be around the young ones with the hunger for work that he once had. His jealousy did not extend to Bishop Mehs's description of Father Alexander's experience of the flesh — tales of youthful carousing, stories that Alexander did not limit to the confessional, and which had dragged him away from parish work to a "safe" academic career: arm wrestling with the Devil.

The water stopped gurgling through the pipes, and a little while later, Odell heard the sounds of Father Milos vaulting down the stairs, on his way to soccer practice at the high school up in Little Rome where Milos was assistant coach. He would be smelling of fresh deodorant and lavender cologne. The thought of Milos and his simple happiness was easier on Odell's mind than this young charge that had been thrown at him. "If you fail this task, Father," Odell said, "it may very well mean the sack for us all. Thus sayeth the bishop."

☥

They sat in silence for a long time afterward, listening to the constant ticking of the clock in the hall. The chimes had made the circuit three times, each sequence calling to Westminster and counting the hour. At the last, the clock struck twelve chimes across the dark halls of the house. Above, Father Julius shuffled about, carting food from the kitchen into the dining room. Father Milos had returned from practice and was making grunting noises on the third floor as he strained at his weight lifting.

Father Alexander's hands trembled as he flipped through the notes again, hoping to find something in the yellowed papers and reams of new computer printouts that some researcher had missed. Deep wrinkles folded across his brow as he read. Odell watched a slight quiver around his lips.

"Fifty years," Alexander muttered over to himself. He dropped the papers on Monsignor's desk and set about rolling up the sleeves of his black shirt. He had more hair on his forearms than Odell had ever seen on a man. "Fifty years, Father, and *this*..." He flicked his hands at the notes sprawled across the desk. "...this is all they've been able to impart. An apparition hanging from the ceiling. Laughter. A moving chair."

"And don't ya forget the crucifix." Odell settled back into his chair and worked at loosening his collar. The second bottle of port had helped to loosen his brain and his tongue.

"Oh yes. A crucifix that spins around on its axis." Alexander slammed his fist down hard on the desk in front of the old man.

Odell, who was used to the ill-spent passions of man, did not flinch.

"Jesus, Mary, and Joseph!" Alexander made for the whiskey cabinet and another round with the tauntalus. They had almost drained all the decanters in the three hours locked in the room together. "You don't need me for this. It's too simple. Any parish priest could go in there and exorcise this ... this..." He slapped again at the papers. "...spook show."

"There's one more thing you don't know yet, Father." Odell leaned back into his chair. The self-gratified look that came over his face was the same one he got after a long night of winning, when he cheated at Scrabble. He made a little cathedral with his fingertips as he drummed them together across his chest. The pause was just long enough to get the young father's attention. One last slap on the back to send him on his way. "There's been a murder there. A body of a young boy was found." As he said the next words, a twitch went across his lips as he forced out the distasteful words. "Hanged, he was. And they found him..." He picked at the latch to the desk drawer with his fingernails. He cringed as he chipped the polish on one finger as he played. "They found him naked, with a rope around his neck, just like..."

"Like the second boy who died there." Alexander said it. He pushed the tension out into the room. "The second one who killed himself out of the shame of what those two had done in that room."

Odell turned away, feeling the cold, bloody taste in his mouth as the priest spoke.

"The second one who killed himself because of the first, isn't that it, Monsignor? Weren't they...?"

"Don't say it." Odell cut him off before he could finish. "We know. And what's done is done, and gone to the grave. But now, we've got a haunt that is killing people, and you have to stop it. No arguments. No excuses. *That,* Father, is your call. Lose it, or be lost yourself trying."

Father Alexander stood, leaning over the spray of manuscripts and old photographs spread across the top of Monsignor Odell's desk. He bowed his head so low that all Odell could see was the crown, and the flexing muscles in the young man's neck. Whatever private battles the priest fought with the forces of evil just then, they were known only to Father Alexander. He sucked in a long breath, held it, and blew it out in a slow and easy stream.

"It's this or I'm out, then, Monsignor?"

"Right you are, son." Odell reshuffled the papers and collected them into one big pile, preferring not to face the young priest for the moment. "And it's a bad one too, I'll tell you. I've been there myself, and you can feel the evil in that room. Why do you think they closed off the whole wing on

36

that floor? Except for those researchers working in the haunted room, that part of the building hasn't been used in almost forty years."

Odell stared again at this fingers and said, "It's in there. And it's bad." The look in his eyes as he met Father Alexander's showed more doubt than the old relic of God was used to feeling. Odell looked glad that it was not he who was going into that room, and into the face of unholy destruction.

"Heaven or Hell," Father Alexander said again. "Sort of gives an all-new meaning to 'Pray for us sinners, now and at the hour of our death.'"

Odell moved his right hand near his stomach in the tiny shape of the cross as he said, "Aye. And death it may very well be."

✟

Saturday, 11:30 p.m.

The hooker was dead at a bus stop where nobody saw anything. She had met her fate in front of an old building, a deserted peep show scheduled to be torn down in another week. Now, all that remained was a chalk outline, a black stain of someone's blood, and a leopard-print leotard stuck to the frozen sidewalk. David rolled up the car window, pushed the heater to HIGH, and drove around the police cars blocking Fourteenth Street. He had more-important problems on his mind at the moment. Like getting out of a murder charge.

The snow had started again. It blew in fast gusts as breezes swept around the marble-fronted buildings along Constitution Avenue. A thick crust of ice shone on the water in the fountain behind the National Archives. Someone had built a snowman on top of the marble rendition of Franklin Roosevelt's desk and he had turned to black, sharp-edged ice.

David liked to drive – it helped clear his head to wander around the dark streets of Washington at night. The car's defroster was fading in and out again. It may as well have been off. The blowing snow was starting to stick in a frosty trim around the edges of the windshield, and his hands were cold against the steering wheel, even through cashmere-lined leather gloves. A quick slap against the heater controls did nothing but raise a cloud of dusty pollen in the heater vents.

He turned right on Twelfth Street to drive by Andy's. David knew better than to arrive unannounced, but the neighborhood was quiet and dark and easy on his nerves at night. All the yups that worked downtown were home, where it was warm. The buildings there were quiet and deserted.

A small park huddled at the corner of Twelfth and G. In the summer, it was where the rent-a-boys loitered, waiting for the men who cruised the blocks from Twelfth to H, Eleventh to F. That night, the park was fairly empty. He wasn't sure if it was the fear of having their throat slit as they knelt to go down on the john, or if it was the single-digit chill factor. Hookers didn't care about getting killed; that was one of the risks of the trade. Keeping warm was another question altogether.

He pulled the Honda around the corner onto Eleventh and waited for the light to go green. As long as the car was moving, he at least got a whisper of warm air out of the heater. Red lights and stop signs were hell to pay.

David never worried about being approached by the hookers, because they sized the johns up by the kinds of cars they drove. No one looked twice at the Urban Guerrilla, unless it was to look up at the sound of another rusted-through part falling off.

At the corner, a lone young boy leaned against an electric switch box, probably hoping for a short circuit to generate some heat. He didn't look too worried about sticking to the frozen metal.

The boy was sixteen at the most, and blond underneath the dirt. The short-waisted baseball jacket he wore did nothing to protect the lower half of his body – the business end – from the elements. David thought it was a little funny and frightening the way the boy snapped to attention as the Urban

Guerrilla drove up. The kid tried to look seductive with his hands jammed down in his jeans pockets, smiling to hide his chattering teeth. It didn't work.

"Shit," David mumbled to himself as he noticed that the boy's cheeks and bare hands were bright cherry red. An hour in this weather would turn the red to frostbite. Then he'd be in D.C. General with the bums, losing toes and fingers, and his livelihood. David agreed with the look on the boy's face: given the prospects, even the Urban Guerrilla was a safe haven for an hour or so. At least it was warm. Well, sort of.

Fighting against his better judgment, he pulled the car to the curb, reached across, and rolled the window halfway down.

The kid didn't wait for introductions or cues. "Take you around the world," he squeezed his face up against the opening, absorbing the air that was only slightly warmer than the outside, "for sixty."

David ran his hand unconsciously across his jeans pocket, checking to make sure he had his wallet, and the Cash Flow card. He regretted the move as soon as he saw the look on the boy's face. The kid thought David was pointing out the equipment to which the child was about to be subjected. Satisfied that he was not short of cash, David said, "Get in."

They had driven two blocks before the boy spoke. "I've got a place we can go if you don't..."

"Is it heated?" David glared over to him. The boy never took his attention away from something just outside the right side window.

"Sort of." He talked to the glass. "I have to get an extra twenty for the rent of the room, though."

"Eighty bucks?" David turned onto Constitution toward the Capitol. "Boy, if you were a dollar a pound, you'd have trouble charging that." He slapped the heater switches again, trying to coax out a few more Btu's. "You got a name, kid?"

"Snake."

David spat a small burst of laughter at the windshield. "Good enough." He turned right onto First. The light was red

39

in front of the Capitol and he debated rolling through the intersection to keep the heat going. As they waited for the green, the boy's eyes never left the Capitol dome. He hadn't been in town too long, David thought. He still had that look the tourists get when the bus rolls by and they get their snapshots for home. "You know where you are?"

"Sure ... yeah." Snake's hands emerged from the jacket pockets and picked at the zipper pull. It wasn't *that* warm in the car. "Been all over town."

"Not to my place you haven't."

Pennsylvania Avenue was quiet. Even the bars were slow at that hour. As they passed the bus stop at the Metro station, a single man, bundled in coats and newspapers, slept on the bench. The boy's eyes followed the sleeping man as they drove past.

"You're kinda young, ain't you?" Snake finally turned away from sightseeing and to business.

"Thanks." David turned onto the side street behind Holy Family. He pushed the remote control and the door leading to the below-ground garage inched up. David felt the remaining warmth leave the car as they waited. "Try to take care of myself." He turned and caught the frightened glances from the kid. "If that's what you mean."

He drove down the ramp and into his slot. Luckily, the downstairs neighbor, the law student from Baton Rouge, had not dragged home an overnight guest to park his Harley in David's space. "Here we are." David pulled the keys from the ignition and waited for the Urban Guerrilla to diesel to a stop. "Home again home again, jiggety jog." He patted the boy on the knee and left his hand on the cold fabric.

"Listen, man." Snake looked up from David's hand to his face. "I don't do *nothing* back there." He nodded in the general direction of his back.

David looked deep into the boy's face, trying to figure out by his accent where "Snake" was from. Judging from the fairly neat condition of the boy's clothing and shoes, David figured he hadn't been on the street for more than a month. A real hell of a season to go into business for yourself, he thought. Now that he had the kid home, he wasn't quite sure what to do with him. He would want payment for allowing David the distinct honor of saving him from freezing to death. Maybe David should just feed him and throw him back out into the snow to freeze tomorrow. "Upstairs." He reached beyond the kid and pushed the passenger door open.

✝

Andy Frank didn't appreciate being thrown from his warm perch on the living room sofa. He made a few defiant digs with his front claws in the carpet, and ambled up the stairs to investigate the bed. He knew what strange humans in the house at night meant. He had about twenty minutes of napping before he would lose the bed and could have the sofa back. David clicked on the lights in the big room and the kitchen. Snake looked up over his shoulder to watch the cat climb into the bedroom, looming overhead in darkness.

"Before you touch any of my furniture or my animal," David spoke from inside the refrigerator as he dug out the mayonnaise jar and a gallon of milk, "I want you to hit the shower." He pulled a half-eaten loaf of French bread out of the keeper. "Leave those clothes on the floor in the bedroom and I'll put them in the machine for you."

Snake leaned back against the counter, trying to look indifferent.

"Upstairs, you can't miss it." He hit a bank of dimmer switches by the phone and the lights came on in the bedroom. "Well, go on. You're working on *my* time, now."

Turning to make his exit, the boy started to say something, but thought better of it. It *was,* after all, David's trick. Instead, he shook his head in disbelief and let out a "shhh" noise.

David stopped him as he got halfway up the stairs. "By the way." Snake stopped, not turning. "Mustard or mayo with ham?"

"Neither." The boy spoke to the bedroom above and continued his climb.

41

David had forgotten what a little pig he had been as a teenager. Living on the street probably made it worse for this kid. Snake finished off the French bread, two pounds of ham, almost all the milk, and half a pack of Double-Stuff Oreo cookies.

He had to push up the sleeves on David's bathrobe to have the use of his hands. The collar was packed in loose folds around his neck. His short-cropped hair, white as the terry-cloth, stood straight up around his head from being toweled dry.

"This is a lot of trouble for one trick." Snake pulled the robe tighter around his neck.

"Sorry." David peered at him over the rim of his coffee cup as he finished the dregs of his reheated morning pot. "Didn't know you were on the clock." David motioned toward the window with the mug. Outside, the snow was falling in a thick fog, building up on the window ledge over the top of the feeder where Andy Frank watched birds for hours, dreaming of Finch Fricassee. "Bet you're losing a lot of business out there tonight."

"Look." The boy put down his empty milk glass. He didn't bother wasting enough to give himself one of those cute cherubic milk mustaches. "I've got to live, you know. Food and rent don't come for free."

"Oh. I'm sorry." David dumped the empty dishes in the sink. "I thought we'd been sitting here playing goddam Canasta for the last two and a half hours." He left the devastation in the kitchen until morning. It was too late to worry about washing dishes now. "If you keep this up, all I'll have left to eat in the house is sardines and soda crackers."

That course didn't appear appetizing to the boy.

David pulled his fuzzy UNC Tarheels blanket and a sheet out of the downstairs closet and threw them on the sofa. "You sleep here." He bounded up the stairs, pulled a pillow off the bed, and threw it down at the boy.

"But ... what about...?"

"Sleep." David started dimming the lights around the apartment. "You'll get your damn money tomorrow. For an overnighter, too." He stood against the railing as the puzzled boy stared up at him, not knowing what he was supposed to do. The kid was too cute, wrapped up in David's oversized terrycloth robe, the hem touching the floor, one sleeve drooping over Snake's hand like a Merlin robe.

"The light switch is next to the phone. If anything in this house, including you, is missing when I wake up tomorrow, I will personally kick you into some time next week. Is that most clear?"

The boy nodded as he tried to form words. Too young for any good banter, David thought. Maybe with some practice...

"And close your mouth." David swept the cat off the bed. "You'll draw flies."

✟

The wind kicked up during the night. It rattled a few of the loose panes in the St. Lawrence window. David wasn't sure if it was the noise or the warm body backed up against him that woke him.

He clicked on the light and sat up against the wall. The kid had abandoned his post in the living room, and David's robe along the way. He had sneaked into the bed and was now curled up against David, hugging David's pillow, naked as the day he was born.

"Oh jeez." David looked around the floor for something to put on. "Don't these baby prostitutes have beds of their own to sleep in?"

As he pulled the blankets back to get out of the bed, he caught sight of the sleeping boy's body, curled up in repose under six inches of electrically warmed eiderdown. He gasped loud enough to wake the boy and clasped his hands over his mouth as he muffled the laughter. He saw the origin of Snake's name. The boy's penis was big enough to count as an additional limb.

At the sound of David's giggling, the boy rolled onto his stomach, and still the thing's head peeked up from underneath his scrotum. David pulled the covers back over him, and clicked off the light.

He was too tired to worry about the kid – he just wanted to sleep. David padded to the sofa like a sleepy-eyed child, forgetting to rescue his pillow from the thumb-sucking hooker upstairs.

He thought again of the news reports, of Michael Hudson found dead in that dorm room. He wondered how long it would take the police to trace the steps back to him. It would take just as much time as it would take them to read that matchbook with his name and telephone number that David gave him at the Lodge.

He turned over to face the inside of the sofa and tried not to think about another run-in with the police. He remembered things that had happened years ago and far away, when he was young and Raymond was eager and in love. It was in Miami – shots fired, arrests, and a night in a musky Florida jail that he could still see and feel in his nightmares. David mentally braced himself for another go-round with the boys in blue, and pulled the chenille closer to his chin to drive away the sudden chill he felt.

The windows rattled again as he wrapped his arms around his chest, trying to get comfortable, singing softly to himself the old school song: "...Hark the sound of Tarheel voices..."

Sunday, 8:00 a.m.

David woke up the same way he did most Sunday mornings – hung over. It amazed him how someone could drink as much as he did and still be such a cheap drunk ... make that an easy drunk. He was nothing if not a difficult fish to land. When he wanted to be.

He staggered into the bathroom, looked at the Great White Telephone, and wondered for a second why he did not have the immediate sensation that he was about to see everything inside him from last night's dinner pass before him in Technicolor splendor. He also wondered why he woke up on the sofa, and who, if indeed anyone, might be upstairs in the bed.

Suddenly, it came to him that he was not sick because he was not hung, at least not in the alcoholic sense of the word. He looked briefly into the face of the ghostly white man staring back at him from inside the mirror. Whiffs of curly auburn hair circled his head looking for a place to land. His eyes were still puffy from three hours' sleep, and there was a print of a goat's head on his left cheek. That was from waking up tied in knots in the UNC blanket with the image of the school mascot sculpted in chenille.

He heard footsteps overhead in the loft and groaned softly to himself as he tried unsuccessfully to remember who it was. His first inclination was to check down below for excess slaps, abrasions, bite marks, and body piercings that had not been there the night before. Satisfied that he had survived the evening unscathed, he pulled a pair of running shorts off the hook on the door and ventured out into the blinding daylight.

"Oh Jesus," he said as the young kid started down the steps toward him, cat in tow. "Where the hell did you come from, and will you go back again quietly?"

"She likes me," the boy said. Andy Frank lounged in the boy's arms, feet stretched out toward David in serene ecstasy as the boy stoked his belly. The cat was the only semblance of clothing the boy was wearing.

David's eyes trailed down past the cat fur muff to the appendage that extended halfway to the boy's knees, and decided no comment was the best venue. "It's *he*. Why does everyone automatically assume that all cats are female?" David scraped his hands across his beard stubble and tried to stagger toward the kitchen. "And can't you find something to cover that thing up with?" He waved his fingers, making a "shoo" motion at Snake's naked body.

The boy smiled without answering and dropped the cat, who scampered away to groom the fur knocked out of place by his new slave. "What have you got to eat around this house?" The boy's eyes didn't linger where David would expect from his other nocturnal houseguests – at the blinding whiteness of his skin set off by a soft coppery mat of red body hair.

"As I recall..." David offered a discarded sheet he had kicked off the sofa earlier in the evening. The boy passed it by as he headed for the refrigerator. "...you pretty much mowed through everything we had in the house last night. When was the last time somebody fed you, anyway?"

"Don't know." The boy was leaning over the center shelf of the refrigerator, scanning the pickle jars and assorted crusty-topped mustard jugs. Even without porn-star tan lines, the skin of his buttocks was much paler than the tawny gold of his arms. The kid was a god in training, if he lived to see next year. Snake stood and turned. "What day is it?"

"Sunday, last I checked." David felt suddenly naked himself, even though he wore the threadbare gym shorts he used when there was nonsexual "company" sleeping over. He felt better as his hand brushed blindly against his pelvis and struck fabric.

He was certainly no member of the Teenie Weenie Club, but there was no use in getting into a manhood competition with a kid named "Snake" who wasn't even old enough to have peach fuzz on his chin. Besides, David didn't like to deal with physical humiliation before he'd gotten the first cup of coffee down the pipes.

"So how much is this little extravaganza last night going to cost me?" David stepped gingerly past the boy, who had gone back to rummaging among the unidentifiable aluminum foil bundles in the vegetable crisper. "I mean, in addition to your coming in here and running through my kitchen like a plague of locusts."

"That's right." The boy set the milk on the counter and left the refrigerator to rummage through the cabinets. "We never did get around to deciding on a price."

"But we didn't do anything, except watch your feeding frenzy." David pulled down the electric coffee grinder and handed Snake the box of cornflakes. "Bowls are in the cabinet next to the sink." He pointed with the top of his head. The boy squeezed by him and pulled down a large serving bowl. David wondered if he shouldn't hide the cat, just in case the boy got a hankering for some meat with his grain.

"Don't make no difference to me." Snake splashed the milk over the cereal. "Some of 'em just want to sit and talk. One guy dresses me up in gray flannels and a blue blazer. I go out with him to dinner. It all costs the same."

"You've got to eat, right?"

"Yeah." A stream of milk dripped down the side of his cheek as he crunched a mouthful of the cereal.

David frowned at him, because he liked the cornflakes to sit for about fifteen minutes and get soggy before eating them. Breakfast cereal, unlike men, is better limp when eaten, he

47

thought. "So why didn't the guy let you keep the clothes?"

"Who?"

"The one that put you in the outfit for dinner."

"Oh. That one. He just has the one outfit. He's *very* particular about the boys he gets. They have to be the right size."

"So how long have you been doing this?" David dumped fresh-ground coffee beans into the drip machine and filled the reservoir with bottled water from under the sink. The pause was too long, and he turned to face the boy, raising one eyebrow in a bristly red question mark.

"Long enough." A look spread across Snake's face, like David was treading out into the area that was marked "staff only."

He decided to retreat. "How about a hundred? How far will that get you?"

"It's not that I'm *going* anywhere, man. I just need to get some food, do my laundry, and stuff like that." The boy looked grateful as he dumped more of the cereal and milk into the bowl and moved toward the dining table. "A hundred is fine. You're a nice guy."

"Funny, I was thinking the same thing about *you*." David followed him and sat at the opposite end of the table. "You look like a good kid. Better than most I've seen and heard on the streets."

"Do this often, do you?"

"You know what I mean." David heard the gurgling of the coffee machine as the last of the fresh brew drained into the pot. "You don't look like you belong out there to me." He poured the hot coffee into the first mug he pulled out of the cabinet. It was purple and had copulating penguins on the sides. "You look too clean. Too much like a kid."

"Man, don't you know that's what the old ones like nowadays?" He dug into the cereal, not looking at David as he spoke.

"And how about you? What do *you* like?"

David got the look like it was "staff only" again.

✠

The doorbell rang while David was loading the last of the dirty dishes into the machine. Before he could warn the kid away, Snake had lumbered over and answered the door, not thinking about finding something to cover himself with. As David ran around the corner into the big room, he caught sight of the nude adolescent waving a comely dark-skinned young man of unknown identity into his house. The visitor just so happened to be wearing a D.C. Police badge on his belt.

"Go finish your breakfast, boy." David turned Snake away from the open door as the woman next door walked by, her arms full of *Washington Post,* her eyes bulging at the sight of the boy.

"I'm looking for Mr. Harriman," the officer said. David had seen the fast glint in the man's eyes too many times before.

"Jesus, Lord, here we go," he mumbled to himself as he extended his hand to the man. "I am David Harriman. Won't you come in, Mr....?"

"Daniels." The man's grip was firm. The grip he held on David with his eyes was even stronger. "Rod Daniels. D.C. Police. I wonder if I might have a few minutes of your time. If I'm not interrupting..." He glanced over toward the boy. "...your breakfast."

David folded his tongue inside his mouth and bit down as hard as he could to keep from asking "Rod" if, with a name like that, he had ever thought of a career in skin flicks. But considering the slightly paunchy fit of the man's shirt, he probably didn't have the body for it. "Not interrupting a thing..." David raised his eyes inquisitively at the man.

"'Detective' is the rank. But you can call me Rod. Is that..." Daniels pointed to Snake with the pen he pulled from his jacket pocket. "...a friend of yours?"

"Hardly a friend, Rod." David led the officer to the sofa, threw the blanket onto the floor, and pushed him down into the cushions. "That's my boy."

"You have a son? You don't look old enough."

"Well, Rod, back then I was a precocious little fucker."

He heard Snake chuckle in the background.

"Run upstairs and get your jeans out of the dryer, son. This man is not interested in seeing your little wee-wee flopping in the breeze."

"Oh, Daaaaaddy." Snake started toward the bedroom. Daniels choked as the boy stepped around the counter into view again.

David patted Rod on the knee and said, "We call him 'Snake.'"

It took Daniels a few seconds to stop choking and catch his breath.

"Where's the mother?" The detective spoke, straightening his tie and brushing imaginary crumbs off his chest.

"Dead."

"Oh?" Daniels dug a notebook out of his other breast pocket.

"Left for Arizona right after the kid was born. Wanted to get in touch with her feminist roots. Moved to a lesbian sheep ranch in the desert outside Phoenix. One day, she fell in the dip tank."

From above, he heard Snake put a pillow over his face to cover the laughter.

David made his lower lip tremble. "It's tough being a single parent, Rod." He stopped and took a deep breath just like Joan Crawford would do at this point. "But enough about my happy family. Why the hell are you here bothering me at this ungodly hour of the morning?"

"Well, David. I can call you David, can't I?"

David nodded and made a waving motion to help the man get to the point.

"We are helping out with an investigation of an incident that took place in Maryland that may have some connections here in the city. It's a little tough, since it's really out of our jurisdiction, but..."

"Incident. You mean like a murder?"

"You've seen the story on the news, I take it." The detective made a disgusted look at him as he continued. "We wondered what you might be able to tell us about that night." Rod was fidgeting for a blank page in the notebook.

"You found the matchbook, then."

Daniels blushed. He must not have been a detective for too long. He hadn't developed a good poker face yet.

"Hold on just a second." David leaned in a whispered aside to the detective. "Let me get rid of the kid so we can talk."

David ran up the stairs to the bedroom, where Snake was squeezing back into his work clothes. He fished five twenties out of a drawer, rolled them tightly, and palmed them to the boy.

"You've really got to find a safer place than that to keep your cash," Snake whispered to him, giving him a light peck on the cheek. "Daddy."

David winced at the sound of the word. "I'm not *that* old and desperate yet, you little wench." He returned the smack. "Run down to the Safeway at Kentucky and C and get some food. If you want to share a dinner, you can bring it back here. If you don't, then have a nice life." He patted the boy on the rump and followed him down the stairs.

"Now, where were we?" He sat too close to the detective, who did not slide away. Snake pulled up the zipper on his jacket and turned to David as he opened the door. "Steaks okay for dinner, Daddy?"

"Better get some sauce for them, too. We're out." He winked at the boy and nodded toward the door. "Be careful crossing the street and don't talk to strangers."

"You don't have to worry about that, Daddy." Snake jiggled the spare key to the apartment before he stuffed it in his pocket. It used to be in the drawer where the money was. He pulled the door softly closed as he left.

"Now, Rod." David could feel the sweat working up under his arms as he tried to slide closer to the detective, patting the man's cupped hands. "Where were we? Oh yes. A murder."

"The Maryland State Police were called by the campus police at Mary Redeemer College about ten o'clock." Daniels stared into a half-empty cup of coffee as he spoke. "The body was found by the first of the paranormal researchers, who arrived for work at seven in the morning, found the body, and called the campus police."

"These ... researchers. They work on the weekend?" David gnawed on a dry triangle of toast as he tried to pay attention to the details Rod was throwing at him. Something didn't seem quite right with the sequence of events. Or maybe it was just his curiosity playing with him.

"They work every day. Seismographic recording. Changes in temperature and humidity. Nothing really elaborate like you see in the movies."

"Did they catch changes in these records for the night before?"

"Nope. Nothing. That's a little odd, but we're looking into it."

"Hmm." David offered his plate of toast to Daniels, who declined. "Maybe the ghosts did him in."

Rod Daniels looked at him and offered his cup to David for a refill. "I don't believe in ghosts," he said. After taking his warmed cup, he said, "What can you tell me about Michael Hudson? Did you know him long?"

"Not long at all," David said. "Actually, we had just met that night."

"Interesting." Daniels scanned the room as he sipped the coffee. "I mean, what with you working for the family and all."

"Yes, but I didn't even know he was part of the family until that night. I just work there. I don't run their social register."

"This is making some heat for us, you know. Cave Dwellers and all. That's why we got called into the case. Some people around town think the state police in Maryland are a bunch of bumpkins that can't do their own investigation, particularly with such an important family."

"I wouldn't know about that," David said. "They don't let me cross the line into Maryland all that often." He pushed the plate of toast away as he smiled and said, "I haven't had all my shots."

Daniels smiled and said, "You say you didn't know Hudson before that night. Had you heard anything about him? Anything *peculiar* around town, maybe?"

David, who was the centerpiece of most of the good gossip around town, said no, he had not.

Daniels leaned back into his chair, scribbling something in his notebook that David could not see. "There is some inference from the oldest brother, Mr. Granville Hudson, that Michael may have had an interest in the occult." He stopped writing and looked directly into David's eyes, trying for confirmation.

David shrugged and let him continue.

"Mr. Hudson thinks it possible that his brother may have had plans to meet someone there for ... some sort of bizarre sexual activity, and things got too rough."

"Interesting conjecture," David said, "but I wouldn't know anything about that, since all the 'sexual activity' took place here in this apartment. And it wasn't exactly what I'd deem 'bizarre.'"

Rod Daniels looked at David for a long while, not saying anything and not taking notes. It was as if he were probing David's bones to try to find evidence that David either knew nothing of what had happened, or that he knew everything by having been there. "And how can you explain this matchbook with *your* name and address that was found by the body?" he said at last.

"Probably the biggest mistake of my life," David said, trying hard to smile in the face of his accuser.

✝

Sunday, 7:00 p.m.

David had a big headache. It had started when he found out that one night's trick was the next morning's murder victim.

It continued as he picked up an adolescent on the street and brought him home. Finally, it carried him through getting caught by the cops over breakfast for both.

Rod Daniels had introduced himself as being part of the D.C. Police's new program to bridge the chasm between the police and the local gay community. He was one of the token gay officers whose job it was to show off what the city was doing for its own. Daniels's office was called when the gay connection was made. Homicide had more than enough other cases on its hands to worry about without a public relations nightmare like a gay Washington socialite found dead in a haunted seminary.

David flopped down across his bed and tried to will the headache away. This was the time Madge should have called. His mother had an uncanny intuition for calling whenever he was in bed, whether or not he was sick or asleep.

He closed his eyes and tried to make the pain stop. It marched around his head, paraded down his back, where it made a U-turn, and came back in the opposite direction. He hoped sleep would make it go away.

He was disappointed in Daniels's visit. Of course, Daniels hadn't believed a word David had said about Snake. By the end of his stay, he was rolling his eyes back in his head, nodding, and trying to make excuses to leave.

On his way out, Daniels had handed David his business card with his home number penciled on the back. He told David that if he remembered anything important, to call. Any hour, day or night. David wondered how serious Daniels was about the night part when he saw the photo of a rather handsome older man in Daniels's wallet. There would be more time for fact-finding later. David had to be in Daniels's office Monday morning to leave a more official deposition.

David fell asleep with sounds of slamming metal doors ringing in his ears. It was the sound of jail cells, he thought, crashing shut. He dreamed in fleeting clips of long dark hallways and of running his finger on dusty tables and leaving dark prints in the dirt. In the dreams, the smears in the dust turned to blood.

✝

When he awoke, the house was dark and he could hear the sounds of plastic bags rattling down below. "William?" he called out into the darkness. In his half-awake state, he assumed it was William putting away the groceries.

The sound stopped and was replaced with that of chopping. He sat up in the bed, rubbed the sleep off his face, and felt his way around the room toward the railing leading down. He walked through the bedroom in darkness from memory, as there wasn't enough light coming through the stained glass window to see. In the colored panes, the yellow flames leapt out at him, along with the bright blue of St. Lawrence's eyes.

As he started down the steps, he saw a light on in the kitchen, where Snake worked among a pile of fat Safeway bags piled around him on the floor.

"How in the hell did you get all this stuff back here?" He peeked into the bags. It was a good general weekly grocery run, even though it was enough food to keep David for the next month. The kid had obviously done this before.

Snake smiled at him, looking angelic, whiffs of steam boiling up around the locks of his blond hair. He gently stirred a large pan of brown gravy that patiently boiled as he went back to chopping a pile of fresh mushrooms.

David reached into one of the bags and pulled out one of the four packs of Double-Stuff Oreos. "Never mind. I don't want to know."

"Not before my dinner, you don't." Snake grabbed the bag out of his hands. "I didn't just spend an entire night's wages on food just so you could stand there and eat cookies. Make yourself useful and set the table."

David pulled glasses and plates out of one cabinet, napkins and silver out of another. He smiled to himself every time he got to use the "real" silver, because it reminded him of Raymond's family and the raid they pulled on the apartment the day after the funeral, six years before. They came in, as legal heirs, and took everything that was Raymond's, including the possessions David and Raymond had bought together. They boxed up their son's life and shipped it, along with all the money, back to east Texas, from where, like locusts, they had come. Too bad they didn't know about the life insurance policy naming David as the beneficiary. Too bad they weren't smart enough to know the difference between the stainless steel flatware they took (it was Raymond's in college) and sterling.

David set two places at opposite sides of the table. For some odd reason, he put Snake in Raymond's old place, opposite his. William always used to sit at right angles to David when they ate. David stacked the four bags of Oreos in William's place.

David cut into the steak, which was cooked just like on television – all red and juicy on the inside, the steaming mushroom gravy a perfect shade of brown, the onions grilled just long enough. "You a fry cook in a past life, kid?"

"Nope. Had to cook for my little brother a long time ago." Snake held his knife and fork like clubs, and circled his arms on the table around the plate, as if guarding the food against sudden attack. He clanked at the plate with the fork while he covered with the knife. David wondered what would happen when Snake had to let down his guard to cut the steak.

"Where's the brother?"

"Home." It was one of those answers you get from interrogating a guilty teenager, or from doing business with your enemies. David got the exact answer to the question and nothing more.

"So where's home?"

"Out there." Snake nodded toward the window. "That's where I live, so don't ask me about any family or stuff like that, okay?"

"Pardon me, I'm sure. Just making conversation." David saw a flash of fire behind the boy's eyes. Whatever the story was on why Snake was on the street, he was keeping it to himself.

"So why'd you come back? You had your money. You didn't need to spend it on me."

"Maybe you needed some companionship. Maybe you needed a date for the evening."

David chuckled as he cut into the baked potato, filling the cavity with sour cream. "Not at your prices I don't, thank you very much. I'm not so desperate I have to pay for it. Not yet." David knew he had gone too far when he saw the hurt look in the kid's eyes.

"Maybe you're right. Maybe I should just get the fuck out of here." Snake threw his napkin on the floor and pushed his chair away from the table. The tears started to come to Snake's eyes and David wondered if they were the tears crocodiles cry, just before they bite off your leg.

"Hey, look. Kid." David jumped up and followed him to the sofa, where Snake was trying to get himself into his jacket. The boy's hands wouldn't go into the sleeves, because they were shaking. "I'm sorry. Come back and help me eat all this food you cooked."

David grabbed him by the shoulders and spun him around. As he turned, Snake's eyes locked with David's. It was that same pleading look he had seen the night before. First, it had been those icy blue eyes staring out from that dirty face, asking him for a warm place to stay to keep from freezing to death. Now that the face was scrubbed and the hair was combed, the eyes clutched onto David and begged for a dry spot of land. They asked for an island where he could grab on to keep from sinking below the water for the last time.

David saw himself in those eyes. At fourteen, thinking he was the only one; thinking that there was something wrong with *him* rather than something wrong with the world.

Snake swallowed the tears and pushed back the emotions that he had let creep out to see the air. "Yeah. The dinner." He dropped the coat on the sofa. "I worked too damn hard on that to see it go to waste."

"So tell me, kid. Snake. Do you have a *real* name, or do I have to keep calling you that for the rest of my life?" David picked up his napkin and cut into the steak again. He tried the cheap American wine Snake bought and decided not to question where or how he got it. Perhaps he could cork the bottle until the next time he had wallpaper that needed stripping.

"Scott."

"Anything else, like a last name?"

"No. Just Scott." The boy went back to guarding his plate with the knife.

"What's the matter? Afraid I'll call your parents and have them come and pick you up?" David polished off the wine in one long gulp, hoping Snake wouldn't insist on pouring him another glass.

Snake snorted, talking through the mouthful of steak he was working on at the moment. "Whose idea do you think it was for me to hit the streets?"

✝

David ran down the street to Blockbuster to pick up some movies while Snake hand-washed the silver and packed it away. David hoped the kid wasn't smart enough to know the value of antique sterling, and that he had bought the story about not putting stainless in the dishwasher because it spotted too easily.

He looked at the Family Favorites corner and found nothing that looked interesting. Snake had insisted on something of a sanguine theme, so David settled on a cult film called *I Spit on Your Grave*. He picked up a couple of packs of microwave popcorn and headed back through the snow, hoping that he would still have a VCR to use when he got back.

He arrived home to find everything clean. The dishwasher was humming. The silver was laid out, all freshly washed and dried. Snake was in the shower, having cranked up the volume on David's shower radio to volume ten with progressive jazz on the Howard University station.

"Question." Snake's voice boomed out through the house as the water stopped. David was in the kitchen fighting with the popcorn packet. "You got anything I can wear? I only got my jeans with me."

58

"Look in the top of the closet. Sweats and stuff are on the back shelf." David gave up on trying to tear open the cellophane wrapper on the popcorn and went at it with the first tool that he saw – a pair of grape shears.

"Holy Jesus, look at the size of that thing!" the kid screamed out from inside David's closet. David had forgotten about the life-size poster of Jeff Stryker taped to the inside of the closet door. "Where'd you get *that?*"

"Never you mind that man behind the curtain, now get your little butt down here and watch this chainsaw movie." The sound of exploding kernels came from inside the microwave oven. He would have to lose the poster later. It wasn't good for an adolescent's ego to see what fame was possible, given a good fluffer and a dick bigger than a baseball bat.

"Where did you get all those geek clothes?" Snake came down wearing a size 50 UNC Athletic Department sweatshirt that David had picked up one night while on a close encounter with the Carolina lacrosse team, and a pair of Raymond's worn-out Harvard gym shorts that were hidden in the laundry basket when the family picked the house clean. He took a small tub of popcorn and plopped into the middle of the floor, leaving David the sofa. His wet hair stuck up all over his head as if he had already seen the "better" parts of the movie.

At Snake's insistence, David had to finish off the bottle of wine with his half of the popcorn while Snake put away a two-liter bottle of Coke. David fell asleep before the third hatchet job and woke up with static on the television, the boy curled up asleep with the cat in the middle of the floor.

David shooed Andy Frank away as the cat growled at being awakened and transported. "Come on, kid." David pushed the sweaty hair up out of Snake's face as he pulled him up off the floor. "Let's get you into bed."

The boy was too heavy to carry all the way up the stairs to the bedroom, so David deposited him on the sofa, where Snake rolled over and went back to sleep, hugging one of the pillows. Andy Frank jumped up on the sofa and found a spot between the boy's legs and curled into a ball of sleeping fur.

"Traitorous bitch." David stroked the cat as he clicked off the lamp, leaving them in the light of the television screen.

✝

Monday, 9:00 a.m.

The explosion was what woke him. David first thought the top of the building had come off, but then realized it was the front door closing. The door slammed so hard against its sill that it rattled the panes in the windows.

"Oh. My. *God!*" Andy Williamson's bellow soaked the room and echoed off the ceiling, making David's hangover pound in his head.

David pulled himself across the bed to find the clock. It was a quarter to nine. He had forgotten about Monday breakfast with Andy. It was their day off that week. "Oh shit." He tried to spit the cotton out of his mouth. "It's Auntie Mame on a rampage."

"David Alexander James Harriman the Third, get your ass down these steps right now, and I don't mean maybe!"

A soft groaning sound came up from the sofa. "What's going on? Are you the cops?"

"You. Stay where you are. David, don't make me come up there. You *know* how I get."

David dug around on the floor for his robe, which wasn't there, as the cat jogged up the steps and made a direct line for his hideout under the bed. "Make room for me, boy." David rolled off headfirst. "Andy, darling," he called down the stairs, "make yourself at home."

"It doesn't look as if you have very much home left, what with this ... this child lollygagging on the furniture."

David reached the foot of the stairs just as Snake was kicking the sheet off himself and standing up to face Andy.

He had lost the sweatshirt and gym shorts during the night.

"Please, God." David tried to make for the boy before he got the sheet off. "Not again."

David watched Andy's face crack and slide off to the floor. His eyes went right to the boy's crotch as he backed himself hard against the door. He pointed at the appendage in question, his hand shaking. Andy's eyes rolled back until there wasn't any color in them. David pushed a double vodka with no rocks into Andy's hand.

"Help me to sit down, dear. Auntie feels a bit weak." Andy took a well-rehearsed pose with the vodka glass he had seen from doing a serious study of Sue Ellen's tippling on "Dallas" every week.

Snake stepped forward to help him to the sofa. Andy pushed him back, touching the boy's chest lightly with his fingertips. "Not you." He waved him away. "That thing doesn't look as if it's been paper trained yet. Tell me, child. Have you given it a name?"

David slapped the discarded shorts at Snake as he led Andy to sit. "Breakfast." He nodded toward the kitchen. "And *lose* that damned wine bottle."

"I think you swear too much." Snake hooked the bottle by plugging the hole with his little finger.

"And I think you need to buy a pair of pajamas before you get us *both* thrown in jail."

"David." Andy deposited the glass on the floor, wiping the rim first, to remove his fingerprints from the evidence. "Could you explain the little nymph over there to me?"

"Don't be ignorant, Andrew. Nymphs are female. As you have seen, the child is nothing if not a satyr."

Snake made too much noise rattling pans in the cabinets.

"Don't ignore me. I want an explanation for this one."

"There ain't one this time. Trust me."

"David. I got you through the problems with the bisexual twins and their dog, right?"

"Haven't been able to look at a poodle the same way since."

"And I bailed you out of jail when you got arrested for singing 'This Land Is Your Land' on the steps of the Lincoln Memorial."

"You got *busted?*" Snake was laying out bacon strips across a hot griddle.

"*You* stay out of this." Andy waved his arms. "David. I do *not* believe this one." He grabbed a handful of David's robe and pulled him close. "Do you know how many fairly lethal sins you've committed with this one, not to mention a couple of federal laws that haven't even been written yet? Jesus. They can take away your Sears card for this!"

"It's not as bad as it looks." David wrenched his sleeve free.

Snake pulled a pitcher of fresh-squeezed out of the refrigerator. "Daddy, do you want coffee or juice with your breakfast?"

"'Daddy,' for Christ's sake. David, I am thirty-four years old, and *you* are younger than me, and you have this ... this..."

Snake wiped the bacon grease off his hands. "Boy toy?"

"See what I mean?"

David barked, "Shower," at Snake and sent him off to the bathroom. After the boy was out of the room, David recounted the story of picking the boy up, bringing him home, getting caught by the homosexual bunko squad, and of the boy coming back that evening with seven Safeway bags full of food. He left out the part about falling asleep with the kid while watching a mad slasher movie, and having a wine from Idaho with dinner.

"You don't mean to *keep* him, do you? What if he hasn't learned not to go potty on the rug? What if he leaves Clearasil stains on the bed linens? What if he waters the gin?"

"*You* are going to make me go potty if you don't get over this Eve Arden impersonation of yours. And what do you mean breaking into my apartment without knocking? What if I had been predisposed?"

"Child, you were *born* predisposed: to trouble. That's the only reason I can think of that you drag home every stray that crosses your path. Besides. You gave me the key so I could feed the cat."

"Yeah. And from that expression on your face, you look as if you've *swallowed* the cat. What's the job this week?"

"Don't change the subject on me like that. Besides, it's for the enemy." Andy smeared a glob of strawberry jam across a triangle of dry toast. "Business is slow at the mill."

"Perestroika keeping you out of work?" David stirred a sugar into his second cup of coffee as the water stopped overhead in the bathroom.

"Depends on who you know." Andy took the toast off David's plate. "No. This one's an outside job. I'm installing a system for a guy."

"Oh jeez, here comes the computer talk. Should I have a Valium before you start with the 386 midget whores? Or is this one 486?"

"Sit down and pay attention. You might learn something for once." Andy poured him another coffee, speaking as he dumped in a sugar. "So this guy calls me at home. He saw the report on '60 Minutes' about that job I did for D.E.A., cracking the codes on the drug dealer's computer system down in Richmond. He says he wants me to install a system for him. A network."

"Sounds easy."

"He wants the file server, cellular modems, the whole nine yards."

Snake plodded across the room, dressed in his jeans, sat at what was becoming his place, and dug into his breakfast. "Sounds like a fairly simple setup. Run a few RJ-11s around the room, wire up a small ring net, and you're in business."

Andy's eyebrows shortened the space between his eyes and his retreating hairline as he looked at the kid with new interest. Computer nerds seek each other out like salmon jumping dikes to spawn. And, once found, they are forever seen at the tail ends of cocktail parties, showing each other interesting cable connections and talking in hushed conspiratorial tones about combinations of the numbers one and zero.

"Small problem with running cables around the 'room.'"
Andy slowly stirred the sugar into the coffee. "He wants me to install it in his car."

Snake dropped his fork with a loud clank onto his plate as he took up a loud round of giggling.

"David, such a prize you have here." Andy picked up a length of crispy bacon with his fork. "Do you have to pay him extra to be so enterprising and friendly?"

"It's part of the discount," David said, winking at the boy and going for the coffee pot.

Andy shot David a scared look — fear that David was actually going to let the boy stay. "Funny. I never pictured you as the mother hen type," Andy whispered across the sugar bowl as the two of them dug into it simultaneously.

"Daddy has to go up to the police department and give a deposition today," Snake said as he mopped around his plate with a piece of toast. "And jiz samples."

"Jesus." David dribbled coffee down the front of his robe as he choked. "Will you stop with that 'Daddy' stuff already.

"You have to do *what?*" Andy sputtered a mouthful of coffee across his plate as he spoke. "You mean they actually want you to..."

"Diddle in a cup," David said.

Snake threw a wizened look at Andy and said no more.

"They want to do a DNA match on my blood and semen, to see if it matches the traces of semen found in ... in the victim's navel. And there's probably skin scrapings under his fingernails, too."

Andy blanched and sat back in his chair, tapping his fingers against his plate, trying to soak in what David was saying. "And are they going to match your samples?"

"As far as I know, yes."

Andy placed both hands firmly on the table and said, "Yes. Now. Let's forget for a moment about your trifles here with this felonious rent-a-kid and think about what we can do to keep your ass out of jail on this murder rap."

"Why is it that everybody is so convinced that I'm going down for this?" David was still dabbing at the coffee stains with his napkin. "I *didn't* kill Michael Hudson, you know."

"I know that and you know that." Andy nodded toward Snake. "And the child here probably knows that, *if* he knows which side his bread is buttered on..." Andy leaned over in his chair, arching his glance down toward the tight fit of the boy's jeans, causing David to give him a sharp rap on the shins under the table. "But they have an arsenal of physical evidence that you and Michael were together at or before the time of his death."

"Yeah," Snake said. "For all the cops know, you could have schtupped the guy *after* you snuffed him. You could have snuck him up to that room, strangled him to death, and then did it, right there in the dirt with that dead body."

David shot the kid a perturbed glance that sent Snake back to a serious study of his breakfast.

Andy made a pointing motion toward his cup as Snake started to pick up the coffeepot and offer refills. "What do we know about the victim, other than the obvious, of course?"

"*Nada.* Except that the brother said Michael had a thing for doing it in haunted rooms. Sounds a little farfetched, if you ask me."

"Suspects?"

"None that Daniels said. Except me."

Andy thought for a long time as he stirred three and a half spoonsful of sugar into his cup. "You're going to fry."

✝

Monday, 12:00 noon

"You like them cream filled?" Rod Daniels leaned over the mountains of papers on his desk, and gazed intently over an open box of pastries at David. "I've got cream filled, if you like them."

"No, thank you." David Harriman pushed himself back into the hard wooden chair Daniels had parked him in. The ribs across the back worked against his spine and made him sit up too straight.

"Let me tell you how it happened." Daniels started flipping through the top file folder on his desk: Hudson, M. As he opened the file, David saw the photograph on top, similar to the one that ran in the newspapers, of young Michael Hudson lying naked on the floor of the deserted room, the rope around his neck. But this photo wasn't cropped off above the waist, and David got a sudden flashback of Hudson's lithe young body and long, slender legs. Now, lifeless and pale, they were disjoint objects, unrecognized as once human and warm. Something looked too posed about the position of the body.

Daniels pushed away the pictures for later, and went for the chief investigator's notes of what was found at the crime scene.

"Says here he was found in a room he wasn't supposed to be in." Daniels read without looking up.

"In a part of the building that is sealed off from the outside, and no longer houses students." David recited the litany. He could almost do it as well as the woman on Channel Nine.

"You've been following the story. Good boy."

"When someone that I know ends up dead only a few hours after leaving my house, making me possibly the next-to-the-last person to see him alive, I take an interest." David smiled at Daniels. "Almost as much interest as I'm sure you take in me. *N'est-ce pas?*"

Daniels grunted into his papers and kept skimming. "We've got our leads on you." Without looking up, Daniels reached across a stack of papers and clicked on a microphone that pointed accusingly at David's face.

David responded by leaning forward and gazing into the pastry box. "You going to eat the chocolate frosted?"

"I shoulda known." Daniels offered David the box. "You didn't look like the cake doughnut type."

David assumed that was meant as a compliment and took the gooey pastry, tore it in half, and dunked the smaller part into his tepid coffee. "Too much oat bran cannot possibly be good for you." David returned to his perch on his chair, avoiding the back, which was about as comfortable as an unsprung bear trap.

"Back to the story." Daniels picked up his pen to take notes. "Did you know Michael Hudson before that night?"

"No. I knew *of* him, but I did not know him personally." David felt as if he were reliving a "Dragnet" episode.

"How is that, David?" Daniels glanced up, only for a second. He gave a brief glimpse of humanity, and returned to his scribbling. David assumed it was his work demeanor, and that Rod was probably an okay guy, once you got him out of the polyester suit and wrenched the loaded gun out of his hand.

"I've been working for the Hudson stores since just before Christmas. Holiday help in the store on Dupont Circle."

"I see. And he met you there?"

"No. Actually, we met at the Lodge. Last Friday night."

Daniels knew the club. David wondered if the young police investigator ever hung out there on the back rail, when he got off duty.

Daniels stopped writing and dropped the pen on the papers. "Were you there alone?"

David hoped Daniels wasn't going to go much further down this path. And he debated just how much he would tell, when asked, about what had happened in David's bed that night. "For what I had in mind, Rod," he added an extra slam of familiarity to the detective's name, "I usually do go out. Alone."

Daniels looked at him for a second, not responding to what he said. "What time was this?"

"Well, I wasn't exactly watching the clock as this guy started to make the moves on me, but I'd say it was between eleven-thirty and midnight."

"What did Michael say?"

"He walked up to me and said that he had seen me in the store, and was surprised to see me in that kind of a place."

Daniels stopped writing again. "'*That* kind'?"

"A gay bar." David started working on the other half of the doughnut, pinkie raised. "I guess I'm more butch than I thought."

He at last got a reaction out of Daniels, who coughed twice and picked up the files and shuffled through the papers. His face turned beet red as he tried to hold back a chuckle.

"Now, David, this part is important. Can you tell me what time you left the club with Hudson?"

David thought for a second. Daniels didn't have to volunteer that the timing of their exit was important to placing him with the death. "It was about a quarter past twelve."

"Are you sure?" Daniels unconsciously tapped the face of his watch.

"As sure as I can be. I don't wear a watch, and there weren't any clocks in the club. I can only guess at the time, because the crowd had a midnight feel to it."

David didn't like the unbelieving look that Daniels gave him as the detective nodded toward the microphone. David responded with: "After you work a bar for a few years, you get to know a crowd. They act a certain way at nine o'clock, and another way at one. I'd say it was between twelve and twelve-fifteen, best as I could tell."

Daniels let that pass. "Where did you go from the bar?"

"Directly to my house," David answered without pause. "Drove my car from Dupont Circle to the Capitol. Didn't stop along the way, except for lights." A sudden sense of uneasiness came over David as he recounted his steps.

Daniels's tone changed slightly as he became more warm toward David with the next round of questions. He was trying to appear sensitive when questioning about a delicate subject.

"How long was he at your apartment?"

David thought, mentally retiming the one hasty drink, the sex, and a phone number quickly jotted on a folder of matches and stuffed into Michael Hudson's coat pocket. "Between an hour and a half and two hours."

"That puts it at about..." Daniels waited, hoping David would fill in the time, which he did not. "...half past two in the morning."

"And from there, I drove him back to P Street, where his car was, and let him out. Next thing I knew, he was in the papers. Dead."

Daniels pulled a sheet of paper from his stack, a page of handwritten notes that had been scrawled onto a duty sheet with a shaky hand. "This your tag number?" Daniels pointed to a number that had been marked through with yellow highlighter. It was the number for the Urban Guerrilla.

"Yes, but what...?"

"One the vehicles that you passed on the way back from your apartment was a D.C. Police unit. When two boys stop in the middle of the street and start making out, somebody's liable to take a few notes." In the column off to the side was the notation "025500." The police had spotted him kissing Michael Hudson in his car at five minutes before three in the morning.

"Now let's go back to your apartment for just a second." Daniels flipped nervously through the investigator's notes, until he found the reference he sought. He shuffled the photographs as he asked, "Was there anything ... unusual about the sex?"

"I hope you're not going to ask me what it was we did, Detective, as I don't think that's any use in your investigations." This was the question David had been bracing himself for. His fingers clutched the arms of the chair as he spoke, until he caught himself and loosened his grip.

David tried to lighten his tone, though it was difficult to do. "I suppose you want to know if there was any rough stuff; if I might have been a little overardent in my affections."

Daniels blushed again. He probably only did it in the bed, with the lights out, under the sheets. "Something like that, yes. The senior Hudson brother says that Michael had an interest in the occult. He may have planned an assignation in that room at Mary Redeemer."

"Nothing *unusual,* as you say. No whips. No slaps. No French maid uniforms."

"And no road trips?" Daniels did not see the humor in David's remark, and nodded again, frowning, toward the microphone.

David, mentally counting on his fingers, said, "I don't think that's physically possible, Detective. Your own people saw me setting Michael Hudson out on the street at three in the morning in D.C. When am I supposed to have driven him up to the school, had sex, and killed him?"

Without pausing for response, Daniels said, "Did you notice any marks or bruises on his body that night, David?"

He had to think back to what he had seen of Michael Hudson that night. Mostly, it was inside the Lodge, which was dimly lit, at best. There hadn't been a lot of time for turning on lights when they got back to David's apartment, and after sex, Michael had re-dressed in the bathroom. "Nothing, as I recall. Why?"

"What can you tell me about Michael Hudson other than what you've already said? Do you know anything about his hobbies or interests?" Daniels was shuffling the photographs, setting aside a small stack away from the others.

"We weren't exactly talking about stamp collecting that night, Rod. While we were standing there in the bar, you might could say he had ideas about licking *something,* but it sure wasn't postage stamps."

"Did you know that he was a Maiden Head?" Daniels put the larger stack of photographs back in the folder and closed it. "You know. One of those kids who listens to that heavy metal music all the time." He dropped the closed folder back into the slush pile on his desk, not noticing stray photographs falling down the side of the stack and across David's nervously crossed hands.

"I figured as much when I saw that tattoo on his butt. I'm sure you have a picture of it in that file." David nodded at the folder. He had a very vivid recollection of the mark across Michael Hudson's behind. It was a skull and two crossed

70

daggers, and a credo that said, "Shit on my dick or blood on my knife."

Daniels pulled the first photo off the pile, turned it, and showed it to David. It was a close-up of some part of Michael's body that at first was not easily identifiable. Upon close scrutiny, he saw that it was a pale white shoulder. There was a print on the skin, too faint to be another tattoo. This one, stained on the boy's pale white flesh as if branded there, was the mark of the S.S.

"Was the kid a Nazi, David? A skinhead?" Daniels held the photo up before David's face. The paper wavered slightly in Daniels's quivering hand. "This would help corroborate what his brother said. About the occult."

David studied the photograph for a long time before he spoke. As long as he looked at it, Daniels held it before him, not moving except for the wavering of his tense grip on the paper.

"I'm very familiar with that shoulder." David answered. "I'd even say *intimately* familiar with it." He took the photograph from Daniels, holding it up to his face for a closer look.

"For the time that I saw his shoulders naked, there was no such mark on either one. I think I would have remembered something that looked like that." David looked at the picture again, wondering in his gut if he had gone to bed with an oversexed, goose-stepping fascist who was out chasing ghosts and devils for kicks. He would never know now, he thought.

"Do you have a place where I could go to wash my hands?" David spoke at last. His fingers smelled of chocolate as he cupped them over his mouth and puzzled what to do next.

✝

Monday, 3:00 p.m.

"You look like you could use this." Rod Daniels handed David a draught beer served up in a half-gallon mug. They took a table in the front of June Cleaver's and watched cars and foot traffic inching by on Twentieth, a few blocks away from the ice-jammed gridlock of Dupont Circle. A few more blocks beyond where David has last seen Michael Hudson alive. Daniels had brought his stack of photos with him, and they stuck conspicuously out of his breast pocket.

"Thanks, Rod." David took the beer and tapped a shake of salt into the head. "Do you always treat your suspects to drinks before they get carted off to jail?"

Daniels smiled and sipped at his Tequila Sunrise. "You're not going to jail." He let the first swallow burn its way down. "Unless you popped him."

David tried to read the look in his eyes. Daniels wasn't letting anything slip, and David figured it was because the cop inside was still working. "What do you think?" David tried the innocent look of the helpless-twink trick. It didn't work.

"I don't think, David. Remember, I'm a cop." He smacked his drink glass up against David's beer mug and took another draw off the tequila. "There's a lot of evidence that's going to link you to the crime scene: the semen in his navel, the scrapings under Hudson's fingernails, and the hair found in his mouth. The red hair.

"You could have played too rough. He was just a kid. I've seen it happen before." Daniels stared at the traffic creeping by outside the window. "But for what it's worth, I don't think you did it."

"How do you figure that?" David cringed as he watched Daniels sip the drink.

"The timing mostly. Your story jives with where our reports put you around the time of death. You got a witness says he saw you let Michael Hudson out of your car and then drive away. It doesn't seem likely you would say good-bye, set him out, and then go back and kill him later." Daniels took another long sip. "And besides. You don't have a killer's face. Murderers don't take kids in off the street. At least not to let them stay." His grin took a little weight off his words.

David decided to let the comment pass. The words were too leading, when taken with the probing look on Daniels's face. "So what *can* you tell me about what happened that night?"

Rod Daniels raked his hands through his thinning black hair, debating to himself what he could and could not say. He flashed a soft, easy smile at David as he pondered. David waited patiently for his response.

"The medical examiner pegged time of death at between four and six in the morning. Death was by suffocation."

"Come on, Rod." David pulled back another swallow of the beer. "I could have done better than that by reading the *Post.*"

"Smart guy." Something in Daniels's eyes asked David not to go on.

"I try." David finished the beer and slammed the mug down on the table. "Tell me something that's going to keep me out of jail."

"It wasn't the rope. The boy wasn't hanged." Daniels reached for the photographs. He flashed the close-up of the head and neck across the table. "There is the ligature mark as if he was hanged, but it's not deep enough. Nothing more than a slight bruise. We'd see more postmortem lividity in a hanging."

David shot Daniels a quizzical look while trying to keep his beer down as he looked at the picture of the dead boy's neck and face.

Daniels pulled the photograph away in response to the rapid pallor of David's skin tone. "Discoloration of the head above the rope mark. Nope. This part looks staged."

"So how did he get it?" David folded his hands in his lap, making himself look like a schoolteacher fighting off a case of *mal de mer.*

"Can't say." Daniels looked at him closely as one eyebrow arched. "You're a suspect, remember."

David felt the gentle slap of the words all the way across the table. "Yeah. I remember." He glanced around the near-empty room. There wasn't much of a midafternoon crowd. Randy Hansen repeatedly polished one empty spot on the bar, his mind elsewhere, probably on his boyfriend-of-the-week. "Maybe we should talk about something else, anyway." He picked up a matchbook from the ashtray and saw that it was printed the same way on the inside as the one he gave Mike Hudson from the Lodge. It was very convenient that most of the gay bars in town had preprinted matchbooks with spaces on the inside for name, address, phone, and comments. The last part was usually added later by the recipient, for future reference.

"Where'd you find it?" David studied the matchbook and then handed it off to the detective.

"It was under a chair near the body, where somebody dropped it. Probably just got kicked out of sight when the victim was moved."

"Could have belonged to one of the researchers using the room," David said.

"Could have." Daniels took a long sip of the drink and wiped his mouth with the cocktail napkin. "Except that none of them smoke."

David felt his own noose tightening around his neck.

"How's your kid?" Daniels collected the glasses and wadded cocktail napkins, heading toward the bar.

"Oh, I don't..." It took David a second to realize who Daniels was talking about. "Oh. Him." David followed the detective toward the bar, signaling Randy Hansen, making a circling motion with his hands that meant another round of the same.

"He's alive. Last I checked." David said. "More than I could say when I first saw him."

"You just be careful with that one." Daniels handed Randy the empties and leaned against the bar. "You don't know what you're getting into with some of those street kids. I do."

"You see a lot of them, I guess." David mirrored his pose.

"Half and half," Daniels said. "Half of them end up in the lockup. They steal. They shoot each other in the head for a five-dollar rock of crack. They jump into bed with the first man who drives down the street and waves a twenty in front of their nose." He shot David an accusing glance over the top of his glass.

"And the other half?"

"We scrape them up. Put them in plastic bags and send the pieces home." A slight flinch came across his face as he spoke. Daniels watched the grenadine rise up through the tequila in his drink, not looking at David as he spoke. "What parts we can find, that is."

David had a habit of twirling one long curl of hair around his fingers when he got nervous. He felt the tug against his scalp before he realized what he was doing. He pulled his hand away, looked at it as if it wasn't his, and took his beer from Randy, nodding a stiffly formal thanks. Randy took the cue and moved quickly to the other end of the bar, out of earshot.

"So who's the man in the wallet?" David brought the mug to his face, but had to pause halfway and recompose his hands. He felt a weakness in his fingers, as if he was going to drop the drink. It was the bit about the plastic bags. He didn't want to hear that. The last thing he needed at the moment was to come home and hear that this street kid had just been run through a giant Seal-a-Meal and sent home. Wherever *home* was.

"Mm." Daniels put down his drink glass in midgulp and dug in his pocket for his badge case. "Danny."

He pulled out the photograph David had seen the day before. An older man, in his midfifties, distinguished and well dressed. The suit had a Saville Row look to it, and the haircut was one of those naturally perfect designs that looked as if it cost more than most people spent on a week's groceries.

David took the photo from him, admiring the gentrified good looks of the man. "Did you say *Daddy?*"

Daniels chuckled and toasted David and the picture. "Used to be. Once upon a time. We've been together fifteen years. Met when I was nineteen. We went to the same school."

75

"Oh Jesus. Not college sweethearts." David handed him back the picture. Daniels carefully placed it back inside his case, with just enough of a flash of the metal badge to elicit a look of alarm from Randy Hansen.

"Yep. I'm afraid so. He was a resident at the university medical center. We met over my twisted knee in Sports Medicine."

"Oh. And a doctor, too?"

"Neurosurgery, finally. He teaches at Georgetown, but he's out on loan this year. Cedars-Sinai." Daniels stuffed the badge case back into his pocket as he finished his drink and slid the glass away.

"So how'd you come to be a gay cop?" David wiped his lips with the back of his hand as he pushed his mug away and dug his fingers to the bottom of the peanut bowl Randy put in front of them.

"I've been on the force all my life," Daniels said. "Came here right out of college. Not too much a phys. ed. major can do, other than teach."

"Funny. I can't picture you snapping towels with young football players in the locker room." David gave Daniels another appraising glance. He wondered again what secrets lay just behind Rod's Wemblon food-proof tie.

Daniels laughed and turned off his cop face for the first time in the conversation. "I followed Danny to Georgetown with the furniture and the books. Started at the academy here, and worked my way up to Homicide."

"Gee. Some accomplishment." David could not hide the consternation in his voice. He had seen enough death and destruction in the past ten years to do him a lifetime. "I'm sorry. Just not my idea of a career."

"That's okay. It's not many people's." He pointed David toward the rack where their coats were hanging. "So when this gay integration program started, I jumped. I thought it was high time I did something for the community besides running around with a pooper scooper, cleaning up the mess."

76

"Very noble of you." David looked at him, trying to picture the ribbing and abuse Daniels had to put up with when he started his job. Police work not being a strongly gay occupation, he knew it had to be tough for Rod to come out to all his co-workers, and then go on to be a "token," and to work in a totally gay unit. "You should be proud."

"It's not noble at all." Daniels pulled up the zipper on his parka. "It's my job." He checked his pockets to make sure everything was where it should be.

For a second, Rod Daniels's eyes bore into David's as they both stood, looking at each other, considering future options. It lasted only a second, because the moment was killed by two words. In David's mind, the word was "married." In Daniels's, it was "suspect."

The detective reached for the door handle, and then stopped. "Oh. By the way..."

David flinched. He was too familiar with these last-minute questions from the police. They were usually the ones that the officer had been waiting for an hour and a half to ask, while working too hard to put the suspect at ease.

"How well do you know Richard Parke?" Daniels let the question run out too fast, as if he was embarrassed to ask.

David knew Richard Parke only as a tangent to his circle of friends. Richard lived on the other side of Capitol Hill, near the Supreme Court. They were little more than acquaintances, and were not on each other's dinner guest lists, because of Richard's predisposition toward chasing and collecting young toughs. Rumor had it that Parke had a very expensive sex life, what with constantly having broken bones set, and paying off straight boys to keep them quiet.

Even though Richard spent most evenings in the bushes around the Iwo Jima statue, he spent his days as a partner in Wells, Farber, Biddey's Washington, D.C., office, where his specialty was criminal law. David assumed that when times were slow out in the shrubs, Parke could always call in a few sexual markers from his client list.

"I know *of* him. Why?" There was a hot buzzing in David's brain as he wondered what the connection was between Parke, an uptight two-face who tried to fool his straight friends with a "confirmed bachelor" act, and the wild-assed Michael Hudson, who seemed willing to do or say anything with anyone anywhere. David knew there was something a few years back about Parke taking on a case for a gang of delivery truck hijackers, but Richard had managed to keep his name and face out of the papers ever since.

"Nothing in particular. Just curious." Rod pulled his parka hood up over his ears as they stepped out into the sharp cold of the January afternoon sun. David's ears went red from the wind and the freezing air hurt the insides of his lungs.

Daniels turned to David, his cop face back on, pointing toward his city car. "Is there someplace I can drop you?"

David looked at the car and then at Rod Daniels, who was fighting a quiet battle to keep all the expression off his face.

Before David could answer, Daniels said, "I've got an idea. You have time for a road trip to Maryland?" It sounded about as spontaneous as the first question about Parke.

"You mean up to that school, don't you?" David started to make small jumping motions, trying to keep his feet warm. "You want to go up to where it happened?"

"Sure. Why not?" Daniels popped the lock on the car and opened the door.

As David was sliding across the cold plastic seat, Daniels's words coasted by his ears. "Never can tell. Maybe *you* will see something up there that somebody missed."

✝

Monday, 5:30 p.m.

Cox Hall was a large, innocuous dormitory that could have been built yesterday or could have been built ten years ago. Now no one could tell, given the conspicuous gouges of ill use

78

that semester after semester of uncaring residents had shown its many walls.

It was a giant X-shaped postmodern monstrosity, built in the middle of a college campus that was, except for its location in time and in the backwoods of Maryland, gothic. The architects had even been so ashamed of Cox Hall's looks that they built the dormitory down inside a small glen, so that the roadway came up to the fourth and fifth floors of the ten-story brick building. Its four arms grew from a central tower, and within its walls a thousand students lived. As they were riding up the elevator to the eighth floor, David remembered that the running count would now be nine hundred ninety-nine.

Two men stepped off the elevator first – an escort from the campus police, who had access to the room, and a Maryland State Police officer who was working with Daniels on the case. They helped to shield David and Daniels from the bitter cold wind that snapped at them from behind as they walked down the outside balcony toward the suite where Michael Hudson had lived. The closer they came to the room, the harder David's head pounded – a warning bell in his head shrieked that something was about to go very, very wrong. Along the length of the balcony, the men walked single file down the long corridor, the two uniformed officers lagging to the back, David trying to move Daniels along faster before his joints froze.

"That was a pretty nice-looking cafeteria on the first floor," David said, more to see if his frozen lips would still work than to make conversation. "Maybe we should have stopped off for coffee or something on the way up. Down there at the Cox Hall dinette."

When they entered, they had passed the dorm's cafeteria. It was filled, even at this late afternoon hour, with lugubrious students, poring over open textbooks and styrofoam cups with tea bag ends hanging over the side.

"Looked like a good place to suck up some dinner," David said.

Daniels's face went green as he turned his face away, trying to refuse to laugh. The joke sailed clean over the state policeman and hit the campus cop. He gave a smirk to David and kept walking. He had probably heard it before. Then he stopped abruptly and jingled a key ring loudly in the air to make the whole party stop. "This'n hyear," the cop said.

Rod Daniels looked at David, smiled, and said, "I suppose you wouldn't have known where Hudson's room was if you'd never been here before."

"Don't play with me," David said. "You don't know how I get." He brushed past the Maryland state policeman and walked inside.

No one loitered around the suite, and all the doors to the rooms were closed – no surprise, with the outside temperatures hovering in the single digits before wind chill. The campus cop found the keys to the room. He fought with the lock before finally pushing the door to, allowing a blanket of dark, hot air to rush out, smacking the men in the face.

"It's just the way your people left it," he said.

"Be careful not to mess up anything." The state policeman had to take off his glasses and clear away the fog that had formed on their lenses. "We're going to have to release all this stuff to the family."

Daniels felt around blindly on the wall until he found the switch and clicked on the light, blinding the four of them with the brightness of the bank of fluorescent tubes overhead.

"Hmm" was all David could think to say as the three others stepped into the room and quietly pushed the door shut. Once closed in, the room was effectively cut off from all outside noises, except for the gentle thud of a stereo playing next door. As he unzipped his coat, David busied himself with trying to recognize the song from just the bass line.

Around him, on every inch of wall space, David came face-to-face with the most raggedy collection of rock-and-roll singers he had ever seen. All male, all with hair that looked to have gone through a blender on the "liquefy" cycle, and all stretched or poured into skin-tight latex pants. David was not the most imaginative person in the world, but he thought, as he looked around the room at the posters, that even the slowest of minds would have had a field day in that room, given enough libido and the right inclinations. First, he saw the blank stares of the two uniformed policemen and then the slight glaze that had come over Rod Daniels's eyes, and he knew he was right: the room was a crotch watcher's reference library. "Where's the phone?" He tried to snap Daniels out of his trance.

Without speaking, the state policeman pointed to the wall, where a bright red slimline with an avocado green cord was mounted. Across the back of the receiver, someone had painted "HOTLINE" in a wavering script, in what looked to be black nail enamel.

David looked around the top of the dresser immediately underneath the phone and found what he wanted: a note pad. He ran his fingers gingerly over the top page and felt nothing but the gritty coating of fingerprint dust that covered almost every surface in the room. If there had been any conversational doodling there, it was gone now. And the top pages were missing. "Is it all right if I use this?" David waved the pad toward his chaperons.

"Here." Daniels handed him a blank reporter's notebook from his pocket, and a fresh number two pencil. "Use mine instead."

David leaned over the dresser and started scribbling the phone numbers there, trying to get the ones that looked as if they might have been written there in the last year or so. None of them had accompanying names or dates, just lots of numbers. "I suppose you've already done this," he said to Daniels, who did not respond to him. Daniels was busy flipping through Michael Hudson's collection of record albums and CDs.

"Find anything unusual there, Rod? Maybe some Montovani or perhaps an Arthur Murray that doesn't belong?" David came up behind him and began reading album covers over Daniels's shoulder.

"*Nada,*" Daniels said. "All the same. Kick-ass rock and roll, from one end to the next."

"How's it organized?" David was standing on tiptoe to see over Daniels's shoulders.

"It's not ... just thrown in here in any order."

"I doubt that." David elbowed him out of the way. "You can't have a record collection this big and not have it organized so that you can find ... Hello." David stopped at one record and pulled the jacket from the queue.

All three men stood behind David and looked down at the album he held out.

"What is it?" Daniels looked at David and then at the record.

"It's *Making Babies, Live on Stage.*" David's eyes glistened as he turned the square of cardboard over and over in his hands.

"I don't get it," Daniels said.

"This is the quadraphonic version," David said. "It was a limited press run from 1977, now worth about as much as the car we drove up here in this afternoon." David clucked his tongue and put the album back, flipping the file closed. "It was one of my favorites from that year – that was before I discovered disco, you know.

"What it tells me, dear Inspector..." David returned the notebook to Daniels, after tearing out his scribbles. "...is that he kept his records in sequential order by year. See. *Making Babies, Live* is here on the left, followed later by Ratt, Poison, and the much-to-be-feared Guns 'n' Roses."

"Interesting," Daniels agreed. "But it doesn't tell us squat about who killed Michael Hudson."

"You're just not looking hard enough," David said. "You police types never do." By then, he was looking over the items on top of the desk and had ransacked the desk drawer.

"We've already been through all of this before, including a complete inventory of everything that's in this room," Daniels said, a slight tone of impatience in his voice. As he stepped closer to the desk, his right foot kicked a small wad of Polaroid film backing under Michael Hudson's single bunk bed.

David could feel a slight twinge of his own impatience boiling up into his words as he said, "Then why the hell did you drag me all the fucking way up here in the middle of the night for no good reason other than to look at the pricey record collection of a dead college boy?" The smile on his face was strained and forced as they stared each other down for a few seconds, before David turned away to the closet.

Inside, the rod was sparsely hung with three or four pairs of jeans and a week's supply of cotton button-down shirts. Michael had a heavy down-filled coat and a leather jacket that was weighted down with studs nailed into its back. The only jacket David had seen Hudson wear – a Polo stadium coat – was missing. As were the shoes. "Did you take anything out?" he said to Daniels. "As evidence, I mean."

Rod Daniels scanned the inventory list he unfolded from a coat pocket. "Nothing from the closet. Mainly personal items from the desk and the dresser, but nothing in there. I'd say the investigation team didn't find anything interesting."

Hidden in the back of the closet was a single Brooks Brothers suit, well pressed and neatly brushed. It looked as if it had not been worn more than once or twice. On the floor, among the leather tennis shoes, the numerous pair of boots, and a pair of yellow shower thongs, there was one pair of dress shoes, not worn enough to have the finish scuffed off the soles. "I'll bet his mother bought these for him," David said.

In the bottom of the closet was the laundry hamper. David stopped. "Did you look carefully at this stuff?" David asked.

"They looked," Daniels was stretching to peer over David's shoulder into the bottom of the closet. "I suppose they had to look in there to find out what all the guy had.

"Where's the underwear drawer?" David stood up and started going through the dresser until he found the paltry collection.

"Now this really *is* odd." David was nervously digging through the few boxers and assorted bikinis in the drawer. All white cotton.

"What's that? He didn't sort them by day?" Rod Daniels flopped down hard on the bed, causing it to squeak loudly as the two policemen sniggered.

"No, just something I've seen before, that's all." David returned to the laundry basket and dug his way to the bottom, coming up with a pair of jeans and a bright red thong that would have offered little more for coverage than thread and hope. "These," he said, extending one in each hand to Daniels. "He was wearing these the night I tricked with him. I know it."

The two policemen backed away from David and banged hard up against the wall, one bumping into the stereo and flooding the room with an instant blast of screeching guitar riffs. They all jumped at the sudden noise as the embarrassed man fumbled to turn off the stereo. When he could not, Rod Daniels yanked the plug from the wall, leaving the room in silence.

"How do you know, David? How can you be sure that *these* clothes are the ones he was wearing that night, and not just clothes *like* the ones he was wearing?"

"Take a sniff." David extended the underwear to Rod Daniels, who gave him a look of alarm, as if David had asked him to stick his nose in the crotch while the victim was still wearing them.

"Go ahead. Smell."

Daniels did as he was instructed, and must have liked what he found, because he drew the tiny triangle of cloth back to his face and inhaled deeply, closing his eyes.

"Now here." David tapped impatiently at the base of his neck as he pulled his parka free and opened the first button on his shirt.

With less reservation, Daniels did as he was told and sniffed David's neck, bracing himself against David's arms as he leaned closer, looking to everyone in the room as if they were slow dancing. Daniels pulled away quickly, a sharp look of surprise on his face.

"That's not much," Daniels said. "You two could coincidentally have the same cologne."

"I doubt it." David closed his clothing and crossed his arms over his chest. "First of all, there's no cologne of any kind in this room, even in his shaving kit. Second, my cologne is only available from Les Galleries Lafayette in Paris." David turned to the two uniformed officers and said, "I fly it in, you know."

He looked around the room and saw that the store's name brought no hint of recognition from any of the men. "That would make it very unlikely..." David folded the underwear and jeans and handed them to Daniels. "...that Hudson could have gotten this scent anywhere other than at my home or off my person that night."

David glanced again at the desk that was unusually clean, compared to the rest of the room. "That means that he may have actually died in this room. Or, that whoever killed Michael Hudson was in here after the murder. And since you've yet to produce any sort of an address book or phone list, we can only assume that they found what they came here seeking."

"Even so..." Rod Daniels played with the end of the disconnected stereo cord. "...you haven't shown us anything to prove that person was not *you*."

David scratched his chin for a second, pondering the loose end of the electrical cord that was waving in his face like a dead snake gripped tightly in Daniels's hand.

"Has the family been in here since the murder?"

Daniels thought for a moment and answered that Granville Hudson had been, the day after the investigation team, to remove any "personal family valuables."

"And how about Parke?" David rebuttoned his shirt and started to zip his coat before the look of alarm from Daniels stopped him.

"David, you have no reason to believe that Richard Parke has *anything* to do with this case, just because I..."

"And I have no reason to believe he does not," David said, pulling the zipper up to his neck and moving toward the door. "I assume that my little performance out there on the balcony and the one in here, finding the clothing worn by Michael the night of his death, got you what you wanted. Can we get back to civilization now?" With that, he opened the door and took long steps out onto the walkway.

Daniels followed close behind, stopping at the suite door to thank the other officers for their time and to send them on their ways. "Okay. I admit it. I had to know if you had ever been here before. Getting you up here to see if you could walk to his room was the easiest..."

"Let's get something straight, Detective." David Harriman leaned backward over the balcony, picking up momentum with the anger in his voice. "All you had to do was ask. There was no reason for all this perpetration with getting me up here for nothing. I have a life, too, you know." He spun around and spoke out to the cold wind that was blowing against his face. "Or do you cops forget that, when it's convenient?"

David could feel a hand press against his back and a soft voice saying, "Sorry."

"Talk to the brother," David said at last. "I think that line about meeting someone for a trick in the haunted room is a bunch of horseshit. Somebody's trying to lead you on."

"What makes you say that?" Daniels bundled deeper into his coat and stood beside David on the rail, looking out into the darkness.

"Remember, I had a few hours of experience with Michael Hudson," David said. "He was good, all right, but he was pretty much a one-song wonder." David pushed away a lock of hair that was blowing into his mouth. "Michael wasn't *that* creative."

Rod Daniels either smiled into the wind, or he grimaced at the cold against his skin. He took what David said and did not respond.

"Something's not right here." David leaned over the eighth-floor balcony of Cox Hall, into the night wind. "Something in that room just doesn't look right to me, and I'll be damned if I know what it is." Off in the distance, he thought he heard voices coming to him across the air, but he assumed it was the chill of the evening whistling through the heads of the pine trees that grew all around the campus. Inside, his gut ached for him to get out of there. He had a bad feeling about this place. Real bad.

"You mean other than the clothes?" Daniels stood with his back to the balcony rail, shoved his hands down inside his coat pockets, and shivered with the cold.

"Something's missing in there, or something's been added, and I don't know which. Didn't you notice? No dope. No booze. Not even a bong." David leaned out, jamming his hands deeper into his pockets as he looked over the tops of the trees toward the horizon. "Doesn't match up with the stories I've heard told around the store about Michael's reputation. You don't get kicked out of Betty Ford and have a room that clean of paraphernalia."

Far off, on the other side of the campus, was the silhouetted outline of a giant statue of a nun, her back to them, her arms spread out in prayerful hope. David looked at the statue and thought again about the place they had just been.

Who or what, David wondered, had turned their back on Michael Hudson and left him dead in a strange room with a noose around his neck? He thought he heard the voices again on the tips of the air. It sounded to him like a laugh. He closed his eyes, assuming it was coming from one of the rooms nearby, and as he did so, the sound was gone. In his mind he thought again of what he imagined in that room: Rod Daniels holding a dead snake. He shook the thought away and opened his eyes.

"Where did they find him?" David tried to keep the cold wind from numbing his face. "Was it far from here?"

"Over on the other side of campus," Daniels said. "At the seminary, over there." He nodded behind himself, toward the statue that loomed over them in the darkness. "The parapsychological researchers found him, early the next morning, when they came in to set up some new sound recording equipment. A day later and we would have had the whole crime on tape. You might not be standing here now."

"Research? In a deserted dorm room?"

"I don't know anything about it," Daniels said. The serious set of his face told David that he was telling the truth, and not to ask further. "It's something run by the Church, and we're not to stick our noses into it unless it's *directly* tied to the case. That's the instructions from the governor here and the mayor back home."

The buffets of wind cut off part of Daniels's words as he slapped his hands together, trying to get warm. "What do you say we go downstairs now and suck up some food?"

David looked one more time at the silhouette of the statue, standing above the trees in the darkness. Then, he looked at the detective and wanted nothing more than to be at home, preferably soaking in a hot bath, alone.

"You get me back to D.C. tonight," he said, "and I'll treat you to the best white garlic pizza in town."

Rod Daniels stepped away, back down the hall, jiggling the keys to his car over his head.

Tuesday, 10:00 a.m.

David found one thing that he and Snake held very strongly in common: cussed stubbornness. Even though snow was pouring down outside, Snake insisted that he be allowed to walk home. David insisted that he drive the boy to wherever it was he lived. David, with more arguments and a greater sense of patience, won the battle. Or so he thought.

The Urban Guerrilla sloshed down the mucky blackened ruts of Pennsylvania Avenue toward the Capitol. The best compromise David could get from Snake was a drop-off at a public place close to where the boy stayed. Snake would not let David see his hideaway.

"This car's a real piece of junk." Snake pulled a loose piece of foam rubber off the seat cushion and waved it at David, watching it disintegrate into so much plastic dust. "How old is it, anyway?"

"Ten ... no ... twelve years old." David jiggled the gearshift as they waited for the light to turn. "I've had her since I was in college. She and I have been through a lot together." He glanced fondly into the backseat. "Most of the adventures are far too sordid for your young ears to hear, though."

"Ah, gross!" Snake inspected the rear half of the car over his seat's headrest. "You mean you did it back *there?* In the *car?*"

David sniffed at him and nudged the car forward as the light changed. "I was young and in love at the time, young man." He had to slow up for the large car in front of them that could not keep moving in a forward direction. "Something I'm sure you know nothing about at your age. Love, that is."

"So why don't you buy a new one?"

David punched his finger into the sagging headliner that made the car look like the inside of a tent. "Why should I do that? This one gets me from A to B with little or no complaints."

"You know, you'll never get any guys running around town in a car that looks like this. The rule on the street is you're not supposed to get in any car more than four years old."

"Guess you broke that one, then." David looked at him and smiled. "But then, I'm sure your decision probably had a lot to do with my captivating charm and my undying good looks..." He ruffled his hand through Snake's hair as the boy tried to wedge himself, giggling, up against the door.

"I was freezing to death," Snake said through his laughter. "It was either you or walk all the way down to the bus station."

"Gee. With a choice like that, I can see the great mental stress of your decision." David turned back to the road.

After a few more blocks, Snake said, "It's a nice house, though. Looks like a church."

"It *was* a church, brainless." David turned in the direction Snake pointed.

"So." The boy paused for a second, working up the nerve to ask his question. "Where did you get the money for the house? I mean, it looks kind of expensive."

"Casing the joint, were you?" The concept drew a blank on the kid. He probably had never seen any good '30s gumshoe movies and didn't know what it meant. "I inherited some money from my dad when he died."

"Oh. I'm sorry." The boy's voice turned serious. "When was that?"

"1975. I was fifteen years old. The old man was in a board meeting. He stood up to make an objection, and dropped dead on the spot."

Snake did not respond to the story.

"That paid my way through school and got me up here to Washington. I make okay money pouring drinks, you know." He had to stop again and wait for a pair of taxis to slide out of the roadway.

"So who's this Raymond guy?"

David almost let the car skid onto the sidewalk when Snake asked him that. "How do you know about Raymond?"

"Because you say his name sometimes when you're asleep. Is he your boyfriend?"

"He was." David tried to speak calmly about Raymond, and not let the feelings out. Even after all those years, it still hurt as if it had happened yesterday. "He isn't now. He's ... he's gone."

Snake's face went ashen as he turned himself in the seat, putting one hand on David's arm. "Was he ... sick?"

David, realizing what the boy was asking, and seeing the look of panic on his face, said, "Oh no. Hell, no." He added an extra spark of liveliness to his voice as the bad feelings passed. "He was fine. No. It was an accident. In California."

"I'm sorry, David." The kid settled back into his seat. "He must've meant a lot to you, if you still think about him."

"He did." David turned to Snake, smiling. "I'll show you a picture of him sometime. You know, when he died, he left me a million dollars in life insurance."

"No!" Snake looked around the car. "A million dollars, and you still drive this junk heap." He rubbed his hands across the cracked vinyl seats, seeing another imaginary car in his mind. "If I had a million bucks, I'd have a Ferrari. A red Testerosa."

"Wouldn't do you much good, since you're not old enough to drive."

"Yeah, but I wouldn't have any trouble picking up the guys in something like that."

David pulled the car to a stop in front of the National Botanic Garden, in the shadow of the Capitol dome. The hand brake ratcheted up as he yanked the lever and killed the engine. "Listen, son. I'm not going to give you some kind of lecture on how you should live your life, because that's not my job."

Snake studied him with the glazed-over expression teenagers get when adults pass on the wisdom of the ages.

"But I don't want you to think that life is all about driving fast cars and picking up guys on street corners." David looked away and sketched his initials in the dust on top of the dash. "That's not even close."

The boy looked crestfallen as David put a reassuring hand on his knee.

"I picked you up that night because you scared me. I thought you were in danger out there in the cold, and I took you home to get you warm. I didn't bring you home for..." He had to stop as he felt the tears welling up in his eyes. The boy focused on David's hand as his own dug deep into his baseball jacket pockets.

David gave his knee a squeeze and said, "I don't care if you're into boys, or girls, or orangutans. It just doesn't matter to me, Snake." He pulled a Kleenex out of his coat pocket and gave it to the boy. Snake gave his nose a honking blow, staring down at his shoes. "I like you because you are a friendly kid, and, even though I don't like your job very much, you seem to have a fairly good head for staying out of trouble. So far."

"I like you too." Snake spoke to his lap, almost in a whisper. "I like you a lot." He wadded up the used tissue and put it in his jacket pocket. "I don't have many friends out there who don't want something from me." He looked up at David, a single tear streaking down his left cheek. "You know..."

"Yeah, kid. I know." David smudged the tear away with his thumb. It reminded him of something Madge would have done to him as a boy. Madge Harriman was pretty good about spit-washing away tears and stains on boys' cheeks. "And don't ever think that I have you around for that, because I don't. I like your company. You're a bright kid, and somebody's got to keep you from freezing and starving to death out there."

"I know." Snake's voice cracked as he reached across the seat and hugged David. The warm skin of Snake's smooth cheeks pressed against David's morning stubble, and his breaths slowed, almost to the calm, even rhythm of sleep. David put his free hand to the back of the boy's head and felt his hair, soft and fine like silk. They held each other for some minutes, until the heat had all but dissipated from the car, and fog stuck to the windows.

Snake pulled away from him and fidgeted behind him for the door handle. "I have to go now, and check on the other guys."

David felt a punch of worry as the boy stepped out into the cold air, pulling his skimpy jacket tight around himself. "Are you going to be all right out there? Do you have a place that's safe?"

"I'll be okay." Snake dug into the pocket of his jeans and pulled out the spare key to David's apartment. "You'd better hold on to this," he said, handing it back. "I wouldn't want to lose it, or have somebody steal it." The look he gave told David that he didn't want to leave, but that he had to. Something was out there, waiting, even if it was just freedom from a specter too private and scary to discuss with David. Something ominous and foreboding chased after the boy, but David did not know what it was. It was just a feeling, David tried to reassure himself. Unfortunately, most of David's "feelings" were correct.

David folded the boy's fingers around the key as he said, "Keep it for a while. Just in case you want to share a pack of Oreos some time.

"When will you come back?" David patted Snake's hand closed. "When can we do another dinner? I'll even let you go to Safeway and pick out the stuff again."

"Soon." Snake's hand lingered inside the car for a second. Then, with a hard slam, he closed the door and jogged off toward the deserted walkways of the Mall behind them, toward the dark snow-crusted turrets of the Smithsonian castle. In the middle of the block, he turned and waved back to David, looking for all the world like any other kid on his first junior-high class trip to Washington.

David turned the key and brought the Urban Guerrilla back to life. He backed the car out into the street and turned back in the direction of the Capitol and home. "Do me a favor, Lord." He leaned forward and spoke out the windshield, up into the gray snowy sky. "I know you're busy, but could you look out for that one for me?"

☩

Tuesday, 10:00 p.m.

Something that Daniels had said about Richard Parke chewed at David's brain all that day. Or maybe it was the way he weeded it into the conversation that made the words play over and over in David's mind, haunting him, as if there was a clue there that his mind was not immediately picking out of the chaff. He had let it stew all that night until he could wait no longer. Putting on an extra layer of clothing to protect against the bitter cold of the car, David pulled the Urban Guerrilla out of the underground garage at Holy Family and drove up the street to where Richard Parke lived.

He sat, parked along the side of East Capitol Street, outside Parke's house, looking intently at the shallow spot in the snow out front, where Parke's car had waited throughout the storm. Now, the car was gone and the house was dark.

David huffed against the window, watching the breath first turn to fog and then to frost as it stuck to the glass. He wiped away the thin layer of ice on the inside of the glass and became hypnotized by the occasional snowflake that still fell from the dark night sky, like moths around the street lights. This was doing him no good, he thought at last, and he did a long U-turn in the middle of the street and started driving toward the Capitol. He knew very little about Richard Parke other than the gossip. But, if he believed half the stories he heard, there was one place in town that Parke might be visiting.

It was early enough in the year that the giant Christmas tree in front of the Capitol building was still standing, lit with hundreds of tiny white lights, tall and simple in its grandeur. It was nothing like the smaller tree that went up in back of the White House every year, covered with large balls of light and huge, tactless ornaments. David usually avoided the sight of it every year.

He circled the car around the front of the building and by the front of the National Botanic Garden, slowing long enough to look in through the giant windows on the ends of the building to see the scores of poinsettias lining every available square inch of floor. A heavy sweat of moisture stuck to the inside of the windows that reminded David all at once of growing orchids in the winter. He wasn't sure what the thought meant as he drove down Constitution Avenue, toward the White House. Orchids, he thought again to himself. How beautiful they are – rare and yet so easily bruised. He shook the thought out of his head as he inched the speed up in order to get where he had to go before freezing to death.

The dusting of snow increased as he drove, and by the time he had made it to the middle of town, it was again falling heavily. Just past the White House, he saw a ruddy light shining out from the surrounding buildings, as if angels had been slaughtered on the spot and their radiant blood had stained the snow. The large illuminated insignia on the Red Cross building shone out through the snowy night and cast an eerie pink glow as the white flakes fell in front of it.

At the end of the street, Constitution turned into Route 66, heading out into the quiet suburbs of Virginia. But David wasn't going that way. He turned instead onto 23rd headed toward the Lincoln Memorial.

His was the only car going across the Arlington Memorial Bridge as the curtain of snow that fell almost obliterated his view of the road. Below, the choppy waters of the Potomac

River flowed on their way out to sea. Ahead, the lights around the Custis-Lee Mansion led him forward. If Richard Parke was out and about that night, he could be found somewhere in the Arlington National Cemetery.

David stopped just inside the gates and pulled an old dusty tour map out of the glove compartment. Following his scribbled notes, he circled through the grounds, up illegal paths where only government vehicles were permitted, until he arrived at a small parking lot that was secreted away from sight. There, in the deserted cemetery, the lot was almost full, with lonely cars slowly turning white and fading into the snowy background. David pulled the Urban Guerrilla into the last empty space and slid to an icy stop, bumping up against a large granite marker.

He looked around at the other cars, wondering which one, if any of them, belonged to Richard Parke. In a few of them, men sat inside, smoking cigarettes and waiting, their eyes eagerly scanning the nearby bushes for action as they all turned in concert to size up David when he arrived. He couldn't tell if he was interesting to them, or if he was the center of attention only because he was fresh meat on the rack. In either case, he pulled his down-filled mitts over his hands, pulled the zipper up as far as it would go on his parka, and stepped out of the car, his feet sliding on the ice.

Coming around a short bend, he was immediately blinded by the lights that circled around a giant statue. High above his head, young soldiers of a past generation tried to raise a flag into the peppering of snow on the bronzed top of Mount Suribachi. Below, around the base, sentinels waited, loitering around the bushes, stamping their feet and rubbing their gloved hands together. Vacant, hungry eyes followed David as he stepped closer, falling into the icy-hard track worn into the snow by patiently circling feet.

Wordless communications seemed to pass between the men as, one by one, they began to migrate toward the end of the statue facing back toward Washington over the white fogged horizon. There, as he followed the pack like a wolf smelling blood, he saw a small group of men, behind the bushes, standing in a quiet circle. Whatever was going on inside the shield of bodies, David could only guess, but he knew it was the type of action that Richard Parke would be chasing on a freezing January night.

After a minute of hesitation, David stepped closer to the circle, close enough to hear the rustling of nylon clothing rubbing together and the hurried breathing of the last seconds of sex. By the time he was close enough to the group to feel the steam of heat that radiated from their backs, the enclave parted, and a young man of a rather frightening attitude stepped clear, pulling a sweatshirt hood over his head as the snow began to stick to his hair. Without acknowledging the group or noticing David, the young man jogged off into the snow, immediately forgotten by the crowd. David stopped himself and removed his hand from the front of his jeans where he had reflexively grabbed for his wallet to make sure it stayed put.

The next person to emerge from the circle was Richard Parke, bundling himself back into his parka and popping at his jeans legs with his gloved hands to brush away the snow from the bottom halves of his legs. As he stepped away, frantic, anonymous hands reached for him, caressing him as he moved toward David. The sight of all those hands seemingly unattached to bodies, rubbing against Parke, made David's skin crawl under layers of quickly failing insulation.

Richard Parke nodded at David as he stepped by, supposedly the only acceptable acknowledgment of David's presence, as there had yet to be a word uttered by anyone, except the young man who had twice stammered "I'm coming."

Taking the opportunity, David fell into step behind Parke, following closely until they had returned to the parking lot. "Richard?" David's words stopped the man cold, just as he was inserting his key into the driver's door of a new silver Saab. The killing look he gave David was colder than the snow blowing around them as he signaled for David to go around to the other side of the car and wait.

Inside the car David said, "I haven't seen you around in a while. I thought you might have given up on hanging out in the bars."

"Oh yeah." Parke popped open the glove compartment and pulled out a small package of tissues. He took one and began scrubbing it around the perimeter of his lips. "I forgot that you used to work at Tyrone's. What are you doing these days?"

"Part-time work, mostly. I worked Christmas as a counter jumper at Hudson's."

Parke stopped wiping his lips for a long second, and then wadded the tissue and stuffed it in the ashtray. "I don't remember seeing you there."

"Didn't know you shopped at that kind of a store." David tried to imagine Richard Parke paying a thousand dollars for a pair of shoes. Except for the new car, Richard never had any of the trappings that one would expect of a high-powered Washington criminal attorney. He was more the khaki pants and Bass Weejuns type.

"That's just it," Parke said. "You *don't* know me."

David stared out the front of the car as Richard Parke lit himself a cigarette and the two of them sat, feeling the warmth of the electrically heated seats cutting through the cold of the night air. When the back half of David's body was sufficiently warm, he turned to Parke and said:

"I came here tonight because I want to talk to you about Michael Hudson."

The cigarette quavered in Parke's mouth as he reached for it with his left hand. "He's dead" was all Parke said as his right hand reached down to the console and flicked at the keys in the ignition.

"I know that," David said. "It looks like I'm one of the suspects in the case. *The* suspect, it appears."

"That so?" Parke rolled down his window a crack and flipped the almost-new cigarette out into the snow. "I never thought of you particularly as the homicidal type." He rolled the window back up and grasped the keys. The engine started on the first turn.

David didn't answer that one as he pulled the zipper tight on his coat. "What do you know about that night?"

"Which night was that?"

In the next few seconds that passed, David saw the look in Richard's eyes that he often saw shining out of attorneys' eyes – mostly right before they kicked the starving widow into the poorhouse, or right before they tied the helpless maiden to the running buzz saw.

"When was the last time you saw Mike Hudson alive?" was the only question David could bring forth.

"Three weeks." Parke shifted the car into gear. "Maybe four. Can I drop you somewhere?"

"I think it's just kind of funny," David said, "that your name should come up in the last round of interrogations I had with district police."

"They have no jurisdiction in that case." Parke's foot slipped off the clutch and the car died. As he restarted the motor, he said, "I can't imagine how my name would have come up, since Hudson and I were..." Parke's attention went back for just a second to the bushes around the statue. Another queue of men was starting just around the opposite side. "...acquaintances at best."

"And at worst?" David worked the door handle with his ungloved hand. As the door popped open, the blast of cold air came into the car again, and light sprinkles of snow blew in around the seal. In reply, Parke jumped up the control on the heater, and David's last words were almost drowned out by the loud hiss of the heater fan.

"It's been nice to see you again, David." Richard Parke had the car rolling before David had gotten completely out of the door. "Let's not make it so long between visits next time." As the door was slamming shut in David's hands, Parke said, "And maybe in a warmer locale."

The Saab pulled away into the dark fog of snow. Richard Parke gave one last scrub of his lips and shrugged his shoulders as he disappeared into the clouds of white smoke from his retreating car. David walked back to the Urban Guerrilla and kicked the door, hoping that a little added force would knock loose a few ounces of warmth from the heater. He may as well have wished for a trip to the moon.

✝

Tuesday, 11:00 p.m.

The wind kicked up at night and that kept Father Alexander awake. The sound of it, the constant wailing of the breeze through the limbs of the old oak tree outside his bedroom window caused him to roll sleeplessly in his bed, kicking the covers away.

A single steam heat radiator by the window spat in the darkness. Boredom maybe, or warnings that the priest shouldn't get comfortable in the old house, or in the strange cold city. Alexander had learned in his practice never to get too cozy and never to turn his back on the ways of evil. That thought suddenly brought a stitch of pain to the scar at the small of his back. He hadn't been looking once, in that house in Mission Dolores, when the fireplace poker swung around and caught him in a rabbit punch. Alexander never made that mistake again.

The cold of Washington seemed unruly to him. And the stifling heat of the house, of pipes clanking far below in the cellar, of the steam hissing around radiator pipes, and of everyone running around sheathed in cassocks and wimples, made him uncomfortably warm. In his own room, Father Alexander cranked the knob on the radiator almost as far as it would go toward OFF, and left a small crack in the window, which sent a bitter, icy draft across the head of his bed and cooled his brow. But still, once he was behind the locked door of his cell, Alexander shed the black casings of his trade and lounged at his desk or on his bed wearing nothing but his white boxer shorts, and the ragged wish bracelet tied around his right ankle.

100

At midnight, a gentle tap at the door caused him to stir from his fits of restlessness. His feet were tangled in the sheets that he had kicked to the bottom of the bed. Alexander tried to get out of them as he leaned across the nightstand, groping for the lamp, and saying, "Yes? What is it?" When the light clicked on, it took a second for his eyes to get accustomed to the bright.

The mutter on the other side was almost too faint for him to understand. "Just a minute," he said, shuffling across the room, pulling the latch on the door, blinded once again from the even brighter light from the hallway.

Father Milos stood on the other side of the door. He gasped once and stepped back, almost bumping into the second-floor banister. Alexander could see Milos's eyes run down his denuded body, not lingering at the boxers, and then coming back up to Alexander's face. Milos, who spent most of his free time bouncing a soccer ball against the garage wall or grunting over free weights in his room, looked surprised at what he saw, maybe shocked that it was on display, but not otherwise interested.

"Excuse the lateness," Milos said. "But there iss a kole for you." He pointed into the dark bedroom, toward the telephone on which one red light blinked. "From Lozangalez."

With that, Father Milos turned and hightailed it back down the stairs, stopping only once to look over his shoulder as Alexander absently yawned, scratched his rump, and closed the door.

"This is Tucker," he said into the telephone, after he picked up the receiver and jabbed at the blinking light.

"So how's it goin' out there, kiddo?" The voice on the other end was that of Father Michael-Lee, God's practical joke on the liturgical world.

"Not bad. Not bad." Alexander settled back down into the crumpled mess of his sheets, and crossed his ankles over the cool metal railing of the foot. "I haven't been up to the place yet. I'm getting some strange vibes about this one, though."

He nestled the telephone into the crook of his neck and crossed his arms behind his head, using them for a pillow. "I think it's going to be another tough one."

"You take it easy out there." Michael-Lee, who was twenty-six, spent what few hours he was not busily inflating whoopee cushions being the mother hen. "Remember the trouble you got in last time..."

"How could I forget," Alexander said. "Is Bishop Mehs speaking of me again, or am I still...?"

"...Among the personae non grata, I'd say. But that's only if you include the bishop sending off to the Vatican Library to get research materials on articles of excommunication. Maybe something about cutting your photograph from the picture of the graduating class at the seminary. You know. Minor hints."

"Well ... at least he's not still mad."

Father Michael-Lee laughed the kind of laugh he used right after he pulled the plastic vomit in the sacristy trick.

"So what can I do for you at this hour..." Alexander stretched to look at the desk and noticed the digital clock that had just clicked to a quarter past twelve. "...of the morning?"

"I need some help with a sermon," Michael-Lee said.

"Since when have *you* ever needed help? Remember the one about comparing God to a tuna casserole? *That* one really packed 'em in."

"Different this time."

"Oh yeah?"

Father Michael-Lee paused, and then said, "It's not *exactly* a sermon..."

"More like...?"

"Okay. You got me. It's a eulogy."

Alexander rolled over, speaking out into the dark and leaning up on one elbow. "That's even easier. Pull out the old number sixty-nine and use that one. It's always worked for me."

"Different. Besides, I don't have the face to pull a three-Kleenex-box eulogy. This one is Hollywood."

"Bad news," Father Alexander said.

"It's worse. I have to perpetuate a lie. Family's orders."

Alexander sat up on the side of the bed. "I think I see where this conversation is leading," he said. "Would this perchance be somebody I know?"

Again, the pause. In a few seconds of silence, Alexander listened to the white noise fading in and out on the line, and in his mind, he could see Michael-Lee with that constipated look on his face, as he tried to wrench bad news out and into the air. Michael-Lee had not yet developed a good bad-news delivery voice.

"It's Dane Andersson."

Alexander almost dropped the telephone. He knew Andersson's work: one of the ensemble players in the Lina Vera movies – including one role as a gay expatriate soldier in the Greek army who deserts to the island of Lesbos to be ... Greek. And Alexander had a fairly good idea of the cause of death of the unmarried thirtyish actor.

"A parishioner of yours, was he?" Alexander had to clear his throat a few times before he asked.

"Toward the end he was. Found a sudden interest in the religious life, and the hereafter. *Very* sudden, you might say."

"Then it was...?"

"AIDS."

"And what's the lie the family wants you to tell?"

"*They* say..." Father Michael-Lee did a bit of harrumphing himself before he went on. "They say he was exposed while he was on location in Spiros. Intravenous drugs. But that he was afraid the stigma would stop his career, so they all kept it quiet."

"And you know this isn't true?" Alexander could suddenly feel the invisible walls of the perpetual confessional close around him. It was one of the bad perks of being a priest. You had to be ready, any hour, at a second's notice.

Father Michael-Lee stammered and said, "That's under the seal. I can't say."

Alexander settled back into the bed, snuggling around the pillows, as if they were going to give him comfort. Their consolation was as cold as the wind that blew across them from the cracked window. "And why did you call me with this?"

"I thought you ... I thought you would want to know." Michael-Lee tried to stick some authority to his words as he said, "I thought it would be important to you."

"It's bullshit to me," Alexander said, cutting him off. "It's false and it's covering up a man's life."

"Some people have to live like that, Alex. You know that." Michael-Lee was his closest friend in the Church. They went through seminary together. They moved to the same parish in Southern California after graduation and stayed in touch even after Alexander gave up parish work to go on the road. Michael-Lee certainly knew all the stories that circulated about Alexander, but he had never, in the many years they had been friends, asked what had transpired, or if they were true.

"I just thought..." The phone line was quiet again for a moment. "I just thought you would like to know."

"You'll do okay," Alexander said. "Give 'em the number eighty-six about being a pillar of the community, and make a fast cut to the eats." He was feeling suddenly that he did not want to continue the conversation with his friend. Maybe tomorrow. Maybe after he had had a chance to get some sleep and stop worrying about his job in Maryland. "You worry too much."

The line was quiet. Michael-Lee was forcing him to speak at a time when he wanted to be silent. He could feel the pressure of that moment coming to him over the lines.

"Are you there?" Alexander said.

"I am," Michael-Lee said. "But sometimes I worry if you are. You can't afford to be either a part-time man or a part-time priest right now, Alexander. It could get dangerous."

"Listen. I want you to do me a favor." Alexander reached over and clicked off the lamp, suddenly feeling very naked and alone in the room. The darkness gave him a false sense of shelter.

"Name it. As long as I don't have to go see Mehs and plead for mercy for you."

"Not that. At least not yet," Alexander said. "But would you run down to Mission Dolores and torch a few candles there for me this week? It looks as if I might need it."

"Sure thing. And you won't think bad of me for what I've got to say in Andersson's eulogy?"

"Just give 'em what they want." Alexander reached down and pulled the rumpled sheets up around his chest. "It may be the music that their souls are praying to hear." The fabric was slightly cool as it fell across his chest. "Good night, Michael."

"You take care of yourself and watch your backside."

Alexander put the receiver down and rolled over, facing the window. As he lay there, he thought he heard a hint of a laugh, floating on the snowy wind as tree limbs made spidery shadows against the opposite wall.

✝

Wednesday, 10:00 a.m.

It was bad enough there wasn't work to do in the store to keep David busy. Worse, they wouldn't send him home.

The call came down about noon, that Granville Hudson wanted to see him at the M Street offices. David left his comfortable position at the shoe polish fixture and walked over, the wind biting his face for the five-block walk from the store to the corporate headquarters. The ride up to fourteen was longer than usual, because the elevator stopped on every floor, letting off another gaggle of homely secretaries on their way up from the Korean take-out in the basement. Each carried a heavily oiled bag of grease burgers and fries.

The offices for Hudson International took up the entire top floor of the Sherman Building at 1700 M Street, Northwest. Granville had the office with the balcony that looked directly down into the pigeon-infested turrets of Saint Matthew's Cathedral.

105

Double mahogany doors blocked the end of the hall, and a small brass plate beside the entrance to Granville Hudson's office said, "Ring for Entry," engraved in the kind of script usually seen on wedding invitations. David pushed the button as instructed, and an elderly secretary came out and admitted him into the inner sanctum of the Hudson family fortune.

Granville Hudson was one of those men who has to have three different wardrobes in his closet. He had the business look, with a selection of suits that he bought all at once from the same store (on sale) so that they were exactly alike. The casual look was an accumulation of every Ralph Lauren ad in print. And, he had his after-hours look.

From the darting glances that were knocking David up against the doorway as he stepped into the room, he assumed the last wardrobe had something to do with stretching dead animal hides tightly across Hudson's fat thighs, riding a cycle, and drinking cheap beer out of the can.

Francis Xavier Hudson, the youngest surviving Hudson boy and the merchandise buyer for the store, didn't speak, but stood there, holding the door open, staring at David. "Afternoon, Frank," David muttered, pushing past him and into the room.

Francis Hudson wasn't that bad a looker, either, David thought. Even though he was only three years younger than the oldest brother Granville, Francis was in excellent shape. The word on the sales floor was that Francis jogged around the Hudson block in Georgetown at six in the morning and again at nine in the evening. (The family owned a square block of the most expensive real estate in town where they all lived in happy nepotism, each in his own house on opposite corners. All four houses backed onto a common roque court and Olympic-sized lap pool.) There seemed to be one rather strong family trait that ran between the three brothers, one that David had first enjoyed at the hands of their youngest brother Michael: they were all quite skilled at undressing men with their eyes. Michael hadn't been too bad at using his hands, either.

David stopped and turned as Hudson slowly clicked the door shut. "I'm sorry about what happened to Michael. He was a great guy."

Francis Xavier Hudson put one hand on David's shoulder and led him across the room. His fingers lingered too long at the nape of David's neck, which gave David the creepy sensation that the younger Hudson brother was practicing a new choke hold on him.

"He was a doped-up loudmouth," Francis said. "And that was his good side. He'd been kicked out of every drug rehab program in the country. He even spent the night in the drunk tank down in Arlington." Francis Hudson spoke as if he were referring to some stranger he had read about in the papers. "Sometimes it was hard to believe it was *my* little brother." The buyer turned away and muttered, "Too bad he had the papers to prove it."

Granville Hudson leaned back in the oversized leather chair behind his desk, far enough back that his crotch was level with the top of the desk. When the two men came closer, he popped his feet on the floor and jogged around the desk, pointing David into a new leather-covered wingback chair.

"Come in. Have a seat." He pushed David into the chair with both hands. In a second, the insincere smile flaked off his face and he nodded Francis into a smaller chair in the back of the room. "I'll get back to you in just a second." Granville said to his brother. "This won't take but a minute."

"I was just telling Francis..." David's voice cracked and he had to start again. "That I'm very sorry about what happened to Michael."

Granville Hudson settled himself back into his chair and touched a button on his phone, turning it off. He looked back as though he didn't quite understand what David was talking about.

"Our mother..." He swept his hand to one side, toward a large painting of a porcine woman swathed in yellow and white, with a shock of glowing orange Lucille Ball hair falling down over one eye. In one hand she held a glass of what looked to be mint julep, and in the other, a small rat-faced dog. "Our mother is not taking it well at all. You see, Michael had become her favorite child, even though he was such a problem." Granville Hudson's eyes darkened as he mentioned his favorite subject – money. "Michael was a very *expensive* problem."

Hudson shot an accusatory glance at David as he said, "Our brother was a homosexual. As you no doubt know. But, he *was* the youngest. The..."

"The last *fruit* of the vine." Francis finished his thought. Granville gave his brother a look that knocked him against his chair and shut him up.

"You were the last to see our brother alive that night, so the police tell us." Granville made steeples with his hands as he leaned backwards in his chair.

"Not quite," David said, trying to sit up straight and not touch the clammy surface of the chair. "After me, there was whoever killed him."

Granville Hudson's eyes glowed almost red as he said, "Yes. Of course."

Granville continued: "We were wondering if he said anything to you. Anything of importance to the family. You know. As a remembrance." The insincerity of Hudson's voice was punctuated by the way his eyes focused first on Francis, then David, and back to Francis again.

David leaned away from the desk and his inquisitor, trying to mimic the man's look as much as possible. He knew that Granville was searching for something other than filial memorabilia. Hudson wanted to know if the boy had dropped the dirt on the family about some shady activity or another, while in the throes of drug-induced ecstasy.

"This is such a heartbreak to us." Francis picked up the thought. "Anything that you can tell us about our brother would be of use."

"Except for the part about his proclivities. We are *not* interested in that." Granville cut him off with a wave of his hand.

David saw the same hungry look in both brothers' eyes. Maybe it meant nothing. Maybe it was genetic. Whichever, it was the same look he got from Michael Hudson, an hour before the two of them were rolling in a sweaty mass on the sheets of David's bed. "Nothing that I recall."

"Now I know the police have asked you all this before, but I wondered if I could go over a few questions one more time." Francis rose and began pacing around the office. "Of course, you don't have to answer if you don't want to. Think of this as a favor. For me and Granville." He flashed a cold look at his older brother, who appeared to be off on another thought, miles away.

"Shoot. I don't mind if you don't."

"Good." Granville Hudson snapped back to attention. "Let's start at the beginning." A strange fire ignited with those words that Francis did not appear to notice. David saw it – a leering, lecherous look. "Tell me. What exactly did our brother say to you in that bar, and what did he do? In public, I mean ... where people may have seen?"

David suddenly realized that he was about to have to answer the sex questions that Rod Daniels had conveniently skirted in the "official" police interview.

✝

Wednesday, 3:30 p.m.

David Harriman never trusted anyone's coffee but his own. He kept a supply of fresh beans in his freezer, the bottled water under the sink, and brewed the potion through all-natural filters made from unbleached paper. The taste was fantastic. Still, he sat at his dining table and watched Rod Daniels dump three sugars into his Jamaican Blue Mountain dark roast and then turn the whole concoction dirty white with a heavy dose of powdered nondairy coffee paint.

"The last thing they said as I was heading out the door was 'Oh yeah, we forgot to tell you. Today's your last day.'"

David stirred his coffee and spoke to the spoon. "Said they didn't need me in the store now that the holidays were over, but would I like to come back and run bar for them, if they need me for parties at the big house."

"You told them to drop dead, I hope." Daniels's face showed pleasure at the noxious sludge he was pouring down his throat.

"I didn't say anything, just took my check and left," David said. "It'll probably bounce, considering my luck this week."

"It's going to get worse before it gets better," Daniels said. He peered over the rim of his cup at David as the rising steam from the coffee made wispy lines of heat over his face. "The lab results are back. Positive on all three. You left DNA fingerprints all over the body, and somebody at the District Building is going to want to know why. Not to mention the Maryland State Police."

David did not speak as he wondered for a quick second how he could get a plane ticket to South America. He'd heard Venezuela was very nice that time of year.

"They're going to want you downtown again for questioning," Daniels said, placing his cup lightly into its saucer, but still holding onto the handle with one hand. "Fingerprints, too."

"You mean they honestly think I...?"

"Those Maryland cops could believe anything, David. You have to remember that we've seen it all in homicide. And a little accidental death brought on by somebody having too many drinks and getting too rowdy is *not* at all unusual." A slight blush came across his face as he said, "For the goon squad, that is."

David leaned back in his chair, almost biting a hole in his lip to keep from screaming out at the detective. Instead, he took a long gulp of the coffee, held it in his mouth for a second until he couldn't stand the heat, and swallowed, feeling it singe its way to the bottom of his stomach. Rod knew he wasn't the killer – the timing made it impossible, but too many fingers of physical evidence pointed back at him. The only way to put

Michael Hudson to rest and to get the cops out of his hair was to find the real killer, and fast. And whether or not he had the help of the D.C. Police didn't matter. Rod Daniels was just another clumsy, plodding bureaucrat.

"I don't like it," David said, passing Daniels a plate of fresh coconut macaroons he'd picked up at Bread and Chocolate on the way home. It was his present to himself for being unemployed again. Somehow, they were suddenly lacking flavor. "Those two were grieving the death of their brother just about as much as the newscasters did when they reported the story."

Daniels stirred his cup silently, mulling over the tale David had just given him of his afternoon in Granville Hudson's office. "They weren't exactly torn up about the whole ordeal."

"They were more concerned that no one saw us *doing* anything in public that might embarrass them, or what Michael said about them. Didn't even seem to care about what happened when we got back here."

"Yeah." Daniels took a second macaroon. "If it had been me, I probably would have asked something direct, like 'Did you kill my brother?'"

David peeked at Daniels over the top of his cup as he took a long swallow, debating whether he should ask the next question. "Look. I know it doesn't have anything to do with the case, but do you think there's something shady going on with the Hudson boys?"

"What do you mean, *shady?*"

"I don't know." David tried one of the cookies. They were soft and fresh, and reminded him of warmer days in summer. He glanced out the window at the advancing black of the night sky; at least it had stopped snowing.

"Something about the way they both looked at me," David said. "It gave me the creeps."

"I know what you mean." Daniels brushed his hands together, discarding unseen crumbs. "In the interrogation, Granville Hudson spent half the interview with his hand resting firmly on my knee. Every now and again he would give it a little squeeze." Daniels's face went bright red. "Condescending bastard. Not exactly appropriate behavior for a grieving brother, I'd say."

"Hey. You don't think he's..." David made a swishing motion with his right hand, trying to paste an innocent look on his face as he asked Rod Daniels if he thought water was wet.

"If he's not, he's stupid." Daniels reached across the table and refilled his coffee. David cringed as the detective dumped another load of creamer into his cup. "He's a Saturday night regular at the Eagle."

"I knew it." David warmed his cup. "I *knew* there was something leather-clad and randy-looking about him." David tried to imagine Granville Hudson loitering around the Eagle, trying to look "genuine" in a pair of black leather chaps, and studded bands strapped to his biceps.

"But wait a minute." David set his cup down with a loud clink. "How would *you* know who's a regular there?"

Daniels's face went red again as he tried not to look nonplused, sipping his café au lait.

David had a lot more fun trying to picture Daniels's bare bottom sticking out of a pair of oiled leather chaps, of Rod Daniels calling him "buddy" or, God forbid, "pardner." Rod was too embarrassed to continue the conversation as he dug through the macaroons, poking them with one finger. David decided to let it drop, and to pull his cowboy outfit out of mothballs for a future drag to the Eagle, just to see the sights. Rod was probably a lot of fun with enough well-worn leather stretched over his thighs.

"Can you tell me what they told you about that night?" David hoped that he was not again digging into confidential information that could get Daniels in trouble with the department, especially considering David's new status as the Typhoid Mary of the homicide set.

"Granville Hudson was at home in Georgetown with his girlfriend Tanya Williams that night."

David cackled a laugh at him. "He has a girlfriend?"

Daniels slid the cup away. "And not just *any* girlfriend. This one's granddaddy owns the *Washington Star.*" He sloshed his dregs around the cup a few times before he continued. "Granville was married once, too. Mother Hudson had it annulled after a year and a half to keep the blushing bride from spilling the beans on Granville and the Japanese houseboy."

"Eighteen months without consummating their marriage vows, eh?" David laughed, wondering to himself how much Mother Hudson had paid to get that one okayed in Rome.

"Francis..." The detective grimaced. "Francis is a little skittish about all this. He sweats a lot when you start to ask him questions." Daniels took the last macaroon from the plate and tore it in two, giving David half. "Says he was having dinner with friends that night and had too much to drink. He camped out in their guest room until the next morning when he returned home."

"Has *he* got a girlfriend to corroborate the story?"

"Girlfriend, yes. And the friends, of course."

David, taking the cookies, led Rod away from the dining table to the living room sofa.

Daniels continued. "The girlfriend was at home, asleep in Francis's bed at *his* house in Georgetown, at the time. She took the call from the Maryland State Police when they called the next morning with the bad news."

"Have you talked to Richard Parke yet?" David tried to change the subject quickly, while he had Daniels on a roll.

"What are you trying to do, get me fired?" Daniels settled back into the sofa. He raked his fingers through his hair. The look on his face showed internal questions – wondering if he had already told David too much.

"Just trying to make some sense of this whole mess." David slid closer to him on the sofa. So close that David was almost speaking into his ear. "You know." He spoke as softly as he could without whispering. "I have trouble sleeping at night, because of this."

Daniels's mind worked quickly to edit out what he could and could not say. "Parke and Mike Hudson were 'regulars.'"

His words stammered, as he tried to pull away from David's hold. He gave up the battle too quickly.

"What do you mean by *regular?*" David pulled back. He knew he was getting what he wanted.

"You know. Fuck buddies. Probably about every week or so, to hear tell. They met at..."

"I know where they met." David stopped him. "Parke only goes to a couple of places in town to find companionship."

David knew that Michael got a little exuberant in bed, but he had a tough time imagining him doing the kind of rough stuff that Richard Parke liked. Also, Michael was a little too vocal about his inclinations for Parke's liking. Richard preferred the tough straight guys who would do it just for the cash or who used the "boy, was I drunk last night" excuse.

Another thought suddenly entered David's head. "How about the roommate in the dorm? Anything on him?"

"Didn't have one," Daniels replied. "The last one didn't come back after midsemester break. I don't think they got along too well."

"Can't imagine why." David scooted to the opposite end of the sofa, satisfied with the information he had. His little test worked, and Daniels passed, giving him what passed for the truth. "Living with an outspoken homosexual kick-rocker on drugs, up there in the mountains at that cloistered Catholic college, next door to a seminary. Sounds like an ideal learning environment to me."

Daniels was silent for a long time. He sat staring straight ahead, mentally flipping through his own notes. "Poor kid," he said at last.

"Which one?"

"The roommate." Daniels gave David a look that said he had already expressed his grief for the loss of Michael Hudson. That had happened someplace quiet, away from the tax-paying public. Rod could do nothing for Michael now but finish the case. "What the hell kind of an introduction to gay people is that?"

David thought about the scores of gay people he knew all over the world; some good, some bad. They did everything: cured illnesses, sold real estate. Dealt drugs, built computers, worked in furniture factories, were rock stars with millions of fans. David couldn't think of a good *or* bad introduction to gay people. They were all just people.

"Why don't I wrap up the rest of those cookies for you to take back home?" David jumped up, rattling them on the plate as he made for the kitchen. Daniels shot him a look of disappointment. He had been milked for what David wanted, and was being given the bum's rush.

"Yeah," he said. "Sure." He went to the closet and helped himself to his overcoat. As David returned with the waxed bag of macaroons, Daniels looked at him and said, "You want to come around to my place and help me cook dinner some night?"

David studied Daniels's face for a long time, trying to gauge the intent of that invitation. Either Daniels was still pretty naive, or he was getting better at lying from questioning too many suspects.

"Sounds like fun." David put a heavy crease in the folded top of the cookie bag. "You solve this case and we've got a date."

Rod Daniels's face went all red again as David said, "Married men *do* date on occasion, I take it."

✝

Thursday, 3:00 p.m.

It was the first time David had been to a job interview where the first thing someone said to him was "Now take off your clothes." Usually, that didn't come to him until about the second week on the job.

The office where he sat with Jim Barnette was gray. The walls, the ceiling, the furniture, and the boss's skin – all gray. Sounds of heavy breathing echoed around on the backs of the walls, as if two giants had stopped by to boff on the roof. No such luck: it was the speakers lining the wall around the movie screen in the theater next door. Jim's place, Cinema Verite, showed skin movies twenty-four hours a day in the scrubbed-clean halls of the theater-bookstore.

Jim's father had started the business as a strip joint for men who wore raincoats on clear days. Jim took over and brought the southeast Washington club, parked in the middle of the worst side of town, uptown.

"I need you weekends at Finders-Keepers. You'll be on the back bar." F-K was the second of Jim's three enterprises. The third, in true homosexual diversification of capital, was a coffee shop in Amsterdam that was a gourmet emporium of the best marijuana Western Europe could grow. "But I need some fill-in, too. Here."

David knew what that meant. He knew Jim didn't need a projectionist to change the videos every hour and a half. He needed strippers for the weekend shows. *That* was why David was there, standing in an open office, pulling off his jeans as comely young men with exaggerated hair and at-titudes to match passed in and out with papers for Jim to sign.

When he was bare, David stood at attention, trying to focus on a point on the wall, rather than catching Jim's inquiring glances at his body. He also tried not to blush, even though he could feel the red climbing up his face to the top of his head. He thought the room became noticeably brighter as he threw his clothes in a pile on the leather sofa and stood, his winter white skin reflecting every light in the room.

"Not bad." Jim Barnette looked at him like a careful buyer about to put money down on a piece of broken antique furniture. The look in his eyes said David was a fixer-upper. At least that was better than saying he was a cream puff, which they both already knew. "Not bad at all. In an open-shirted sort of way. How *old* did you say you were, David?"

He lied downward a couple of years and said he had just turned thirty.

"Well. You know a few of our customers are into the old ones." Barnette opened a desk drawer and pulled out a pack of Dunhills, lighting one. As he spoke, the cigarette bobbed up and down between his lips. "I *know* you're good behind a bar. I saw you mixing drinks at Tyrone's. You're one of the best in town, they say. Maybe *the* best." He flicked the cigarette at a large marble ashtray on his desk. "You ever do any dancing before?"

"Honey, I was disco when disco wasn't cool." David tried crossing his arms across his chest, but he felt as if he were posing for the underwear pages in the Sears catalog.

"Was it ever?" Barnette laughed and coughed out a blast of smoke that went down the wrong way. He pulled a white towel from a neatly folded stack on the credenza behind him. He threw it at David as he said, "Let's take a walk. I want you to meet my boys."

☦

David saw at once what Jim meant when he said that a few of the patrons liked the old ones. All of the other performers in the show that night had still been in diapers when David was passing his first driving test. They all had butch little stage names like Brad, Buck, and the dreaded B.J. They were all eighteen, not a year younger, not a year older. They all looked younger than Snake.

"You know what the difference is between a good dancer and schlock, David?" Brad, the first serving of the midnight show, was pulling a skin-colored bikini up over his apple-shaped bottom. When he bent over to step in, his legs automatically went into an aerobic switch, unconsciously practicing the routine.

"No, but I'm sure, from that expectant look on your face..." David bent his head to get a better view of Brad's backside and the gentle arch of his spine as Brad pulled on the second skin and settled all the equipment in place. "...that you're going to tell me."

Brad gave him a quick flash that told David the comment sailed right by and didn't even touch a bleached-white hair on the boy's head. "The difference is in the oil." He dug into his kip sack and brought out an unmarked bottle, handing it to David. "Here. Rub this on my back."

David, realizing he was being tutored by one of the better male strippers in the city, took the bottle and did as he was told. He rubbed a handful of the oil into Brad's shoulders and started working his way down from there.

Brad's head started to roll around under David's grip as if it was about to come unhinged and fall to the floor. He started this little gyrating motion in his hips and David watched Brad's toes spread and flex as he made soft moaning sounds.

David was lost in the reverie of trying to make his fingers fuse with the knots in the muscles of the boy's back. Brad leaned up against the wall, taking the police frisk stance, bowed his head to his chest and spoke as David kneaded his back. "What does that smell like to you?"

David stopped, looked at his fingers poised midway down the dancer's back, then to either side, wondering what he was talking about. "Smell?"

"The oil. What does it smell like?" Brad turned and faced David. His eyes had a glazed look as if David's fingers had been playing the right chords and maybe he wanted to see if they could work up a little tune.

"Doesn't smell like anything." David sniffed his hands. The palms were still red from working Brad's flesh.

"Exactly. A real pro uses unscented natural massage oil that soaks into the skin and won't leave a mess."

"I see." David lifted his eyebrows as he grinned. He could only guess how Brad picked up such handy information. He wondered for a second if there would be more tutoring, but Brad busied himself with the rest of his abbreviated costuming.

Brad started working on his chest, applying even more oil than David had put on the back. "Some of the guys like to use baby oil because it's cheap." Brad was speaking to his left nipple as he pinched and tweaked it between his oily fingers to get it taut. "Makes you smell like a baby, though."

"Perish the thought."

Brad gave him a look like he agreed. David decided to give up on jiving with the kid.

"We had one in here that even used Vaseline on his legs, till it gave him the zits so bad he had to stop working."

David tried to imagine how long it would take to wash off a healthy swath of petroleum jelly after each show. "So what's he doing now, waiting for the zits to clear up?" The thought made him feel incredibly old. He was actually standing naked in a dressing room, swapping acne war stories with an eighteen-year-old.

"He's still around. Jim put him on the afternoon show during the week. That's where you get put if you can't dance, or if you can't get it up on stage."

There is a moment of intense panic that follows seconds after a jaywalker steps back up on the curb, realizing that he was an instant away from being made road pizza by passing traffic. David felt that sensation in the bottom of his stomach as he watched Brad dig another bottle out of his bag. "Get *what* up?" It was a stupid question. Sort of like asking the firing squad if they were using live ammunition.

Brad answered him by stepping over and applying an oily hand to the part of David that *had* been asleep — until David had watched Brad lubricate himself for his part of the evening's show. Brad gently cupped David's scrotum with his small, warm hands as his oily chest pushed David's erect penis up against his stomach. "This."

"No, no, no. Jim never said anything to me about putting lead in the pencil. All he said was that I had to go out there and dance to the music for ten minutes, and take off my clothes." As he stepped backward, he saw the imprint of an exclamation point his equipment had made on Brad's front.

Brad's laughter cut through David, making him feel even more naked than he already was. The erection fell like a cartoon character who had been hit on the head with a giant mallet. That caused Brad to laugh more.

"Come on." Brad slapped him hard on the rear, making a noise that echoed around the room. "Just watch me, and do what I do." He led David toward the door. "And don't worry about the hard-on thing. We can take care of that."

David picked up a towel, wiped the excess massage oil from his penis, and followed behind the exclamation point that walked, bare-butt, down the stairs to the first floor and the stage.

✟

Friday, 2:00 p.m.

Adolfo was a deejay. No other name, just Adolfo. He was the kind of man who would go to Sears to buy Michelin retreads for his Jaguar convertible: no class. He had traded in his Range Rover when he jumped ship at Boys! in Georgetown, six months before. Now Adolfo was the spinner of wax and the stretcher of videotape at Underground, the new het disco in town, at the end of what had, in the years before the riots, been *the* fashionable downtown shopping district.

The last time David had seen him was the night of the annual green and white ball, the last of the big A-Gay "color" parties of 1989. Even then, Adolfo's career was fading faster than an old fluorescent light tube. His nickname was "Flash," which he had imprinted on the license plates of the Rover that Boys! leased for his use. Finally, his act had become more of a fritz, so he dropped the moniker, switched formats, and moved on to larger crowds.

One of the advantages to being a bartender is that you get to know every other bartender, waiter, and busboy in town. And with them, you are privilege to all the bar gossip that comes with them. Underground was pretty new and there wasn't much dirt yet on the place, other than which doormen could be bribed to get you in. (There was a two-hour wait most weekday nights. You only got in on the weekends if the bouncers liked the looks of you, or if you knew somebody on the inside.)

David slipped a double Dive Bomber in front of the deejay, who didn't bother to introduce himself or order when he

120

came in and sat down. Adolfo had been hanging out there long enough. He was one of the "regulars." Jim had already warned David about Adolfo's drinking habits.

"How's it going at the new place?" David busied himself with dusting off already-cleaned bottles and polishing fresh-scrubbed glasses as he spoke. He didn't want to appear too eager.

Adolfo grunted at David, shrugged, and dropped the first dram of whiskey into his beer. "Same."

"Anything new that maybe I should see?" David took the jigger away and dropped it into the blue water of the sterilizing bath.

"Depends on what you're looking for, David." Adolfo pulled a ten out of his pocket and dropped it like a spit wad on the bar in front of him. David let it lay where it fell. "What can I get you?"

"You can get me a name." David didn't bother leaning forward or whispering as he spoke. No one would have been interested in their conversation anyway. "I need to know what you can tell me about Granville Hudson and his brothers."

"Who?"

"Granville Hudson. You know. They own Hudson's, downtown."

Adolfo finished off the glass and tapped his index finger on the rim of the glass, signalling the time for a refill was at hand. "Never heard of him. Why do you want to know?"

"His kid brother is dead. Somebody, you should pardon the expression, offed him."

"Oh. *That* Hudson." The light of recognition came on behind Adolfo's drooping brown eyes. Somebody must have told him once that expression made him look cute – like Bambi. Somebody lied. Adolfo picked up the money he had dropped on the counter, as if picking up a strange piece of litter from the street. In one swift move, the money disappeared into his pocket. Adolfo looked to each end of the bar to see if anyone was listening as he spoke. Since there was no one else in the room, eavesdropping would have been particularly difficult. "Why don't you come see me at work?" Adolfo dumped the second dram glass into the fresh beer. "You might like the sights."

"Haven't you heard? I'm a parent now. I can't be staying out too late like I used to."

"Get a sitter." Adolfo wiped his mouth on his coat sleeve, turned on the stool, and walked out the front door.

"Chatter, chatter, chatter," David said as he leaned over the wash sinks. "I wish to hell he'd shut up and let me get a word in edgewise." David laughed and put the empty beer glass upside down onto the rotating scrubbing brushes. He pumped the glass up and down until it was clean, then dropped it into the blue bath. "Sounds like a bar drag is in the works to me."

✞

Underground was on the second floor of what used to be an old bank building downtown. There was another mega disco on the first floor called the Bank. Underground was over that. It wasn't exactly David's choice for Washington nightlife: the room was mostly filled with grody teenagers wearing black. They weren't *exactly* teenagers, most were a few years older. They did all wear black, though, and they were, in David's opinion, grody. Plus, there was a rather unusual mixture of ambisexuality to the place, as large groups of people either danced or groped each other in time to the music, with little concern for the gender of the person who they felt up.

It was early in the evening, so there was still room to walk among the crowd. The music was a lot of the same stuff that was playing on MTV at the time. The newer, more popular cuts wouldn't get played until later in the evening. On the video screen, a bald woman was unzipping her skin and stepping out of herself while singing about a boyfriend who left her in favor of a chopped Chevrolet. Looking at her, David had to side with the boyfriend.

Adolfo worked behind a Plexiglas screen that was smeared with dried beer stains and scratched from a few too many

122

glasses and bottles hurled at him by unruly fans. The club was barely three months old, and already it looked like a combat zone. Adolfo worked with his back to the crowd, deafened by earphones that were not connected to any of his sound equipment. David banged on the glass, but the deejay either didn't hear him, or if he did, Adolfo wouldn't turn around.

David realized that the deejay was going to be of little help from the booth, so he decided to search the room to see what he could find. Against the opposite wall, standing in *his* favorite spot by the entrance to the bathrooms, he found it. A dark smudge of violence, all wrapped up in brand-new Polo sweats.

Vinnie the Popper was pretty well known around town. If there was a car to be snatched, or if there was something you saw in a store that you wanted but didn't want to pay for, Vinnie was the guy you called. He had been a regular of David's back at Tyrone's. He did a job for a senator once when the senator wanted to make a young girl disappear but didn't want any blood to be spilled, or at least not on him.

Vinnie drank more beer than was good for him and never had enough cash on him to pay his tab. David had covered him more times than Vinnie cared to remember, but David figured it was time for a little memory refresher.

David took a fresh Iron City Lite from the bar and pressed it into the Popper's hands. "Hello, Vinnie." He tried not to stand too close as he spoke. Vinnie seemed okay with the concept of gay boys, but not quite so good on physical contact.

"Dave, my squeeze." Vinnie's face stretched across the longest row of gold teeth David had ever encountered. It was probably the same look the Popper gave you right before he put a new hole in your head with a Craftsman power drill. "Haven't seen you around since Ty's closed his doors. Where you working, man?"

David was not ready to tell the kingpin of Washington shoplifters that he had worked inside one of the hardest-hit shops in the city, so he lied and said that he was just hanging out, doing favors, and watching the tube.

"Favors, you say?" the Popper's skin shone under the flashing disco lights like a spit-polished pair of boots. "Sounds like my line of business."

"Could be." David leaned back against the wall and tried to look cool as sweat began to soak through around the arms of his shirt. He knew what was bulging in the Popper's pants pocket, and that the Popper didn't like any hasty moves that might make his shooting hand get an itch. "I'm here looking for a friend. Thought you might have seen him around."

"I see people." Vinnie tilted his head back and poured the contents of the beer bottle into his mouth. He took all sixteen ounces without swallowing but once. The bottle didn't make a sound as it hit the floor and rolled out of sight on the black carpet under their feet. "Lot of people don't see *me,* though."

"I know what you mean." David didn't want to try the drinking trick to see if he could match the man, so he leaned back farther and pulled another card from the deck. "So where you doing your drinking these days, now that Tyrone's is closed?"

Again, the smile. The Popper's teeth were locked together in a grin that capped a steam vent of some other emotion. David hoped, for his sake, and for the continuing communion with his balls, that Vinnie's emotion was a good one.

"You're a good boy, David. For a faggot. I like you."

"You ain't so bad yourself, Vinnie."

"For a drunk mopper that will shoot your nuts off for a dollar."

"Anything you say, Vinnie." David smiled a nervous grin as he glanced around the dance floor.

The Popper laughed and turned to David for the first time. "This friend. What you need him for?"

"Just want to know what he's up to, that's all. His brother's dead."

"Brother a friend of yours?"

"He was for about two hours."

"You white boys are going to have to learn the right way to fuck." Vinnie's hands went toward his pockets. David tried not to let it show that he was clenching his teeth. "Two hours ain't shit, boy." The chuckle was actually a low-pitched growl, from what David could hear over the sound of music in the room.

The long fingers kneaded the fabric covering the gun in the Popper's pocket as he spoke out into the crowd. "Your friend got a name?"

"Granville Hudson."

"You mean like the stores?" Of course Vinnie would know of him. He indicated so by lifting one foot up off the floor and pointing to the pair of alligator Braganos he was wearing. In the dim light, the skin looked real. "Yeah. I know him."

"So what's the story on him?" David studied the alligator shoes with interest. "Does he hang out? Especially anywhere he wouldn't want to get caught?"

"How would I know that, brother? I ain't his baby-sitter. Besides." He pushed away from the wall and started to step away. "Couldn't do much sneaking around town with that 560 of his. A real Superfly. I could catch some tight trim in a ride like that." There was a silvery glint of longing in the Popper's eyes like a dieter gets when he talks about chocolate.

David thought about the car again as Vinnie disappeared into the crowd. Black with blacked-out windows. All the chromium trim done over in gold plate. There was very little chance of seeing that car parked in a back alley behind somebody's dive beer joint, and Granville Hudson was too much of a tightwad to keep a second car for rambling around places he didn't want his friends to know he went.

The music stopped for a second as a loud scratch came over the loudspeakers which brought David's attention back into the room. A lot of the dancers had lost their balance from the sudden change in the music.

David looked into the deejay's booth, where Adolfo was waving in his direction. He had finally seen David. Adolfo pointed to the other corner of the room, opposite the door.

David pushed his way though a crowd of flailing dancers, swimming his way to the other corner. As he got to a clearing he saw the back of Francis Hudson going out the door and down the stairs in the middle of a group of people. David fought to get clear of the dancers, some of whom tugged at him and pulled him to stay on the dance floor. As he finally broke free, he saw Francis disappear through the door.

It took the coat check twink a few seconds to find his jacket. He threw a dollar across the bar and ran down the stairs and through the crowd waiting at the bottom to go up.

Out in the street, once he got away from the building, everything was quiet. A fine dusting of snow had started to fall again.

"Shit." David stamped his feet on the frozen sidewalk in anger. As he got to the corner of F and Twelfth, he saw Francis Xavier Hudson driving north, up Twelfth Street, alone.

David walked up the block to where he had left the Urban Guerrilla parked facing up Twelfth. The nice thing about having a junk car in the city was that you could park it just about anywhere, and you could be fairly certain that it would still be there, intact, when you returned. His cold fingers fumbled with the keys as he tried to get the door unlocked and get the car moving toward home. It had been a wasted trip to a boring disco that he never would have gone to, were it not for Adolfo.

The Urban Guerrilla, as always, started on the first turn of the key. As he double-clutched to get rolling, he banged his fist hard on the dash above the heater. He knew it wouldn't do any good, but he felt like hitting something defenseless.

Three blocks away, he saw that the silver Mercedes with Francis Hudson inside had sat through the red lights at the little hooker park three times. Hudson was speaking to someone outside the car that David could not see. He gestured across the passenger seat, waving his arms as he spoke out the open passenger's window. Whomever he was talking to did not step out of the shadows of the bushes.

David wanted to wait and see what got out of the shrubbery and into the car, but he saw Hudson look in his rearview mirror and see, David supposed, the white exhaust coming out of the Guerrilla. Hudson turned right on New York Avenue and circled out of sight.

David thought it was probably time to go home and see if he had a home left, what with a kid on the prowl with a key to his apartment. He thought for a second of the news reports of one senator's problems with opportunistic young men. The senator came home one day to find a brothel running out of his dining room, and the *Washington Inquirer* waiting, Polaroid in hand, to scoop up some dirt. Fortunately, David didn't have to worry about being re-elected, just whether or not he would have a stereo and VCR when he returned. Maybe there was enough time, though, to stop off at Schneider's and pick up a bottle of Courvoisier to warm his cockles on the way home.

He did a U-turn in the middle of the street and headed south. There was still a line halfway down the block from the Bank, even as the snow began to fall harder and make a white crust on the black outfits of the kids waiting to get in.

127

Monday, 2:00 p.m.

David wondered if the guy was Episcopalian or Catholic. You never could tell just from the black shirt and the white dog collar. Lutherans and Methodists were fairly easy to spot; they always looked slightly out of place wearing clerical uniforms. Not this guy. He looked like he was born in black and white — just about twenty-five years ago.

The priest came in and sat at the opposite end of the bar, barely able to wrap his bowed legs around the stool. He had one of those faces that told you he drove a Jeep on a beach somewhere, and his cheeks were so pink from the cold they looked as if someone had painted big red circles on them. His hair was short and blond, and his skin was too tan. He was a real babe — a bod for God. David was going to give the man the benefit of the doubt as to why he was sitting at the rail at Finders-Keepers in the middle of the day. It must have been part of his community service work to get out and visit around the neighborhood.

As David walked over to him, the young priest looked up at him with guileless eyes and ordered a Heiney. The priest's eyes sparkled too much as he said the word, David thought, as if the reverend was interested in more than beer. Without responding, David pulled the cold green bottle from the cooler and set it on the bar in front of the man. A few drops of cold sweat from the bottle began to collect on the bar, soaking into the coaster David pushed toward the young man with a flick of one finger. "You need a glass?" The bottle nudged one step closer.

The priest took the bottle, ran the lip against the palm of his hand, and turned it up, gurgling down the brew. Obviously not.

"Haven't seen you around town before." David tried to make it sound as if Washington was such a small town that he could possibly know every homosexual that crossed the tracks to the worst part of town to walk in his door. "You've *got* to be new."

"How could you tell?" The young man smiled back at him, wiping a few stray drops of the Heineken from his lips. He looked as if he wanted to tell David a whole lot more.

"The tan gave you away, for one." David leaned against the back rail, letting the reflection from the glittery design on his t-shirt cast a glare into the young man's eyes. On the front of David's shirt, the Rolls Royce monogram was tastefully done in gold "diamond dust."

The priest blushed slightly, returning to the muses of his beer.

"So tell me." David was anxious for the conversation to continue. This guy was the first live customer he'd had all afternoon. "How far down does it go? I mean, you look like a big strapping man of the cloth..." His eyes strayed down the front of the man's black shirt and blazer. "...as it were."

David's fingers dug into the rail as he said, "I was wondering where the tan stops, and where God begins." He nodded toward the crisp white collar that was a pleasant contrast to the priest's warm skin tone.

"In Christ there is no East or West..." The empty beer bottle rebounded off the rim of the garbage can behind the bar and went in on the first bounce. Two points. "...In Him no South or North." The priest gave him another beguiling look and extended his hand. "My name's Alexander. Alexander Tucker."

"Glad to meet you, Alexander." David pumped his hand, trying to match the hearty grip. "David Harriman. You can call me David. What do I call you? Father?"

"Please." When the priest said it, it came out more like a cloaked version of *puh-LEEZ.* "That's my work name. You can call me Alexander."

"If I have to." David pulled a wet towel from a lower shelf and started working on the edge of the bar near the customer. The spot wasn't dirty, but you could never be too careful. "I've always wanted to be able to call a man Father or Daddy, or one of those diminutives. Even if they *are* too young for it."

The laugh that came out of the priest was an original, David had to give him that. It was refreshing, and much warmer than any he had heard in some time. The sound of Father Alexander's laugh made him chuckle along with his own one-legged joke.

"I'm surprised you have time to make the rounds in here, with an opening line like that." Father Alexander made a waving motion with his fingers, indicating he was ready for another hit from the cooler. "Must be good for tips."

"Take a look in the corners." David directed his attention around the empty room. "Even *my* lines won't pay the rent in here on a day like this."

David reached behind himself without looking, and pulled up his juice glass half full of flat cola. He could feel the priest's eyes following the sweep of his arm as he pulled the glass around to drink. He liked the sensation, but felt an unsure twinge in his gut when he thought about who was shooting the glances. David wasn't sure if he was lithe enough to dodge heavenly lightning bolts, just in case Somebody didn't like his making a move on a man of God. "You got a new parish, or are you just in for the weekend?"

The second beer knocked too hard against the wood as David set it in front of him.

"Looks like it's a bit longer than the weekend," Alexander said. He glanced woefully down into the neck of the bottle, studying the bubbles of froth before going for the attack.

"They tell me that I'm not the parish type." The sudden shadow that passed behind his eyes was gone as quickly as it had appeared. "I'm a paranormal researcher." He said it with the same tone of voice one would use to speak about the weather. "I'm working on a little problem up at St. Aloysius."

"Shit," David muttered to himself as he wiped a long spray of cola from the front of his jeans. As he jumped for the towel, he stepped over the rolling glass that he had just dropped to the floor.

Father Alexander looked at him with total calm. He probably got that kind of a reaction from people all the time.

"Paranormal, you say." David swiped quickly at his jeans and shirt, feeling the cool stickiness of the liquid soak through the fabric. Diamond dust was not at its best when it was wet. "Like..."

"Wraiths. Specters. Demons. The occasional table knocker or household pet possessor. Ghosts." Alexander upended the beer bottle and paid no attention to the wet spot growing on the front of David's jeans from the spill. "There's a lot of business for it in California." He lifted the bottle and gazed intently at the inside, where the beer used to be. "It's a fairly spook-infested piece of land out there. I don't get a lot of vacations."

David could feel that the conversation had turned suddenly. In a way, he felt that the words had turned the attention to him, even though the priest had said nothing overtly accusing. His demeanor hadn't given away any sign that he had been reading police reports on David or that someone at St. Aloysius had let out that David was one of the suspects in the case.

"Interesting line of work, Father." David tried to back away as a new look came over Alexander's face. It was the look an overly evangelical minister gets when he knows he has you in his grips and is about to lay down a "witness," knowing you cannot get away.

"Please. Call me Alexander." He pushed the empty beer bottle toward David with the pads of his fingers, instead of slam-dunking this one into the trash like the first.

"How much do you know about the case?" David stammered, trying unsuccessfully to look casual about the inquiry.

"Only that it's been going on now for fifty years or so, and that no one has been able to get rid of the problem yet. I understand it's something of the local ghost story of choice." Alexander raised one eyebrow inquisitively.

"Oh. You mean the ... the ghosts." David was able to at least get one lung working again as he tried to will his body to relax.

"It started in 1936," Alexander said, warming up to his third beer. "Have you heard the whole story about it?"

"Not that I recall." David busied himself with trying to wash the sticky cola off his fingers.

"There were these two seminarians who lived together there. New to the school. First year." Alexander gave David a knowing glance as he continued. "There were ... rumors about them. Even early on that year."

"You mean like they may have been romantically inclined?" David leaned across the counter, resting his chin on the draught pull for Budweiser.

"Exactly." Father Alexander's face went beet red as he turned for a second back to his beer. "Finally, news made its way to the headmaster of the school, and they were called in..."

David stood up, tucked in the back of his shirt, and said, "I think you boys call it 'counseling.'"

Alexander picked at one corner of the bottle's label as he said, "Right again. It wasn't long after that ... one of the boys ... he died."

"And I take it from the look on your face that it wasn't natural causes," David said. "What happened to him?"

"He ... impaled himself." A sudden moistness came to the young priest's eyes. "Two weeks later, the second student was found hanging from a rope, suspended from the ceiling."

"Dear God." David pulled himself another glass of Coke from the tap and drew one for the priest. "I suppose they thought that was the only way out ... back then."

Alexander took the soda from David and said, "What do you mean *then?*" He took one short sip and continued:

"After that, there were reports of strange goings-on in the room for years. Finally, none of the students would agree to live in the room. Some spoke of loud laughter and rattling doors in the middle of the night when no one in nearby rooms heard any disturbance."

"That would certainly make *me* want to find someplace else to live," David said.

"Two years later, the entire wing of the building on that floor was sealed from the inside. Except in legend, it was never spoken of again."

"Until last week," David said. "When there was the..."

"It was a murder, David." A flash of fear came across Alexander's eyes that he tried unsuccessfully to cover.

So that was it. He *did* know what was going on. And this whole friendly charade had been just that — a cat-and-mouse game with David playing the supporting role. Daniels had sent a priest after him to get information. A humpy one, but a priest nonetheless.

"His name was Michael Hudson." David raised his chin from his chest where it had fallen as he tried to think of what to do next. His voice became cold and faraway. "He was nineteen years old, a student at Mary Redeemer. He was gay."

David's eyes dared the priest to look away. Alexander did not. Instead, the priest's lips moved to say something else, but they did not. Alexander's fingers trembled as he picked up the glass again.

"According to the district police, I may have been the second-to-last person to see Michael Hudson alive that night." David fought to keep his voice from breaking. There was nothing left to cry about now, except fear, and a little anger at this kind of setup. "The next person who saw him was the one who killed him."

"I'm sorry." It wasn't the normal voice that a priest uses when he says that, usually at a funeral or in the hospital room over the dying. It sounded more like he meant it. "Were you close?"

David stooped over to pick up the dropped glass from the floor. His words hit the floor as he spoke, bounced back up and slapped him in the face. "We didn't have time. I don't know," he said. "That night was our first date."

Alexander didn't say anything in reply. He scraped at an invisible moustache as he dug in his pockets for money to pay his tab. "I have to go up there and attend to this," the young priest said. "I don't think it will be easy, because..." He looked away as he pulled out a five and dropped it on the bar, asking David with his eyes if it was enough. David wondered if it was.

"I'm staying with one of the monsignors in town," he said. "I don't know how long I'll be here, but I'd like to see you again." If Alexander hadn't been dressed in that outfit, David would have taken the priest's line as a setup for a date. His voice was too friendly, especially for someone so closely connected to the Michael Hudson case.

"Sure," he said, coughing back all the emotions in him that were fighting to bubble up to the surface. "I'm always here." He thought it best not to mention his once-a-week duty as a stripper at Cinema Verite.

"So what do you figure? *Was* it the ghost in the room that snuffed Michael Hudson?" David leaned back against the bar and tried to look casual as he asked.

"I doubt it," Alexander said. "For whatever hurtful power a spirit may have, there's little to be gained by its killing a young man." He folded his arms back into his overcoat as he said, "The victory comes from leading the soul into perdition by his own hands."

As Alexander snuggled his fingers into his gloves he said, "And we both know that Hudson's death was *not* suicide."

David, feeling the lead of the priest's candor, said, "I've been to Michael Hudson's dorm room at Mary Redeemer College. Even from there, you can feel evil in the air. You can hear death."

Father Alexander looked at him as if he knew exactly what David meant. A slight flinch passed over his cheeks as he flexed his fists once more into his gloves.

"See you later then." Father Alexander turned clumsily, tightening his coat around him until, from the outside, he looked like a normal man.

"You watch your backside out there," David muttered to himself as his fingers stroked nervously over the wet spot on his jeans.

✝

Monday, 4:00 p.m.

January was a slow month in the sin business. Even though the monsignor was obliged to spend two hours every afternoon sitting in the confessional, there was seldom a taker who came into the darkened booth to bare their soul and become as one again with the Church. It was on those slow afternoons that Monsignor Odell spent a few quiet hours with his own meditations, or he scribbled a few notes for the upcoming week's sermon. On this day, he came straight to church with the stack of mail that Father Milos had left for him on the hall table. The new issue of *Vanity Fair* was on the top of the stack.

He had just gotten into the "Vanities" section when he heard the door on the other side creak shut, and the single click of the latch on the door. As he silently dropped the magazine to the floor and crossed himself, he heard the familiar shuffling of legs and feet as the repentant parishioner on the other side knelt in front of the portal between them.

Odell slid the cover open as he always did, muttering an incantation he had learned early on that had stuck with him over the years. The melodic words had the feeling of comfortable old clothes to him as he spoke each syllable:

"Draw nigh unto the Lord and lay upon Him the burdens of your heart, that you may go from here anew and walk in the light of His blessings."

He leaned over closer to the wall, peering down through the portal to the kneeling man on the other side. He had seen the top of that head before, and recognized the warm musk of the cologne that crept through the iron grille, like incense. He felt a quick moment of panic as the young man settled against the shelf just below the monsignor's line of sight, the thick, manly hands clasped in prayer, with an odd-looking plastic rosary entwined among his fingers.

"Forgive me..." the young man said. "It has been..." There was a short pause while the penitent mentally counted to himself. "...six weeks since my last confession."

"Are you sure, Father," Odell said, "that I am the one you mean to hear this confession?"

The young face of Father Alexander Tucker looked up from its prayers. Shiny lines of wetness shone in the dim light of the other side, running down the man's face. Odell noticed a slight quiver about Alexander's lips as he spoke.

"You are the one here who knows me best," he said. "And one of the few who knows why I am here." He stopped, smudged the tears away from his cheeks. He was sitting so close that his movement caused the plastic beads to click lightly against the grille. "Yes," he said. "You are the one."

Odell took a deep breath in, and then let it out slowly as he settled into his chair, looking down to see his fingers nervously fidgeting with the fabric of his cassock. He lifted his hands, looked at them as they rubbed together, feeling the cold damp between them as he said, "Then go ahead, son. I'm ready."

"I have impure thoughts."

That was the one Odell was afraid he was going to hear. Now, here at last, all the rumors that had floated across the country in advance of Father Alexander were about to come out. He felt his fingers turn inward, making small fists as he knocked his knuckles together. As if he didn't already know, Odell said, "About what, son?"

"A man."

Odell rose from his chair, turned his back to Alexander, and muttered to himself and to God, "O Lord Jesus, who commanded us to love our enemies, lead them and us from prejudice to truth; deliver them and us from hatred, cruelty, and revenge; and in *Your* good time, enable us to stand reconciled before You..." At each stanza, he silently beat one of his balled fists over his heart until its racing stopped. He pulled a handkerchief from his pocket and dabbed the sweat from his face as he took his chair. "I'm sorry, Father," he said. "Go on."

"I made the pledge to the Church the same as you, of devotion of myself to our work," Alexander said. "But there are times ... terrible times when I want to..."

"Acquiesce?" Odell finished the sentence for him.

"Today, I went to this place," Alexander continued. "While the others were busy, I took off on my own and went to a bar. A place where men..."

Monsignor Odell held up one hand to stop the explanation. "I know that you went, Father. Though I wasn't sure exactly *where,* I had a fairly good idea that it wasn't just to pick up a paper or mail a letter."

"Is it that obvious?" Father Alexander looked surprised.

Odell chuckled and said, "No. Not exactly. But there's a look to your eyes some days. A hunger for food that you've been trying to stave off for too long with just bread and wine." He could see Alexander's shoulders fall slightly as he spoke. "So tell me, Father, how long have you been in our little club?"

"Five years," he said. "And I was a postulant for five years before that."

"And in that time, have you ever..." Odell wasn't sure exactly what to call what it was that Father Alexander had once done. "...strayed?"

"Not in that five years," he said. "I put that part of my life behind me when I took my vows. And that is why it haunts me now, that I would come here, and the feelings would arise in me again. Feelings that I cannot..."

"Act out?"

"It sounds as if you know a lot about this sort of thing."

"I know a lot about what goes on inside the head of a young priest," Odell said. "It's so easy at first. You're full of the fire called down from Heaven. The parishioners like you. Your sermons are interesting. You haven't yet come to hate parish hall spaghetti suppers."

Odell was relieved to hear a small chuckle come out of Alexander.

"After a while, you get settled in some place. You get a vestry that won't give you up if the Pope himself tried to pry you out. You get ... comfortable. That, boy, is when your mind starts to work on you, digging up all these feelings from your before-life. And suddenly you become very human once again."

"But, Father, I don't want to..."

"Don't deny your humanity, boy. God knows, there's a lot about you that doesn't wash in my book of the way things run, but it's not my place to say. You have a job in the Church as do I. It's difficult, and it requires a lot of strength from you."

Odell put one hand against the grill, as if he were touching the top of the young priest's head.

"You have to go out there and fight the evil one directly. Hand to hand. I have to stay behind here and fight what he does to men's hearts and souls – what he's done to yours just now."

"But there was a man there, Monsignor. A man who worked in the bar." Alexander looked up again, the tears returned to his face. "When I talked to him for just those few minutes, I felt those old feelings coming rushing up to the surface. Feelings that I thought I had turned away from years ago. Can you understand that, sir?"

Odell fibbed and said that he could. "You know where the Church stands on this, Father, so I'm not going to lie to you and tell you it's going to be all right, because it isn't. But what I am going to tell you is that, one day, you will have to come to a decision as to which road you want to take: your vocation or your physical longings."

"But..."

"And before you protest, let me tell you that I've had this discussion with plenty of priests before you were dropped into my life. Only most of 'em had problems with young women in tight skirts."

With that one, they both chuckled.

"Go in peace, son," Odell said. "Somehow, you and you alone are going to have to come to grips with what you feel inside, and how that relates to your job as a minister of God. If it's any consolation to you, I think you're a rare find today." He looked through the screen to the slightly more relieved face of the priest looking back at him. "You are a young man who wants to do a good job, even given your ... adversity."

"Thank you, Father."

"Now. If I could just get you to start wearing socks."

"No ten Hail Marys or Apostles' Creeds for this one?"

"Not this time, son. I save those for the more minor offenses like sloth, greed, murder..."

Father Alexander was pulling his cloak around himself as he stood. "And lust?"

"I try not to deal with that one, myself," Odell said. "I'm way too old for all the machinations involved. Should you ever want to get out of the ghost-chasing business, though, you can take a seat on this side of the booth for me. We can make Tuesdays lust day, and you can have 'em all!"

"Thank you, Monsignor." Father Alexander had his hand on the latch and opened the door.

"Go in peace, son." Odell spoke to the empty confessional Alexander left behind. The aura of his spicy cologne lingered. "And pray for me, a sinner."

✞

Monday, 9:00 p.m.

"Bitch! I thought you said you knew where this place was!" Brad was screaming across the back of the seat of an over-packed Celica winding its way through dark suburban streets.

He jerked his arm as he was speaking and punched David in the ribs.

"If you don't sit your little white ass down and shut up..." B.J., the object of Brad's tirade and the driver of the car, turned completely around to address his opponent, ignoring any obstacles coming at them at sixty miles an hour. "...I'll set your ass out and you can *walk*."

David was on the bottom layer of the backseat of the car. He and four young strippers were out on a road trip. On "loan" to a place called Billy's in the upper stretches of Maryland, the crew had the night off to do a show at the out-of-town club, while the fans back at Cinema Verite were entertained with an all-star cast of boys from the featured films of the week. Unfortunately, no one in the crew knew where Billy's was, exactly, except B.J. He became the appointed chauffeur.

As Brad jumped up and down on David's lap in time to the bumps of the road and the grinds of the radio, David swore to God Almighty that he would never share a car with four eighteen-year-olds again as long as he lived.

As David tried to will his penis back under control against Brad's humping up against him, Brad turned around, looked at him, and said, "David. Pleeeez!" David wasn't sure if that was an admonition or a come-on, and tried to ignore it, even if the Peacemaker had other ideas of its own.

"I don't think this is the place where you're supposed to turn," Buck said, in the front seat. Behind him, Eric kept poking him in the ear with his finger, screaming something about changing the station on the radio.

David jiggled under Brad's weight and tried to find a comfortable position in which the center hump was not grinding into his back half as Brad tried a round of completely clothed pole-vaulting on his front.

"Do you think you could sit still for a minute?" David said to Brad, who got even more excited when B.J. looked away from the road and almost drove the car up the front yard of a Rockville ranch house. "You're starting to churn all my butter under here, and I won't have anything left for the show."

The last sentence suddenly stopped all the three dozen conversations floating around the car, as all the boys let out in concert with "Now it's time for our all-male, all-nude, all-hard-on finale," followed by assorted pockets of giggling and sardonic leers toward the backseat. David had already heard Jim say those words so many times that every time he heard the Madonna song that had been labeled his "theme song," he wanted to jump up, tear off his clothes, and start waggling his weenie around the stage. This caused certain problems when he heard the song out of context – like when he was mixing drinks at Finders-Keepers or, worse yet, when Snake found the song on the bathroom radio and turned it up as loud as it would go. Snake worshipped Madonna the same way David, years before, had knelt at the altar of Donna Summer. Snake was still very young.

At the next intersection, the car turned onto Route 15, heading north away from Washington, and on deep into the hills of Maryland. It was Eric who spoke up first, saying, "Isn't this the road out to Pennsylvania?"

"Yep." B.J. steered the car off the exit ramp, touching the pavement with only two of the four wheels. "If you follow this road all the way up, it'll let you out up around Gettysburg. Between here and there is that ghost place."

"Ghosts?" Brad jumped around once more. "Where?"

"Saint Something-or-other," Eric said. "It's a Catholic school up in the woods somewhere up here. There's a room in there that they say's haunted."

Suddenly, David's penis decided that it was time to go to sleep. David looked sheepishly at Brad, who turned around to give him the "what the hell?" look at the sudden change in the seating arrangements.

"Somebody said there was a murder up there," B.J. said. "Wouldn't want to go anywhere near a place like that."

"You just wouldn't want to go near any place that was a school, that's all," Eric said.

141

"That's not true." B.J. turned around to speak again, almost taking the whole contingent off a bridge. "I happen to be a very strong college athletic supporter."

"Yeah," David said, trying to cover his embarrassment with Brad. "You've usually got your hands clamped around some jock's jock."

Another round of laughter spread throughout the car, followed by a bolt of immediate silence. The smell that came to David's nostrils made him understand what had killed the conversation. Somewhere among the tangle of bodies in the backseat, someone uttered a plaintive "Oops."

"What the hell is that smell back there?" B.J. turned around again, making the car jump over onto the right shoulder. All the passengers screamed in unison as the long branches of white pines scratched up against the windows of the car at a mile a minute.

"I'm ... I'm sorry," Eric said. "It slipped." He sheepishly fumbled to get the top screwed back on what remained of the spilled bottle of Aramis, the contents of which were now inching through the carpet toward David's feet.

"Slipped, my ass." Buck was crawling to get away from Eric and trying to take a place of honor on David's lap beside Brad. "Smells like a whorehouse back here. Jesus. Somebody open a window."

The acrid smell of the cologne quickly filled the car, and once the heating system picked up the smell, a little heat was added to it. The final mixture, combined with Brad's full weight pressing down against his empty stomach, made David want to gag.

"I think..." He leaned forward and rested his forehead against Brad's warm back, which did little to ease the torture. "I think I'm going to be sick if I don't get out of here."

"Don't you dare vomit in my car." B.J. started to turn again, but as he did, Eric and Brad screamed, "No," and tried to push him back around.

"And how in the hell am I going to get that smell out of the back of my car? What is my mom going to say when I get back tomorrow and the car smells like somebody's been fu—"

"There it is!" Brad jumped once more, soundly into the middle of David's groin, causing David to bite down as hard as he could on the back of Brad's shirt, trying unsuccessfully to take a little skin with him. "That's the place! Stop!"

B.J. found a sudden burst of strength and heaved his right foot onto the brake pedal while stamping equally hard on the clutch with his left. The small car did an immediate nosedive in the middle of the road, and the overload of the extra bodies inside was the only thing that kept it from flipping elbow over asshole the rest of the way to Gettysburg. Once David had pulled his face out of Brad's back and was able to breathe again, he saw that B.J. was turning the car into the lot of a small, poorly lit building that had, in a past life, been a garage. Now, all the windows were covered over with a light gray paint, and a sign on the door said, "ADULT BOOKS – OPEN 24 HOURS."

"Jesus, Lord" was all David could think to say as windows opened all around the car and the subzero winds blew into his face. The cold bite of the air was a welcome relief, as it temporarily eradicated the smell of the spilled cologne from the inside of the car, and the cold slap in the face kept David from being ill down the waistband of Brad's loosely fitting sweatpants that sagged just at the base of the boy's tailbone.

"I think I'm going to like this one," B.J. said, speaking in a tone that was the verbal equivalent of licking his lips at the sight of a hot steak dinner.

"Yeah. I wonder why," Eric said as the car circled around to the back of the building where they could enter without being seen from the front door that was ten feet away from the highway. There, at the unlit back end of the building, sticking out of the shadows, was the back fender and shiny hubcap of a new Mercedes sedan. One of the big ones; and this one had D.C. plates.

"Well, I'll be damned." David's attention went to the window, as he almost pushed Brad off him and into the floorboard.

143

Before he could say more, B.J. had pulled the car to a stop beside the back door, and the cadre of strippers was piling out into the cold like the inhabitants of the clown car at the circus. David, being too angled and long to gracefully climb out of the back of the small car, had to sit on the doorsill and then boost himself up to standing. As he did so, his nose came right up against Brad's chest as Brad stepped into David's face to speak so that the others would not hear.

"You and me," Brad said. *"We* are going to share a dressing room on this one."

"Doesn't exactly look like the kind of place that puts on the ritz for the performing staff." David looked around himself at the four boys standing around, stamping in the cold, as an exhaust vent above their heads perfumed the air with used cherry-scented disinfectant. At least it was better than the smell of the car. "More like Grand Guignol, I'd say."

Brad gave him a vacant look and went ahead of the group into the building. "Whatever you guys do," he said, as they passed through the portal from the evening darkness to the room that was dark as black velvet, "hang close and don't talk to *anybody.*"

As he passed through the veil of damp heat into the building, David heard a sound he recognized from his past, a sound that jangled in his brain over the sound of the tinny speakers hidden in the ceiling, crackling out the all-night radio station banter. Somewhere, out there in the darkness, was a man, impatiently rattling his pocketful of quarters, waiting for new quarry.

✝

Monday, 9:30 p.m.

David didn't actually meet Billy that night. B.J. did all the talking for the group, and was led behind a door labeled PERSONNEL ONLY, and did not emerge for almost an hour, supposedly with the cash for the group's performance. The show was to begin at nine, and it was a quarter of before B.J. returned, leaving the group to roam around the building for sixty long minutes, fending for themselves.

Billy's joint *was,* in a former life, a garage. The old grease-stained counter was still there, holding up a cash register that was covered with a couple of decades of black grime. All the numbers had been worn off the keys on the machine and they were now uselessly covered with a layer of plastic food wrap, David assumed to protect against further damage. The cash drawer hung open with nothing but a thick wad of ones inside, and a couple of fives. Behind the counter there was a hand-lettered sign that said, "NO BROWSING," and below that, one that said, "$2.00 MIN. COINS TO ENTER."

Beside the register, there was a machine for counting out quarters. As men were buzzed into the front door of the building, they dropped a couple of dollars in silence; the attendant cranked two rounds of coins off the machine for the customer and crammed the wadded-up bills into the open till.

The man working the front counter had a young body, probably about half past twenty, but a face that looked to have been lurking in around dark corners for at least forty years. When he spoke, his lips jiggled the cigarette that never moved from his mouth, and a rattle of coughs came out of him, three words into every sentence. He smelled of day-old smoke and last week's sex.

David extended a five to the man with one hand, and held up two fingers with the other. The man handed him a handful of quarters and three damp ones which David crammed into his pocket, trying not to reason how the bills came to be wet.

Circling around the room above his head on the shelves that once had held cans of oil and boxes of spark plugs, David saw thousands of pulp novels of every genre, crammed in together and rotting themselves to brown. The books were covered with inches of dust and looked not have been touched for years. They were the justification for calling the store a *book* store to the police. Since the overwhelming percentage of the stock was in regular novels, albeit untouched, there was less chance of harassment from the constabulary, just in case last week's bribe check bounced.

On the next shelf down were the magazines, all shrink-wrapped in clear plastic, all with pictures of men and women, men and men, women and women, and one with men, women, and a dog. Each showed a different variety of sexual activity, and all had names suggestive to the activities at hand: *Shaved ... Lesbian Dildo Bondage ... A Military 3-Way ... Blacks on Blondes.* David tried not to let his eyes linger too long on the magazines with pictures of the muscle-bound naked men with names like *Hud* and *Golden Guys,* and passed instead through the low doorway into the "Exhibition Area" in the back.

There, David saw a maze of little booths, extending out through what had once been the garage bays of the building. After almost stumbling on his first step down into the room, his foot slipped on the oily floor as he moved along, trying to feel his way in the darkness around the walls.

The first thing he passed in the corridor was a lit display case that showed the films that were "on exhibit" in the room. According to the sign, one could select from any of the seven continually running videos, and each machine would accept up to two hundred quarters at a time. David wondered how much time fifty dollars in coins would rent in one of the booths as ahead of him he heard the metallic sounds of coins dropping into the machines. From the distance, he heard the screams and grunts of a dozen different sex scenes all blasting at him at once from every corner of the room. And below the sounds of the video copulation, the muted shuffles of lethargic feet in the slippery hallways.

Rounding the corner and into the darkness, David resolved himself to find a safe booth and drop his two dollars, waiting for his time to go on stage. For a second he mused that he had never gone to this great a length to keep a job before, but as this was at least an adventure that kept him away from the city and near enough away from trouble, he decided to relax, and chalk it all up as a new and probably never-to-be-repeated experience.

The first booth he passed was locked shut and inside, the sounds of the video were turned low and he could hear two sets of shuffling, and bodies knocking up against the close-set walls of the booth. From the sound of it as he passed, someone had ignored the "ONLY ONE PERSON TO A BOOTH" sign just beside the doorway.

David continued feeling around, jumping back only once, when his groping hand fell across warm naked skin that was covered with coarse, curly hair. With a gasp, he turned down another corridor, not waiting around to find out exactly to whom the skin was connected, or why it was, at that moment, naked.

The next booth was unlocked, and an unseen occupant inside slid the door open an inch as he passed. In the dim light from the video screen inside, David could just make out the plaintive eyes bidding him enter, and the three fingers holding the door just so. When their eyes met, an instant of recognition came across the eyes in the booth, and the door slammed shut. For the second time that night, David said, "Well, I'll be damned," and moved on.

He finally found an empty booth and settled himself inside, pulling the lock tight on the door as he stepped in and dropped a quarter into the slot. Immediately, a woman was screaming at him from the screen, as she busied herself with two men, each working on a different orifice. David fumbled around and found a switch to turn off the sound and then turned, looking to make sure it was safe to sit on the narrow bench in front of the video screen.

He dropped three more quarters into the slot and pushed the SELECT button until he found a screen with nothing but static. Before he could compose his thoughts, he felt something warm and heavy resting on his shoulder.

David turned around to see the largest scrotum he had ever seen in his life resting against his cheek, as his nose rubbed halfway down the length of ten inches of erect penis that was extending through a hole in the wall into the next booth. He jumped away, watching a flinch as the testes slapped back against the wall, and laughed under his breath at the notion of another man's penis sitting on his shoulder like a parrot in a cheap pirate movie. He flayed his hands around the lock and jumped out of the booth as quickly as he could move, leaving the video screen to play its silent static for another two and a half quarters.

Finally, realizing that the booths were probably not the safe haven he had thought, David settled on a dark corner away from the black lights overhead that lit the scribbles someone had sprayed on the walls with neon paint to help the customers to see their way through the room in the dark. He pushed himself up as tightly as he could, uttering curses at all of his traveling companions who had immediately disappeared into the little rooms as soon as they had arrived.

From his corner, he could see the first row of booths he had gone past, and had a clear shot of the only door in and out of the room. While he stood, thinking up a thousand reasons to quit this job and not one reason to stay, he saw the IN USE light go out on the second booth, and the READY light come on. A few seconds later, the door crept open a half foot and a figure snuck out, making hastily for the exit. From behind, David recognized the man immediately from his travels through a snow-laden Arlington Cemetery. Richard Parke stopped in the brightly lit doorway long enough to fold himself back into his parka, and to wipe his lips with a tissue which he then deposited on the floor.

David leaned back against the two walls that supported him, thinking to himself. This did indeed seem to be the place to be that night, he thought, keeping mental notes of all that he had seen. The only one missing from the picture was the dead body of Michael Hudson, propped up in some corner, waiting for someone to take it home.

David waited, hoping for a few more minutes of peace before someone made the moves on him, so he could see who else was going to come out of that booth where Parke had been.

After about two quarters' worth of time, the door inched open again and another man stepped out. In the darkness, David didn't at first recognize him. As soon as he was out of the booth, the door snapped shut again, and latched from the inside. *Three,* he thought to himself as he crossed his arms over his chest. This Richard Parke was a kinkier boy than even David had given him credit for.

The second man moved toward the door with less hurry than Parke had. This one pulled a parka hood over his head as he slowly made his way to the door. There, he stopped long enough to run his slim ebony hands briefly over the front of his jeans, pausing just long enough for David's eyes to focus on the shiny black alligator boots the man wore. David knew real gator hide, even in the dark. That's one thing Hudson's had taught him: the unmistakable difference between the real stuff and "Croco-Calf."

The third time, less than a quarter later, the light over the door switched to READY and the door swung open all the way. One leg stretched out into the hallway as David heard a voice above the racket shouting out, "David! Show time!" It was B.J. David had just enough time to see a suit pants leg and the gold tinsel of the fake family crest embroidered on the top of a Bragano black suede opera pump. $349.95; special order only.

"Come on, man," Eric called out through the darkness. David could hear their voices coming closer as the door to the booth he was watching slammed shut and the light changed to IN USE.

"Shit," he mumbled to himself as he pushed away from the wall and wandered into the direction of the approaching voices.

"Hey. Where's the cabbage man?" B.J.'s grating voice took on a particularly nellie tone as he screeched out to be heard over the electronic grunts and groans that filled the room.

"Yeah," Eric joined in. "All head and no butt. Come on, man, put down whatever you've got in your hand and let's get to work so we can get the hell out of here."

"Will you two *please* shut the fuck up." David came up behind them, grabbing them both by the seats of their jeans, causing a round of screaming usually saved for the spook house at the fair. "Let's get onstage and get this over with." He looked at them both and said, "There *is* a stage, isn't there?"

"Sort of," B.J. said. "It folds down off the wall by the bathroom, kinda like one of those apartment beds that hide in the closet. Nobody can go to the shithouse while we're doing the bit."

"Gee," David said, looking around in the darkness behind him. "A captive audience." He pulled them toward the door and the light.

"Not so fast, Harriet." Eric turned and started climbing into David's shirt. It was one of Eric's more irritating habits to literally undress men as he spoke. "We can't go on without young Brad, you know." He then turned and screamed, "Bradley!" out into the room.

A few seconds later, they heard a muffled "All right, all right," followed by animal-like grunting and a deluge of sex words that David had not thought were in the young man's vocabulary.

"He does that every time he gets off." Eric rolled his eyes and did an abbreviated impersonation of what they had just heard. "He got thrown out of his last apartment because he kept the neighbors awake. I guess you get used to it, though." He cast an accusing glance at David and popped the top button open on David's shirt. "Don't you, dear?"

"Could we *please* get this over with," David said. "I've got knitting to do at home." He closed the button as he shouldered past the two giggling strippers. "And don't you children have a curfew on school nights?"

✝

Tuesday, 11:00 a.m.

"Finders-Keepers."

"Hello. Could I ... Is David available, please?"

"You got him, doll. What you need?"

"This is Alexander Tucker, David."

David had to stop for a second and figure who it was that had called. When the face finally connected with the name, he said, "How you doin', Padre?"

"Actually, I was wondering if you would consider doing me a little favor."

David leaned back against the cash register, cuddling the phone under his chin as he gripped the side of the bar. He wasn't sure he wanted to know what the favor was, and even less sure that he would want to do anything involving this priest. "What do you need?"

"I have to take a little trip."

"Don't you still have use of the Pope's car?" David said. "I'm sure you could get a chauffeur to take you..."

"This is something that the Vatican does not need to know about," Alexander cut him off. "It's the job, and I need to go on my own. Without having the monsignor looking over my shoulder."

"I see." David turned around and looked at himself in the mirror as he spoke into the telephone. "And let me guess where you need to go in Maryland."

"I need you to drive me up to the seminary. Alone. And you can't tell anyone we're going."

After David dropped the telephone, he picked it up, mumbled, "Sorry," at the priest, and said, "When?"

"Tonight?"

"No way. I'm working tonight. And besides..."

"It shouldn't take but a couple of hours," Alexander said, as if David's predicament meant nothing to him. "You don't have to wait around. All I need is a ride up there."

"If that's all you need, then why don't you just hire a taxi?"

"Please, David. I really can't explain it all to you right now. This is important to me. I need someone right now who will ... who will understand. *You* understand, don't you David?" If the hint had been any stronger in the priest's voice, he would have put an arm through the telephone lines and beat David on the head with a pine board.

"Can I ask you something flat out, Father? Are you getting the hots? Because if that's the only reason you want me to drive you all the way to Bumfuck, Maryland, to chase your ghosts around..."

"David. You're the only person I know in Washington who is not connected with the Church. I need you to help me, because I don't want them to know I'm going. Things will go better if they don't stand around and watch over me."

"Okay. All right. You win. I'll drive you. But I've got to warn you right off: you'd better dress warm, because the Urban Guerrilla is not made for long-distance winter travel. And you had better keep your hands to yourself on the way up there." David turned to face the wall as he said, "The last thing I want is God giving me a case of boils or grasshoppers for messing around with one of His. You got me?"

"They were locusts."

"What the hell ever."

"Done deal," Alexander said.

"Hey. Watch it." David caught himself shaking his finger at the telephone as he spoke. "That's one of my lines."

☩

Alexander leaned back against the pillows on his bed, wondering what he had just done. He closed his eyes and tried to make the tension between them go away, but all he could see in his mind was the tall, auburn-haired bartender standing up against the cash register in that dingy bar, leaning forward and saying, "What'll ya have?"

He fought hard to slow the pounding of his heart as images flashed in his brain of what he wanted, other than the beer, and as he did so, he thought he heard the laughter again.

He sat bolt upright on his bed, looking around the empty room. All was quiet in the house downstairs. He had heard them all go out an hour earlier. The walls of his cell loomed over him as he sat on the bed, listening for the sound that would not come again.

In that instant he realized that he had played into a game. The opposing team had already found a weakness and was whittling away at him, even from far away at the secluded seminary and that dark room. He wondered if the call from Michael-Lee was part of this game, along with this resurgence of urges he had not felt for years.

Alexander lay back on the bed and clamped his hands over his eyes, trying to make all of the thoughts in his head go away. The longer he lay there, the stronger they became, until he had no will left of his own. The image of the bartender played over and over in his mind. The softest touch of the man's hand on his. The brush of their lips. The sensation of his warm, pulsing breath against Alexander's neck as they rolled together on the white sand beaches of his dreams.

Alexander bit down hard on his lower lip as he felt one hand work down his chest, lingering first at his navel, and then lifting away the crisp elastic band of his white boxer shorts.

✝

Tuesday, 5:00 p.m.

"I don't usually travel like this, you know." Father Alexander folded himself out of the long black wool cape that covered his vestments, and pushed the wadded roll of fabric behind them onto the backseat of the Urban Guerrilla, where it landed on top of David's emergency pair of Wellies that were just Alexander's size. Inside, the cape was blood red satin, and looked to be little comfort against the heavy winter storm. "Back home, I have a perfectly nice little car that gets me around without all this..." He looked around them at the dusty and torn seats and said, "...subterfuge."

Alexander pulled his cassock free and kicked his legs out of the folds of black cloth. Underneath, he wore a pair of well-worn jeans with bare spots on the insides of the thighs. Even with a foot of snow on the ground, his bare ankles showed out in the inch between the cuff of the jeans and his penny loafers. He had a braided string band tied to his right ankle. It was one of those surfer charms that you tied on and wore until it fell off, making your wish come true. This one looked fairly secure for the moment.

"Nice work, if you can get it." David tried to see out the side windows, but the failing heater left a light frosty skim across the windows, blocking David's view. It was already too dark to see anything but the road ahead and the occasional light from houses set far back from the road. They were out in the mountains now, beyond the need for street lights. "Did Rod Daniels put you up to this?"

"Up to what?" Father Alexander suddenly looked like an altar boy, as big circles of red spread across his cheeks. David didn't know if it was from the cold outside, or if he had caught the priest in a lie. "You mean my asking you to drive? Hardly."

"Just seems funny, that's all."

"I was doing some research." Alexander settled back into the seat. The cushions crumpled stiffly as he sat back against the cracked vinyl. "Old court records on the inquests of the original deaths in that room at St. Aloysius. Autopsy records." He blushed again as he said, "I thought of you."

"Gee, thanks, Padre. With friends like you..." David leaned over against his door, unconsciously trying to move away from the priest. He still hadn't decided if the priest was a mule for the cops.

Alexander looked at him for a long second before answering. David could see a private conversation going on behind the priest's eyes, a debate of some sort. After a long pause as David shifted gears to inch around a course of narrow curves, Alexander put his hand on David's leg and left it there. The motion at first felt like the generic move a consoling priest would offer, but David *saw* something else. Something in Alexander's eyes spoke words to him that did not jibe with the man's vocation. When David threw the look back at Alexander, the priest again did not look away or flinch. He had a lot of gumption, David had to give him that.

"You're gay, aren't you?" David said it more as a dare than as a matter of fact.

"Depends on your definition." Alexander pulled his hand away with a deliberate ease that made it seem as if he was not reacting to what David had said. Still, there was an unnamed tension in Alexander's face. He looked at David as if that last jab had hit sensitive skin.

"Don't play semantics with me, Alexander. Either you are or you aren't."

"Why is that important to you?" The priest leaned back further into his corner, drumming his fingers together.

"Because you're a priest," David said. "You're supposed to be married to the Church, and to leave all this earthly stuff behind. Isn't that it?"

"True," Alexander said. The darkness of the afternoon surrounded them, but there was still enough light for them to see. Yet it wasn't as if they were sitting together in a lit room as confession time started. "I left behind my physical affections when I took my vows." The cherry spots on his cheeks grew darker. "I love all people the same, as is my calling. What happened in the past is ... well ... it's passed."

"Don't you miss it, though? The affection ... the touching?" David jabbed at the clutch, shifting down as the car strained up a steep ice-slicked hill.

"I have the work of God to caress me now," Alexander said. Another short burst of pain crossed his face that David could not interpret. Perhaps it wasn't as easy as he described. Perhaps there was more to the story than Father Alexander was willing to volunteer. David was not in the mood just then to find out. He only wanted to get in out of the weather, in one piece.

"Sounds too tough to me," David said, placing his hand over the priest's. The man's skin was very warm against his. Father Alexander patted David's hand friendlily as they sat together in silence. "I bet they give you a rough time about it, too," David said. "Not many gay priests around that I know of."

"I am a minister of God first," Alexander said. "And a man second."

David felt the welcome swaying of the car as they made turns and stopped at lights. He drove on, pretending to himself that everything was going to turn out well at the end. David looked at the priest and knew to himself that it would not.

In the silence, he felt the continual comforting pat of Alexander's hand against his. It was a quiet sentinel in the darkness. That gentle motion of the priest's hand was an anchor David could hold onto and keep from sinking deeper into his own growing fear.

David spoke to the darkness of the cold night ahead of him out the window. "Don't you worry that you'll slip up one day, and want to go back to it?" He swayed to the right, against the priest's shoulder, as the car turned a corner.

"Holiness is not just a luxury of the pure." Alexander spoke in rhythm to the patting of his hands. "And Church is not a museum for saints."

David smiled to himself as he remembered the line. It was something that his grandmother had been fond of saying to him, years ago. "No," he said. "It is a hospital for sinners." They both smiled and said no more.

They rode the rest of the way up the mountain without speaking more than the coupling of two hands in the night.

✞

Five in the afternoon was not the appropriate time to go calling, Alexander thought as the geriatric Honda skidded to a stop at the foot of the snow-packed hill.

David looked irritable and tired from the drive up from Washington against rush-hour traffic. "Should I try to get in any closer than this?" He leaned over the steering wheel, trying to watch the direction the car slid. Finally, it stopped, a little sideways in the wrong lane.

"This is fine," Alexander said, collecting his equipment off the floorboard. "This is close enough for you."

"Staying home and forgetting this night ever happened couldn't be far enough away for me," David said. "You sure you don't want me to come in with you?" He popped the transmission into reverse, set the brake, and cautiously stepped out of the car, dancing on the ice. "Careful, kid." David's voice, suddenly tinged with a nervous lilt of moonlight and magnolias, jumped with the cold as Father Alexander stepped out of the other side of the car. "It's a bit treacherous out here."

"You don't know just how close you are to the mark on that one." Alexander wiggled his fingers into his new leather gloves and settled his feet into the borrowed pair of bright yellow boots.

"It's dangerous, David." Alexander double-checked his bag and held onto the side of the car as he made his way around to the path leading up the hill.

"Oh, and what do you call driving the Beltway during a snowstorm? Fun?" David followed close behind, giving Alexander a little nudge in the rump as the priest took the first step up, staggering to remain standing on the ice.

"Easy there." The young man's voice was soothing as it crooned into David's right ear. The priest was more firm underneath the vestments than the loose-fitting clothing suggested.

"You be careful," David said. "I don't want you to fall out here. God knows I couldn't pick you up and carry you back to the car."

Alexander stopped and looked at David with an appraising gaze, shrugged, and moved on.

At the crest of the hill, Odell's scribbled directions told them they were on the remote back side of the Mary Redeemer College campus. Most of the lights were out in the classroom buildings as they walked alone, two black dots in a field of white. Behind the library, they walked down another embankment and into a stand of trees, all heavily banked with snow in their boughs. The scene reminded David of a flocked Christmas card.

Alexander prayed intently, to make the sound of a friendly voice. His words reverberated in their muffled ears, the tones ringing with the rhythmic cadence of his galoshes as they crunched against the hardened ground. Except for those prayers, neither of them spoke.

In a clearing, they came to a large stone altar that was used in better weather for outdoor masses. The lichen-covered carvings that, in summer, told the story of the Last Supper were now caked in layers of snow frozen on snow. A single set of bird's tracks meandered halfway across the top. Above, straight over the altar stone, the statue of Mother Seton rose out of the trees, and with her outstretched stone hands, seemed to hold dominion over all that watched and waited that night.

Out through the trees and up the other side of the hill was the building Alexander sought. Carter Hall stood alone, the oldest dormitory, just at the edge of the seminary campus. They took a low stone wall that separated the college from the seminary in one broad step and kept moving toward the gothic spires of the remote cloister. Alexander stopped once, glanced around at the vacant, sleeping campus behind him, and continued, hastily crossing himself once and repeating the Hail Mary for providence.

"You shouldn't get much closer," he said to David as they came within the shadow of the silent old building.

"You've got to be kidding. I've come all this way up the mountain and you're not even going to let me catch the matinee?"

Alexander stopped and turned so quickly that David walked directly into his chest. "Now listen to me. This ... this thing is responsible for at least two deaths that we know of. It *feeds* off the suffering of others. You don't know how these spirits can be. It will eat you alive."

David stood up against Alexander and said, "I doubt that. You have to remember that I'm not quite the Bible-thumping believer in the spirit world that you are."

"David ... you can't. You simply can't go in there. Don't ask me to explain further." They had reached the back door. The entrance, cut into the back side of the building, was covered with the dead appendages of ivy that would completely obliterate the doorway in summer. The door was almost indistinguishable from the outside walls, and was easily missed by those who didn't know it was there. Alexander's key jumped into the lock and turned easily in his hands. "It's not just you that I'm worried about."

As he spoke, a sudden blast of wind shot around the side of the building, making David almost lose his balance.

"I can't have any distractions while I'm in there," Alexander said. "I'm afraid that my..." He had to turn away for a second as his fingers tightly gripped the doorknob. "...my inclinations will be used against me if you go in there."

David looked deep into the eyes of the frightened priest and replied, "Oh." He put his hands on Alexander's shoulders, patted the thickness of the priest's cloak, and said, "I've been given the bum's rush a lot of times, but I have to say yours is the best one I've heard yet."

Alexander grabbed at David's arms as he was about to step away. "Come back for me. In the morning." There was a pleading look about him as one hand almost went to David's face and was then pulled away by unseen forces in the priest's soul.

"Sure," David said. "Sure thing. We'll do a breakfast someplace warm, okay?"

Alexander looked at David as few men ever did and said, "Take care out on those roads."

"You, too, Padre." David coughed once and turned away. Behind him, in the silence of the night, he could hear Alexander's feet shuffle on the stone steps as the exorcist climbed up into the building, ready to do battle.

✞

Once Alexander had passed through the outside doorway and started the climb to the fourth floor of the dormitory, the sound from the outside was muffled in soft howls of wind that cut around the sides of the building. He stopped for a beat, listening, just to make sure that the sounds he heard were only the wind whistling around the carved facade. Satisfied with what he heard, he continued.

Inside the building, the fourth-floor wing had been completely sealed off. A false wall had been built at the apex of the cruciform building. On the inside, where the seminarians lived, hung a painting of the Virgin surrounded by votive candles. On the outside, where the ghosts lived, the stairwell smelled old and dank. Alexander paused to listen to the soft echo of his feet sliding across the dusty stairs.

It was on the third-floor landing that he felt it first: a cold wind that was sealed within the building. There were no open windows or doors, other than the one by which he had entered. He thought for a second that he heard the whisper of his name in the air that played around his head, teasing him, tickling around his legs to see how much fear was inside him.

"Alexander," he thought he heard it say to him. He shook his head, disbelieving, and continued up the stairs.

Halfway to the next landing, he heard it again. "Alexander," it said in a slow, whispering tease. It knew his name already, he thought, as he paused before taking the next step.

A strong buffet of wind pounded against him, almost pulling him over the banister as he started to move. He grabbed the railing and tried again.

A shadow passed before his eyes – more tricks. He had seen all of this before and knew that the ghost was testing him, feeling around beneath the young man's bones to find out how quick and easy this prize would be.

"I know your ways," Alexander called out into the darkness. "We are not afraid of you this time."

He stopped and listened into the darkness. Above him, on the other side of the door that opened onto the sealed corridor, he heard a slight scratching at the wood. There were short clawing noises, as if a small animal was trying to get out. Then they stopped, and Alexander stood in silence, waiting.

It was time to return the favor of running a few tests, Alexander thought as he reached blindly into his hip pocket and pulled out his purple silk stola. In the darkness, his fingertips caressed the silk embroidery on the sides. The touch comforted him as he felt out the designs in the darkness. As he slipped it over his head, he touched his lips lightly first to the golden Alpha, and then to the silver Omega. His lips felt the change in the texture of the fabric as he passed over the burn marks, left from the house in Beverly Hills.

Again, the thoughts of his failure there flashed before his eyes, and he pushed them away. He could not show a sign of weakness or remorse when dealing with evil. He *had* to win this battle. He *would* win.

"In the name of Christ, I command you out of..." A stronger blast of wind, chilling as ice, picked him up and threw him down to the next landing. The ends of the stola flapped around his neck as he fell, bundling him up like a winter scarf. He thought for an instant he felt a slight tug on the ends. Another warning.

Alexander sat at the bottom of the stairs, brushing the white dust off the legs of his jeans. He leaned back against the wall and straightened the stola against the front of his shirt. Popping his hands hard against his thighs, he tried to push himself to his feet. "So *that's* the way we're going to play, is it?" He felt around on the floor until he found the black doctor's bag he had brought with him. He shook it once to make sure nothing was broken inside, and took another step up the stairs.

A foul stench floated down to him from the fourth floor. Like something that had died and was left in the sun – or the ovens of Hell – too long. It was a smell he was familiar with, but one he could never get used to in this business. Whatever was living up on the fourth floor of this building wanted to make sure that Alexander did not get to it.

He wondered for a second about how the past exorcists had been ineffective. He realized then, as he jerked his head to one side trying to avoid the smell, that his predecessors had no power over the spirit. It was not afraid of them. At least he had this one on the run already.

Father Alexander steadied himself against the wall and pushed away toward the stairs. His back ached as he made the first step up – he hadn't landed correctly. At least this one didn't try to set him on fire like the last one did. At least not yet.

The prayer that was playing over and over in his head came out of his mouth as he pulled his weight up, one tread at a time. One foot slid across the steps as he recited each line of the prayer...

Blessed Mary ... Mother of God ... Pray for us sinners ...

Now ... and in the hour ... of our death...

Floating all around him in the air, he could hear the sounds of the laughing voice, singing his name over and over. "Alexander. Alexander. Alexander." The name floated around him in a relentless singsong until he thought he could not stand to hear it again. The spirit mocked him. It knew secrets about the priest already, and they had not even met, face to ethereal face.

At the top of the stairs, the voices and the laughter stopped. All of the wind was gone, except for a faint whine of the air blowing around the corners of the building outside. It was so quiet that he could hear the small particles of ice blowing in the air and scraping up against the outside door far below. So quiet that his own breathing was suddenly deafening in his ears.

It was too quiet, he thought.

His trembling fingers reached toward the latch on the door. Again he stopped, wondering what electrical charge was connected to the other end that he should get such a greeting on his way up. A soothing voice inside him – the intuition he counted on when he worked – told him the door was safe. On the other side, in the sealed corridor, his nemesis waited, clutching fingers as close to the door as his. The chill of touching the cold brass knob relaxed him, and he leaned forward to take a firmer grip. He was about to turn the handle when the door jerked away and unseen hands grabbed his arm, pulling him face-first down onto the fourth-floor hallway. The door slammed shut behind him, barely missing his legs as the sound of the slamming door echoed throughout the abandoned rooms of the sealed corridor.

Father Alexander slipped into unconsciousness, feeling around for his sacristy bag that had been left behind, locked on the other side of the door.

✝

Tuesday, 5:30 p.m.

David leaned against the outside wall, waiting for the nerve to start the trip back down the hill and across the campus to the Urban Guerrilla. Something in the urgency of Alexander's voice made him linger behind, waiting for some sign that it was safe to leave the priest and return to civilization. In a few minutes, he heard the sound of a door slam somewhere high up in the building, and assumed that was his sign.

David pulled the door open and peeked inside the dusty hallway with the stairs leading up into the haunted regions of the old dormitory. A single light bulb suspended from a C-hook over the door flashed on and off, as if not making a good connection, and lit the small corridor in lightning bolts of harsh white light. David took one step into the hallway and, with a sizzling sound, the light over his head was gone. He stood in darkness.

The wind behind him blew the door shut with a thud against his back, bumping him further into the room. He stumbled forward and fell upon a cold metal railing that tilted upward. With one foot feeling the way, he was about to push himself up the first step when he heard a voice come to him, soft in the night. The sound was familiar, but somehow out of place in the dark corridor.

"David?"

He froze in place, trying to assign the sound to a face. He was zipping through his mental notes of everyone he knew as he heard, "Is that you? I'm glad you're here, David."

"Snake?" He jumped back with a gasp, as if someone had punched him in the stomach. He felt the hot touch of a hand against his in the dark. "Is that *you?*"

"I'm here, David," the voice said, and with another sizzling sound, the light flashed on again, though dimmer than before.

In the light, David could see Snake, standing at the foot of the stairs, dressed in Raymond's ragged Harvard gym shorts. He dropped David's lacrosse sweatshirt as he took one step forward, his dirty bare feet scratching against the dusty floor. Inside the gym shorts was something that David had not yet seen. Or at least not in its awake state. Snake exhaled, almost hissing as he covered the space of the small foyer in a step, plastering his hands to David's chest. The skin burned where Snake's hands touched him, even through the layers of his clothing.

"Daddy," Snake said, as his hands made their way to David's belt and quickly pulled it open. Snake's tongue lashed out, leaving a warm damp spot on David's fly. The breath seared through the fabric of his jeans.

"No!" David pushed as hard as he could against Snake, knocking the boy against the handrail. Snake let out a soft grunt and slid to the floor.

As David flailed with his belt to refasten it, he looked over at the boy. There was a muddy redness to his eyes and his hair stuck around the sides of his face in greasy clumps. His face was puffy and swollen on one side. As Snake reached out to him, he saw scabrous cuts and needle tracks down the lengths of both arms, punctuated by those slender hands and pale fingers that writhed at him like eels. "Daddy, pleeeeease," he said, standing and stepping out of the gym shorts. Snake turned and bent over, spreading the cheeks of his buttocks with trembling fingers as he again said, "Pleeeeease!"

David screamed so loudly that his lungs hurt as he turned and fought to get the door open. His first try met only with resistance as he heard the child's voice behind him, pleading. With his second scream, David shook the door until it came open in his hands, and, without stopping to look back, he ran out into the snow and across the campus, the sound of the boy echoing in his ears.

He was running so hard at the stone wall that he forgot to jump and caught his shin on it, falling down the hill, rolling in the snow. The ice running down the back of his coat made him scream again with pain. After taking a few yards on his knees he was up again and running, down the hill toward the car. As he passed the altar, he heard the voice again, laughing in his brain, cajoling him and calling him Daddy. As he slapped his hands against his ears, hoping the laughter would go away, he didn't see a tree root sticking halfway out of the snow. He tripped and fell down the hill leading away from the altar.

When he opened his eyes, a tall pink-skinned old man with bright white hair stood over him. Beneath his overcoat, David could see the purple shirt and clerical collar the old man wore.

"Heavens to Betsy, boy. Where are ye off to in such a rush?" He stopped David's rolling and helped him to his feet.

For a few seconds, all David could do was tremble and cry. Words would not come to him.

"I would say you look like you've seen a ghost, but I think you just might tell me I'm right."

David's jaw flapped as he pointed in the direction of the seminary campus.

A sudden steeled look came over the monsignor as he said, "Are *you* the one what drove that car yonder up here?"

David nodded.

"Then he's already in there?"

"Who are you?" David was finally able to control his quaking enough to speak.

165

"Never mind that. I've got to get up there to him before it's too late. He doesn't know how bad that thing is." The old man's voice faded away as he wadded his cassock up around his waist and trudged off, trying to run in David's tracks. "I heard ye leaving. About as quiet as the battle of Jericho, you two. I *knew* he'd try something like this..."

"Wait." David yanked on the old man's arm trying to stop him. "You can't go up there. I saw it."

"What did you see, boy?"

David stammered and flushed, trying to put into words what had happened to him in the dormitory. "Well ... I don't exactly know *what* I saw."

The old priest made a "pshaw" sound and continued tracking through the snow.

"You can't go in there," David said. "Not alone."

"And please don't think that *you'll* be going in there, too, will you?" The old man looked at him with one eye squeezed shut. "Ah. Now I know. *You* are the one." Odell took the stone wall in one step and kept moving.

"Which one?"

The old man blushed and pulled away from David. "Never mind. Now you should just hightail it back down to your car and get back into town where you belong. This is no place for the likes of you!"

"Listen. You don't understand." David crossed in front of the man, not letting him open the door to the hallway that had again blown shut.

Odell elbowed his way past. "No. *You* don't understand. You have to go and you have to go now." He pulled open the door and stepped into the again well-lit hallway.

Above them, they could hear crashing furniture behind the walls. Screams and the sounds of splintering wood were followed by the dead thump of a body being dropped to the floor.

"You hear that?" the monsignor said. "You are the weak link in him. You bring up the weakness that the spirit uses against him. You have to go, or Father Alexander is dead as sure as you and I stand here."

166

"No." David pushed past the old man and walked back into the room, feeling a rush of adrenaline as his eyes glanced nervously to where he had earlier seen the naked image of Snake reaching out for him. "I don't believe it. A ghost can't kill you. These little noises and flickering lights are one thing." He chased the monsignor up to the first landing where the old man stopped, not letting him pass. "But if Alexander is in trouble in there, it's going to take the both of us to get him out."

"No." The old man spun him around and pointed him back down the stairs, his cape flying around in a wide circle as he spoke.

As David turned, he heard a strange sucking sound and looked down to see Richard Parke, naked from the waist down, laughing up at him. In one hand, Parke held a long gutting knife dripping blood onto the floor.

David took two steps down and saw there the naked body of Snake, convulsing in the dust as the last of his life pumped out of the gash running across the boy's throat. Parke grabbed one of Snake's legs and rolled him over with another sucking sound of steam and blood escaping from the wound. Viscera splattered over the tops of David's boots. Parke propped up Snake's lifeless hips and positioned himself between the boy's thighs.

David gasped and looked up to the priest, who showed no change of expression. The monsignor looked at David and then at the empty floor below and said, "Whatever shadow you see, you don't see. It is a ghost the thing has brought out of Hell to frighten you."

Stumbling off the steps, David inched his way around the wall toward the door, staying clear of the scene before him as Richard Parke reached behind himself to take up the knife again, raising it over his head, ready to strike the boy's back. With his other hand, he inched his recalcitrant penis toward the lifeless boy, coaxing it with gentle stokes and small giggling sounds.

"Go!" Odell shouted, pointing toward the door. "Run away from this evil place. You see nothing but what it wants you to see." The monsignor turned and started up the stairs again, crossing himself to a new chorus of screaming from behind the walls.

David felt his way to the door and pushed against it with all his weight, falling forward into the snow that burned his face. He did not stop running until his sobbing body slammed against the cold metal of the Urban Guerrilla.

✝

Tuesday, 6:00 p.m.

Four hands held him up against the wall as Alexander's eyes fluttered open. He wondered, from the unflinching grip that fairly dug into his muscles, if they had once been human hands. He couldn't tell in the dim light of the hallway. Whatever it was that held him there remained cloaked in the darkness and dust of the abandoned rooms. They pushed him hard up against the wall, and the jolt of his head hitting the plaster shook him awake.

He licked at the trickle of blood that ran down one corner of his mouth, across his lip. He had either hit the floor hard when he fell, or someone – something – had punched him in the face.

Through the cloud of darkness, he could hear heavy breathing. He could hear the sound of it blowing toward him, but could feel no breath touching his skin. Satisfied that the panting was not his own, he listened to the exertion of invisible specters that held him against the wall. What is so bad in this place, he thought, that the forces of evil would exert such energy trying to keep him away? Alexander said a short prayer for strength and tried to work one hand away from the wall where it was pinned.

"Blessed Jesus, Son of God," he began. He felt a slip of the tenons that held him. "Blessed Savior of all who come to You with repentant minds and contrite hearts..."

One of the hands released his arm and delivered an invisible punch to the center of his chest that knocked all the air

168

out of him. They let him slide from the wall, back to the floor, where he curled himself into a ball, fighting to get the air back into his lungs.

As he lay there, the coolness of the floorboards numbing his cheek, he felt a sharp tug at his stola. Both ends yanked in opposite directions, cutting off what little air was making its way down into his body. The fast motion caused him to bite down hard on his tongue as he was dragged back up into a standing position.

"Father Sister Father Sister Father Sister." The voices around him started again, mixing the words with taunting laughter. It knew about him, then. And it was going to use what it knew against him.

Alexander pulled at the ends of the stola as hard as he could, until he heard the fabric rip in the clutches of the spirit. "Name yourself." He gasped the words into the darkness as he fought to keep from falling. He would not show weakness now that he had their attention.

The laughter stopped, as did the touch of the four hands on his body.

"I command you in the name of God Almighty to name yourself so that I may know who is my adversary."

In a fleeting second he felt one of the hands brush against him, as if in a caress. He knew it was no use to move away. He had seen the attacks in California. And he had felt the grasp of that demon's claws across his own naked body, even as it followed him back to his home and jumped him in the shower. Alexander could not run from that which he could not see. For fifty years in that building there had been enough running, and secrets, and building walls where there should be none. Now it was time for him to stand, and clean house.

"You will tell me your name so that I can drive you from this place and back to your Hell."

Again, he felt the hand run across his body. A nudge against one of his breasts, and then a hand cupped the cheeks of his behind. "Sisssssster" was the only audible response.

"Be present, O merciful God, and protect us through the hours of this night..."

He heard a loud growl just before he was knocked backwards, ten feet down the hall, hitting the wall full force. Prayers and supplications angered the demons, he knew. And that anger made them weak. It was also becoming apparent that this spirit, more violent than any he had fought before, meant to kill him if it could.

"I want a name!" he said, trying to pull himself up from the floor. He got about halfway to standing when the four hands pushed down hard against his shoulders and twisted his head upward.

A sharp voice came back to him. A voice long dead that may not have spoken to living man for those fifty years. Dirt rolled among the mold and stench of the sound as the demon said, *"Thettragramaton."*

The hands loosened their grip on him again and Father Alexander sat down hard on the floor. The name was familiar to him, but he could not place it. He remembered it from way back, when he was still a seminarian. The voice began to chuckle as Alexander thought.

Seminary. That was it. Elementary Hebrew class. The *Thettragramaton,* "YWWH," was a Hebrew word for Jehovah. The spirit was toying with him before it came in for the kill.

"Obmutesce maligne spiritus." He hoped he remembered the quote correctly. It wasn't all that often that he had to play language games with ghosts, but if the spirits of the two dead seminarians wanted to play first-year Hebrew, he decided to hit them with a little grade-school Latin, and hope they hadn't died before they had the class. The line was from the Book of Mark: "Speak no more, wicked spirit."

Alexander fought to grab on to something to keep himself from levitating off the floor as he felt the hands lifting him into the air. A low angry growl hovered around him as he helplessly flailed at nothing, trying to stay close to the floor. *"Quod tibi nomen est?"* he screamed out into darkness. "What is your name?"

The hands shook him in the air, until he felt that his arms would come disjointed. The growl increased to an unearthly scream of torment as he felt the fingers working furiously against his helpless flesh.

"Asmodeus." The voices, suddenly two distinct sounds instead of one, screamed back at him from every corner of the hallway. "We are Asmodeus."

Alexander felt the blood rushing from his head as he fought to stay conscious while the shaking continued. He tried to move away from the touch of the fingers which turned to sharp pinches on every inch of his body. Asmodeus, he knew, was the demon of fornication. He had taken control of the spirits of the two boys who had killed themselves years ago in the abandoned room.

They had died for what they thought was a grave sin, and that sin now fed the unwelcome demon. Alexander's only chance for survival was to counter the power of Asmodeus with that of purity.

He began to see bursts of color before his eyes, and was about to blank out when the shaking stopped and he was dropped, eight feet to the floor. He pulled himself up, favoring his right knee where he fell, trying to support himself against the wall.

Across the corridor, he saw an image come to him out of an unused room. It was a vision, unlike any he had ever seen in his dealings with the spirit world.

At the end of the corridor, walking toward him, was the image of the Virgin Mary. A white light emanated from her robes; her eyes, the clearest of blue, called him to her in a soft, beguiling way. Beautiful dresden fingers reached for him, curling in welcome, and she smiled.

The torments around his head fell away as he stumbled toward her, repeating his prayer, "Blessed are You amongst women..."

She smiled in recognition of the words, and extended one golden hand to him, inviting him to step into her warmth and love.

Father Alexander was not sure if he was being called to heaven as she pulled him closer. He half expected a chorus of angels to sweep down and carry him away, as all in the corridor was quiet. His sensations of the evil spirits were gone as Mary waved him closer, inviting him to her, and to rest.

Just as he was about to touch her hand, he looked down to the hem of her robes and saw the scaly end of a tail extending beyond the fabric. She was an illusion from Asmodeus. He had transformed himself into the image of the Virgin to fool Alexander into moving closer.

Father Alexander screamed in pain as he felt the cut of an invisible blade ripping through his chest. It tore into him, probing his muscles, until it reached the tender fibers of his heart. There, it stopped and wrenched another scream out of him as someone unseen twisted the knife one turn through his heart. Father Alexander was lifted from the floor by the pain, and then fell limp.

As Alexander fell, he heard nothing but his heart striking its last mortal beat. The sleep that followed enveloped him; it was the slumber of the angels.

✟

Tuesday, 6:30 p.m.

Alexander Tucker opened his eyes to find himself floating in an ocean of stars. All around him were the planets and constellations, following their unending circles around the sun. He was above them all and with them all, until he saw before him the face of God.

Well, it wasn't God, exactly. Or at least he *hoped* not, as the face had an alarming similarity to that of Monsignor Liam Odell of the Diocese of Washington, D.C. Alexander had always assumed God to be a bit more ... Presbyterian.

The voice that came to him, thick with Scottish brogue and heavy with concern, called, "Come here, boy."

A hand, thin and pale, reached for his. The fingers shook once, an accent to the command for him to come forward when Alexander lingered too long. "Be quick with you, boy." The voice sounded more urgent than was necessary in that place of rest – wherever it was. Nothing seemed urgent to Alexander just then. Everything was soft, and easy: a beige cloud.

Grasping onto the man's hand at that moment seemed a likely thing to do, so Alexander put his fingers – young, thick, and strong – into those of the monsignor. The old fingers wound among his and pulled tight in knots. In an instant, Alexander was pulled back to the dark, stinking hallway of the seminary. His ears rang with the sound of a distant giggle off in the distance that he was sure only he could hear.

"Never trust a bairn..." The old man leaned over Alexander, who lay spread on the floor like a tossed-away doll. "...to do the work of a man." Monsignor's soothing hands brushed against the aching muscles in Alexander's face. In the touch of the man's cool fingers, Alexander could feel the healing touch of an advent of unspoken prayers.

"I'd thought you was a goner that time." The old man stroked his face once more, and pulled on his shoulders to help the fallen exorcist sit up. "I could feel the breath of life slipping right out of you."

Alexander rubbed a hand uselessly across his face, trying to make his eyes focus. "What are you doing here, old man? You're supposed to be back at the vicarage. Asleep."

"And damned well I would be, too. That is, until you set off half the neighborhood, trying to sneak out with some strange man in a beat-up car. There's some nosey ones that lives around me, and not much goes on in that house what they don't see." The monsignor reached behind him and pulled up the dusty doctor's bag, sliding it close to the young father. "And, I might add, you forgot *this* out *there.*" He pointed down the hall toward the door to the stairs.

Father Alexander examined the bag with his initials stamped in gold over the open clasp. "Thank you, Father," he said, picking it up and looking inside. "I wouldn't have gotten very far without this."

As he tried to sit up, he brushed one hand back across his forehead, trying to wipe away the dizziness he felt in his head from the falls, the shaking, and seeing the demon of lust disguised as the Virgin Mary. His hand brushed across a slick, gritty mark between his eyes. It was oil; probably from the vial he had packed in his bag.

"Unction?" he asked the monsignor, more with his eyes than with the word. He wondered if he was really so far gone that Monsignor Odell had started the visitation of the dead.

The old man nodded softly. "I told you. I thought you were taking the walk through the valley on me."

"I think I *was,* there for a second. Until you pulled me back to this God-forsaken place." He stood up and tried to knock some of the dust off his clothing. "Remind me to sit down later and calculate if thanks are in order for that, or an admonition from on high."

The monsignor laughed and slapped the boy across the back. "So where's the spook show I drove all the way up here in the middle of the night to see?" The cheerful tone of his voice disguised the concern he had for the young man. His eyes dodged nervously as Father Alexander tried to move his arms and legs without showing any pain.

Alexander was about to call upon the saints for help when a sudden blast of freezing wind that smelled of death pushed them back against the wall. Alexander fluttered his arms against the force of the gale while the monsignor was flattened against the wall – his long black cape shrink-wrapping him to the plaster, outlining his skinny legs.

When the blast stopped, Odell pulled himself free of the wall and brushed the deep wrinkles out of his cloak. "A bit of the windbag, this one. Isn't it?"

Alexander did not answer, but dug into his bag, which had skidded across the floor and was parked between Monsignor's feet.

He pulled a small clay font out of the case. After first kissing the inside of the bowl, he placed it gingerly on the floor, moving carefully as if it were an old and precious relic. Next, he pulled out a jar of salt and poured the granules into the bowl, carefully drawing a cross – white against the dark brown of the baked clay.

Odell couldn't hear the short prayer Alexander said as he poured the salt. He watched as Alexander stopped once, crossed himself, and ground his thumb into the center of the drawing. Reaching back into the bag, Alexander brought out a vial of holy water, and crossed the air over the bottle, muttering again to himself.

As he poured the water into the bowl he said, "May the salt and water mingle together in the name of the Father ... and of the Son ... and of the Holy ... Spirit. Amen."

The outside walls of the building shook with the shouts that came from all around them. "Holy Sister Holy Sister Holy Sister." Voices screamed through the air until Alexander rolled himself into a ball, trying to hide his ears with his arms from the torrent.

Monsignor Odell jumped up as the screaming started, abandoning his position by the young priest's side. The time for being the silent observer was done. "Down, Devil!" he shouted into the room. Odell pointed to one far corner and said, "Go there and stay. That..." He pointed to the corner farthest away from where they worked. "...I command that to be your personal Hell. Go there and do not move."

The walls shook again until Alexander thought the building would collapse. He wondered if anyone on the other side of the dorm could feel or hear, or if the battle was played only for them in that small corridor.

"He." The voice of Asmodeus echoed from far away. "The priest is ours. Go, old man, and let us take what is ours."

Father Alexander met Odell's inquisitive look with the word "Asmodeus."

"Aha." The word was short and clipped as he turned to face back down the hall into nothing. "I should have known it would be the devil of the flesh, sent to torment us."

The walls shook again, and the vibrations almost knocked Odell off his feet. The voice called out to him again. "He is *ours*. Away with you, old man, or we will do with you what we will do with him."

Alexander screamed in torment as both hands grasped his crotch. Father Odell was just as glad not to know what the demon was doing to the priest that he could not see.

"He is *not* yours," the monsignor said. "This boy is a man of God, and I'm here to take him out of this place. Alive and whole." A bead of sweat trickled down his forehead toward his collar as he balled his fists together. "But not before I send you back to Hell, where you belong. And not before those two tormented boys' spirits go to their eternal rest."

The floor buckled violently as Monsignor Odell repeated the Latin incantation. "...I exorcise you, filthy spirit, every invasion of the enemy ... every phantasm, every legion ... in the name of our Lord Jesus Christ..."

"Ours! Ours! Ours!..." the thundering Asmodeus called back to him. Behind Odell, Father Alexander writhed on the floor, his hands skipping over his body trying to fight away the caresses of the attacking demon.

"Why do you stay? ... Why resist, since you know that Christ the Lord has ruined your forces?" Odell stepped backwards through the quaking room to take hold of the priest's hand. "Cower at him who was offered up in Isaac, sold with Joseph, slaughtered in the lamb, crucified in man, and from *this*..." He waved one hand over Alexander. "...emerged the victor." He tried to shield Alexander's body with his own, but none of his actions were stopping Asmodeus.

"Get out while you can." Father Alexander turned to him. Welts like insect bites were raising over the skin of his face. "Don't let him take you down too, Monsignor."

"Bullshit, boy." Odell dropped his hand, stood and turned on the spirit again. "This is what I think of your damned

Asmodeus." Odell twisted his head around as he spat down the hall in the direction of the torments. He called out to the spirit, "You're nothing but a damned liar and a damned cheat. First, you took those two innocents who thought they'd done wrong..."

The laughter in the air started to build around him as he spoke.

"...And now, you want to take my young one here."

"He is *ours!*" the voice called out through the laughter. "We have him. We have *always* had him."

Alexander screamed in pain again as the invisible hands played with the insides of his mouth, pulling his tongue and stretching his cheeks and lips. Odell had to look away to keep his stomach from turning.

"Out, damned Satan." Odell waved his hands through the air, sending bolts of anger out into the room with every motion. "I'll have no more of you here and none of your useless tricks. Be gone from this boy and be gone from this place. To the pit of fire with you..."

The laughter grew to a crescendo and then stopped. Odell caught himself and stepped down from tiptoe, dropping his arms to his sides. His hair stood up around his face in a white halo and his cloak was thrown back over his shoulders, making him look like a wizard who had just cast the cleansing spell.

The shouting had been too much for him and he grasped out, feeling his way down the wall toward the floor to sit. He looked over to see that Father Alexander, though no longer tormented by the demons, still writhed on the floor, his hands shaking much like he had been electrocuted. "Is it over?" Odell asked. He wasn't sure if he was asking that of Alexander or of God Himself. Or of Asmodeus.

Alexander did not answer, as he was trying to work the shaking out of his limbs. God, who never works to the cues of man, did not answer. The reply instead came from the one they were fighting to destroy.

It started as a small red ball at the far end of the room. Slowly, it grew to the size of half the wall, and then, a wave of flames rolled across the floor toward them. As the fire touched the wool of Monsignor Odell's cloak, he had time to say only, "Sweet, Blessed Jesus."

Tuesday, 9:00 p.m.

When he arrived back on Capitol Hill, David went out on the street trying to find Snake, to assure himself that what he had seen *was* just a vision, and that the boy was safe and unharmed. He circled around the places he expected the boy to hang out downtown, around the hooker park, among the deserted alleys behind the quiet office buildings, and in the small park in the center of Dupont Circle. Snake was nowhere to be found, and David prayed to himself that the reason was only because of the quickly advancing cold of the night.

Richard Parke had to be the answer to the puzzle. David started walking toward Parke's house on East Capitol Street, about a seven-block walk from Holy Family. Walking fast in the snow helped to jar the shaking out of his arms and legs that the two-hour drive down from the seminary had not. It probably would have been a better idea to drive, considering the snow peppering down outside, but he knew that there was no place to park nearby, and he'd end up walking just as far anyway. As his boots slipped and crunched on the hard-packed snow and ice, he could still hear the occasional sound ringing in his ears – of Snake calling him "Daddy," and then that laugh. He picked up the pace to try making the sound go away.

The houses on East Capitol stood in a silent, white-dusted row: a uniform line of doorways and stoops standing in formation from the eastern steps of the Capitol building. There were no cars roaming the streets at that hour of the night in the middle of a snowstorm. There was only the occasional lonely Metro bus that rumbled from stop to stop, letting off and picking up tired workers on their way home from the night shift.

David pushed himself down as deep inside his coat as he could go, trying to keep warm as he walked. Still, the cold wind pushed up under its tail and bit at his legs. He stepped quicker still once he got up to East Capitol Street, hoping to get to Richard's house before he started to get numb.

The house was on the corner by a bus stop. Richard Parke's Saab hatchback with the fold-down backseats and heavily Scotchguarded carpet loitered at the curb, covered over with two inches of snow. David supposed business was slow in the bushes on a night like this. Behind the Saab, fresh tracks from another car left white zigzags on the darkening pavement as David stood for a second, watching the tread marks fill with new snow and disappear. He kicked at one of the Z-shaped marks with the toe of his boot and stepped inside Richard Parke's gate, which screeched as it swung on one loose hinge.

A light was on on the third floor where the bedroom was, and one on the first floor in the living room. Through the window, everything appeared to be in its place, almost as if posed. Coffee-table books were stacked just so. All the bric-a-brac were arranged in perfect symmetrical patterns on the shelves. A huge green velvet tuxedo sofa, a leftover from the late 1960s, faced the fireplace, which was framed with blue-and-white delft tiles. As he pushed the bell, David thought the whole room looked like an ad in an outdated magazine.

As the bell rang the second time, a large blond golden retriever shuffled down the stairs and sniffed at the front door. David could hear soft scratching sounds of the dog pawing at the other side of the wood. He rapped on the door a few times, calling out, "Richard," but got no response.

When he began knocking on the door, the dog came around to the window and put his front paws up on the ledge to see outside. When he pressed his muzzle up to the glass and then pulled away, a smear of blood stayed behind.

"Jesus." David wiped the clean side of the glass, as if he could feel the blood through the pane. "The jerk's got mad and kicked the dog." He stood up and banged on the door with his flattened palm. "What a bleeding asshole." He rapped again, knocking out the tempo of the words into the door with his hands. "Richard. It's David Harriman. Get down here and open this door before I wake up all your neighbors."

David figured that would get him down, as there was nothing Richard hated more than being connected to anything "gay" in front of his neighbors and daytime friends.

"Richard. I mean it. I'm not leaving until you let me in. I want to talk to you about Mike Hudson, and we can do it here, or I can tell my story to the police. *They* can come down here and start asking questions that you don't want to answer." The dog was beginning to whine on the other side of the door.

Finally he gave up on knocking and tried the knob. With one turn, the door gave to in his hand. The dog nuzzled his way past David, brushing his damp nose against David's fingers as he sauntered down the sidewalk and out into the street, stopping first to stain the snow piled up beside Richard's car.

As David pushed the door open and stepped in, he rubbed his dampened fingers together, kneading the sensation of the warm wetness across his cold skin. Inside, he turned up the hand and saw that it was indeed blood. He pushed the door shut and saw the bloody marks made by the dog on the back side of the door and called out, "Richard?" in a soft, clinical-sounding voice. Then he muttered, "What an asshole," to himself as he followed the trail of bloody noseprints on the wallpaper up the stairs to the second floor.

"Richard. It's David Harriman," he called out into the silent house, in case someone was waiting upstairs behind a door with a baseball bat in his hand, ready to knock a burglar in the head. "I want to talk to you about Mike Hudson. I think you know something that you're not saying, and it's better if we talk here, off the record."

He stopped on the second-floor landing. Above, the sound of Vivaldi floated through the darkness at him. It was *Summer,* an old chestnut. David had always figured Richard Parke to be more of the Stravinsky or Morton Subotnik type. No accounting for taste, he thought, reminding himself that Richard's appetites usually did run toward the mundane. After all, dirty old men had stopped doing straight hoods in the bushes sometime around 1972.

He stood on the second-floor landing, listening to the runs of the music, so familiar he could hum along. He took one step down the darkened hall toward the next run of stairs to the third floor when he heard it. A sound stopped him and kicked on every alarm circuit in his brain.

He did not hear the sound with his ears. It came into his head as his foot moved across the deep burnt orange carpet. It was a strange echo, a gurgling sound that lasted just a second and was gone. It almost sounded like a man sticking his head out of a pool of water and gasping for air, before going under again. The sound was so fast, it chilled David to his marrow and made him shiver with a sudden deathly frostiness that ran through the house. He knew in that second that he was not going to find Richard Parke in the house that night. Or at least not alive.

He stepped into the dark study on the second floor and clicked on the desk lamp. There, on top of an open checkbook, was a pair of tortoise-shell glasses with thick lenses. The frames were old and chalky, and looked as if they never saw daylight outside the house. Richard was too vain to wear anything like that in public.

David read the carbon copy left behind in the book. The last check had been made out to "Cash." It was for twelve thousand dollars, exactly. The handwriting wasn't quite the same as the three previous checks written in the book. The top drawer of the desk was askew, so David took the invitation to look in. Someone had already done a job of looking for something in there – all the papers were out of place, pens out of their slots, and everything jammed back together in such a way that the drawer would not shut. Someone had been looking for something and then had given up in a hurry.

From the corner of his eye, he saw something odd, out of place with everything else in the drawer. It was almost hidden under the paper clips in one of the indentations in the pen slots. There, from under the silvery curls of the clips, stuck out the brassy end of a key.

David picked it up, cold and heavy in his fingers. The engraving on the top said, "MARY REDEEMER COLLEGE DEPT. OF HOUSING. DO NOT DUPLICATE."

He clicked off the lamp and stood, looking out the large picture window that faced out onto the street. He could see the bright lights of the Capitol if he squeezed himself up into one corner. Below, the dog, having made his rounds of all the bushes and trees on the block, waited patiently at the door to be let back in.

Whatever the sound was that came to him, it came from above. He steeled himself, afraid of what he would find, and crept back to the hallway and the stairs to the bedrooms on the third floor.

A strange smell came to him as he got halfway up the stairs. It was a warm smell, odorous, of men who worked out in the sun all day and sweat through their clothes. David thought it odd for a prim attorney to let his house smell like the inside of a high school locker room, and wondered how many scores of young men had made the run up those stairs and left their musk on the carpet and the handrails.

"Richard?" He whispered the name, realizing he was being foolish. No one in the house remained behind to hear his voice.

At the end of the hall, a light shone out from under the closed bedroom door, and the sounds of Vivaldi moved from *Summer* into *Autumn*. He stepped cautiously down the hallway, feeling along the rail in the darkness until he came to the door.

His hand paused as he touched the knob. Instincts told him not to open the door. His gut told him to turn and run out of the house, that danger was flying toward him like snowflakes falling to the ground.

David's fingers trembled as he reached for the door and peeked through the crack of the opening. Below, he could see the bloody paw marks where the dog, in a playful mood, had pulled the door shut. Dogs are good at stuff like that, David thought. Cats aren't good for much except eating and sleeping. He had to force himself to think about something friendly like dogs and cats to keep his courage up as he pushed the door open.

As his fingers moved the door away, he heard the sound again. This time, he knew what it was when he saw the streaks of blood splattered in long arcs up the bedroom walls: his senses had been warning him of what was in the room, but, as usual, he hadn't listened.

David glanced around the once-white walls at the long rainbows of blood painted across them. At his feet, in the middle of the floor, he saw the fountainhead from which they had come. Richard Parke lay on his back, his legs folded up under him, his jeans and underwear pulled down around his knees. Across his hands and once-muscular thighs, David saw ejaculate that he assumed belonged to Richard. Where the blood had not smeared in his face and hair, David saw more that he assumed came from someone else. In between, some-one had cut a very straight line across the man's neck, from one earlobe to the other, so deep that his head lay back on the floor at an odd cant that went farther than it was supposed to.

The skin was paper white from the loss of blood − a color that David had not seen before in a human, either living or dead. All of the blood had soaked into the carpet and added to the humid warmth of the room. Even so, David's body quaked as if he were standing outside, naked in the snow.

The only thing David could do at that moment was to stand very still and gasp, trying to catch his breath, feeling as if someone had squeezed all the air out of his lungs. Inside his head, his voice kept telling him, "Turn away, you fool," but he could not. As he stepped around the room, he tripped over a low table because he was watching the body as he walked. He couldn't take his eyes away, as if half expecting it to get up and walk away.

David pulled himself away and looked around the room. Nothing seemed disturbed or rifled. He didn't know what had been up there before, so he had no way of knowing if anything had been stolen. He went to the compact disc player beside the bed and hit the STOP button as the refrains of *Winter* were about to begin. Someone had set the player to automatic repeat, so the disk started again at *Spring*. David hit the OFF button and killed the music.

"You should have known this would happen one day." He turned and began chiding the dead man lying in a puddle of drying blood and semen in the middle of the floor.

He picked up a pump jar of Anal Eze from the bedside table and threw it against the back wall. "Damn you," he screamed out into the room as the jar hit. "Damn you all to hell and back." David knew that he had lost an important connection to Mike Hudson's death. Now they were both dead. "Damn you to hell and back." The dead man had answers to important questions, answers that no one else knew. "Twice."

His knees were starting to give way, and David leaned against the headboard of the bed for support. There were O-rings bolted onto the wall just above the bed, with fresh shiny gouges where someone had used chains. He held onto a ring to keep from falling as he wondered what, if anything, would keep him out of prison now.

David stood there, leaning against the wall, until his breathing became slow and regular. When at last he opened his eyes, there was an unusual flash lighting up the blood-smeared walls. He turned to the window and looked down. There, stopped along both sides of East Capitol Street were four D.C. Police cruisers, doors hanging open in the cold, blue and red lights flashing in the silence of the falling snow.

Six patrol officers were jogging up the sidewalk, brushing past the dog and shining flashlights in the front windows. One of the beams caught him in the eyes, temporarily blinding him as he heard the first pounding thumps of fists beating on the front door.

✝

Tuesday, 10:30 p.m.

Rod Daniels's office echoed with a resounding crash as his fist formed a large dent in the side of the metal locker he punched. "I ought to put you in jail for this." He leaned over and screamed into David's face. "I ought to put you *under* the goddam jail and seal the floor after you! How would you like me to show you where John Wilkes Booth is buried?" He pulled back and paced back and forth around the room. Rod's anger at David came in short waves that broke out like surf hitting a jagged coast, and then it subsided for a few moments as he paced, before breaking from him again.

"Rod, I was going there to get information out of him, because..."

"You went there trying to do my job for me, David," Daniels screamed at the blank wall. "Damn it. I've got enough to do on this case without your interfering with my investigations."

"And you weren't straight with me. You were all full of your half-facts and innuendo about Parke and Michael Hudson. You said just enough that you knew I'd..." David gripped the sides of his chair to keep from jumping up and going for his throat. He could feel the heat working up his face as he looked down to watch his fingers flex. He knew he was wrong. And what was worse than that was the embarrassment of being caught at it. The muscles in his arms stretched and released, making him look from across the room as if he was lifting weights.

A bolt of electricity passed between the two men. If they weren't sitting in a police interrogation room with David

186

skirting a second murder charge, it could have been taken for something more. David tried to lower his voice. "You didn't tell me Richard was a suspect. You didn't tell me there may have been more of a connection between Parke and Michael Hudson than a couple of quickies in the boxwoods."

"Wait a minute. Just wait a minute." Daniels spun around, one finger pointing into David's face. "Since when are you on the salary of the district government? Since when are you on *my* investigating team?" The pointed finger balled into a fist which shook furiously in David's face. He slapped his arm away, turning again to face the wall.

"This isn't a game, you know," Daniels said. "We've got two dead men in this case now. If you had walked into that house about an hour sooner, there would be three." David didn't hear Daniels mutter, "And I couldn't take that."

"So you know I didn't kill Parke." David shot the words across the room at Daniels. Harsh and cold, they bounced off the police detective's back and returned to David, filled with ire. David watched Daniels's shoulders make a slight cringe as the detective's fingers stretched over his belt like one of those television cowboys ready to make the fast draw. "How long?"

"As soon as the stiff squad walked in the door." Daniels's voice smoothed. His temper calmed. "Parke was dead an hour before you got there. A good hour. Somebody called 911. Young ... male ... street hood. Or some guy trying to sound like one. We don't know."

"And you know when I got there because..."

"The neighbors." Daniels pulled a chair up under the table. "You were screaming out there on the front porch..."

"To raise the dead." David relaxed, dropped his grip on the chair. Finally, he released his pent-up tension in a chuckle, and then a laugh. He leaned back in the chair and laughed until it hurt his lungs. He laughed until the tears broke in his eyes and he could not stop crying, and wrenching out the pain that had built up in his chest. All the while, Rod Daniels sat, waited, watched David.

Daniels's face cracked its stony composure, reflecting the anger and panic in David's cries, but he sat, his hands resting lightly on the table. "I want you to go home. Get some rest." He crossed to the other side and gently massaged David's shoulders as he spoke. "I want you to forget about this. You're out of it now, and it doesn't concern you."

"I can't forget." David closed his eyes and felt the strong, thick fingers digging into the knotted muscles of his shoulders. "I can't forget that Michael Hudson was alive one night in my house. And the next morning he was a headline on the obituary page." David had to stop as the shuddering cries worked through him. "I can't forget walking into that house and seeing Richard Parke dead on the floor." The thought of all that blood running down the walls made him want to vomit again.

Rod Daniels didn't say anything, but dug harder into David's shoulders, rooting his thumbs across David's tense muscles.

"There's no reason that kid had to die, Rod." David let his head roll against Daniels's thick wrists, responding to the warm fingers against his tired body. "When I set him out on that corner, he was happy and relaxed." He swiped the back of a hand across his face, wiping away tears. "God. He was smiling when he stepped away from the car."

David felt the hands move away from his shoulders as he closed his eyes, pushing the tears back inside where they belonged. He heard Rod Daniels's footsteps as the detective moved across the room to the door, to the safety of a hasty exit from the situation. The detective's breath came out in ragged short puffs for a second as he massaged his temples and eyes. One rolled-up cuff of his wrinkled white shirt had worked loose and hung free and unbuttoned. In another second, he turned, pasted a weak smile on his face, and tried not to meet David's gaze as he spoke.

"I'm sorry."

"Don't be." David steeled himself again, thinking of the whole ordeal, disappointed in himself and at how easily he had been lured into a useless situation that had no future, even before the death of an innocent. Once again, it was love on the rocks for the bartender. "So what happens now?"

Daniels twisted the doorknob and stepped out into the hallway. "Forget Hudson and Parke." He pulled the door closed as he said, "Forget this case and go home to your kid."

✞

Wednesday, 2:00 a.m.

Fear, anxiety, and a hapless teenager had worked on David's nerves too much, keeping him awake later than his usual time. In sleep, he was haunted by the dreams of William, and of their long and impassioned farewell. The whole brief affair had been nothing but one long good-bye.

He also had the dream of the night with Michael Hudson. Always the same, it had ceased being sexy, and grew tiresome since the object of his affections was on ice in the D.C. morgue, waiting for the ground to thaw enough for a proper burial.

As he slept that night, languishing in dreams of the wide blue-and-green hills of his boyhood home in North Carolina, of wind blowing through his hair, and of birds calling their mates from trees, he was pulled to consciousness by a light tapping at the front door. He lay still on the bed, listening in the darkness, wondering if the sound was from his sleep or if it was real. In the world of his premonitions and visions, of his mind's hearing a man die an hour after the man's heart had gone still, David wasn't sure any more what was real and what was a vision.

He heard it again, three light taps of knuckles against the wood.

He didn't know who it could be at that hour of the morning, but assumed it was one of the neighbors in trouble or a problem in the building. He pulled a sweatshirt on as

189

he stepped carefully down the stairs toward the door. The heat was turned back and there was a slight chill in the room.

He opened the door to see Snake standing there, wrapped in his light baseball jacket, shivering. It didn't look like the cold, though. It was shock.

Snake stared straight ahead, beyond David into the darkness of the apartment. His hair was mussed, one spike in the back stood straight up in a white-blond finger. He looked as if he was going to fall down as he looked at David and muttered, "I don't want to do this any more."

David took the boy by his shoulders, trying to awaken him from whatever trance held him, and gently brought Snake into the room. The hallway was stifling with heat compared to the living room. He turned on a light and flicked up the heater control as he silently pushed the door shut.

"You look like hell." He slid the chain and twisted the deadbolt. "Tell me what happened." It was the dead calm in him that spoke, that gnawing ability to stay perfectly cool at the moment when everyone else flies off in panic. He could read trouble in the boy's eyes. Trouble and fear that Snake would not – or could not – put into words.

"Do you think I could sit down first? I'm freezing to death."

David pulled the fuzzy blanket out of the closet to wrap around the boy. "Give me that jacket," he said. "I'll hang it up for you."

Snake unzipped the jacket without looking at the pull. As he opened the coat and moved his arms out of the sleeves, David saw the splatters of blood on the front of what used to be a solid white t-shirt. David dropped the blanket and almost tripped over it getting to Snake. "Oh dear God, boy." He spun Snake around, checking for exit wounds or other damage. "Who did this to you?"

"That? Oh. It's nothing." He swiped at the dried stains. "Not mine."

David didn't wait for further explanation. He grabbed the neck of the shirt and ripped it down the front, pulling it away from the boy's body. Snake jumped back, gasped, and flinched, half expecting a slap to follow.

"Out of the jeans, too. Come on." He didn't mean to talk rough to the kid, but it was the panic working in him, bubbling to the surface. If there was any kind of damage to the boy's body, he wanted to deal with it posthaste.

He was relieved to see no wounds on the kid's chest or back.

As Snake peeled off the layers of clothing and David saw he was all right, the shivering slowed until it was only in the boy's hands. He wrapped the blanket around himself and settled into the soft cushions of the sofa.

"Talk to me." David sat down beside him, feeling all the nerve endings in his skin bristling and alive with electricity. "You knew where to go to get warm. Hell! Why didn't you just come here if you got cold?" He fought not to yell at the kid as he pulled down the sharp tone of his speech.

"I didn't want to interrupt."

"Don't give me your shit, kid. I'm not one of those bumpkins out there on the street. Why do you think I didn't take the key back and throw your ass out of here if I didn't expect you to use it?"

"David."

"Yeah, what?" After his immediate panic wore off, it was replaced with anger. He wanted to give the boy one of Madge's famous speeches, but Snake wasn't his kid. Snake was as much of a responsible adult as he was.

David slapped himself mentally for thinking of Snake as an adult. He was fourteen years old, for Christ's sake.

Snake looked up at him, his face blank but with eyes that begged. "I'll give you everything I have, if you'll let me stay here tonight." He picked up the jeans from the floor, dug his hand in a pocket, and brought out a wad of bills. There must have been five thousand dollars in hundreds and fifties there.

"Lord, child. Where'd you get that kind of money?" David took the bills from him and started unrolling and flattening them out. The hoods on the street would slit your throat for pocket change. David was amazed the kid had survived the trip across town with all that cash on him.

"Some of it I earned. Some of it..."

"You stole." David counted the pile of bills neatly on the floor in front of them. It was $7,950.

Snake's eyes held back the tears as he spoke. "You've got to believe me, David. For whatever else I've done, I never stole. That money was mine. I took it from..." His voice trailed off as he stepped too closely to the topic of his past that he would not discuss.

"You're still shaking. Can I get you another blanket? Some cocoa?" He was dying to ask the boy what had happened to drive him back to the apartment, splattered with blood, but he also wanted the situation to stay calm. No crying children, and no screaming underemployed redneck bartenders.

"There was this guy, you see." Snake's eyes welled with tears and he snuggled deeper into the blanket. Only his head stuck out of the blue-and-white folds. "He picked me up and took me back to his place in Georgetown." He looked away, wiping his face with one flattened palm.

"A trick." Sirens and bells were going off so loudly in David's head that he wanted to get up and run away from the kid. He wanted to scream and kick holes in the walls. He didn't want to hear about what someone would pay to do with a fourteen-year-old boy, but he had no choice. He kept all the screaming on the inside and drew all the emotions off his face, in order to get the story out of Snake.

"Yeah. He said it was worth three hundred to him, and there'd be no sex." He turned and faced David with a look that was too honest. It was the guileless look of a child speaking of things adults should never have to say. A look that burned into David's memory in a place where it would haunt him for the rest of his life. "David, I don't *like* sex very much."

David had to put his whole fist in his mouth to keep from crying out. He took one long breath that pushed tears of anger out on his cheeks.

"He took me into his living room and took off his pants..." He stopped for a second, looking away. "Then he straddled the coffee table ... and sat down."

"What did he want *you* to do?" David was afraid to ask, seeing again in his mind the sight of the shivering kid at his door, and the shirt splattered with blood.

"He wanted me to..." Snake leaned over and rubbed his forehead against his knees. David heard a short burst of crying and stroked the back of the boy's head.

"You're safe now. Nobody here is going to hurt you." David forced his voice to sound as soothing as possible. He wasn't used to being so nurturing to someone. He hadn't done it since he'd had to console Madge when his father died.

"See." David rubbed the cat with his toe as Andy Frank curled himself up against the folds of blanket around the boy's legs, begging for attention. "Even the worthless brain-damaged cat wants to take care of you." The smile in David's voice sounded too fake.

Snake took a long, jerking breath as he sat back up, rubbing at his red eyes. "He gave me a hammer and a nail," he said. "And told me to nail his balls to the table."

David had to turn away to keep the boy from reading his face. He wasn't sure if he wanted to vomit first, or faint as he grabbed instinctively for his testicles, rolling himself into a ball on the edge of the sofa.

"There were these nail marks on the table where it was done before." Snake continued speaking as David writhed on the sofa, trying not to lose his dinner, trying to wrench his right hand off his penis where it was locked like a chastity belt.

"And there were these marks on the sack. Scars..." Snake spoke in a monotone, as if reading a description out of a book. David rolled his face into the cushions and screamed into the sofa, trying to muffle the sounds.

"When I drove the nail through the skin ... this blood shot out ... all over the place. It was on my hands and on my jeans. Some of it got in my hair."

David was panting, trying to catch his breath, realizing that hyperventilation was only going to make him pass out faster.

"When the nail was halfway into the table, that's when he ... he got off. I took the money and ran out. Left him there. I couldn't look back."

David lay back against the cushions, sweat rolling off his forehead. His eyes had rolled back in his head and he couldn't get them to work right. "Did you get any of the blood or semen in your eyes or mouth? Do you have any open cuts or scrapes?"

"No. I'm careful about that stuff."

"You need a bath."

"Took one before I came here. I had to think what to do next. You were the only one I could think of to talk to." Snake sat back against the sofa. Telling the story had taken the tension out of his body, and most of the shaking from his hands. "They'll laugh at me," he said at last.

"Who?" The statement woke David up, brought him to full attention.

"The other guys. They'll say I chickened out."

"Bullshit. You know how much nerve it takes to ... to do that?"

"They pick on me anyway."

David realized there was more to the story than just the bad trick. "Because you're younger?"

"Not all that young, you know."

David had a sudden insight that, at fourteen, Snake was over the hill for one whole set of johns, while not yet even in his prime for another.

"No," Snake continued. "They pick on me because I'm the only one who doesn't do it with girls." The last part trailed off so that David could barely hear what he said.

"What do you mean *do it?*"

194

"You know. Like you." Snake's face went dark crimson as he mumbled, "They call me names and stuff because I only like guys."

"Sorry to disappoint you, kiddo, but I *have* 'done it,' as you say, with women. I prefer men."

"I know."

"Do you think that makes me any better or worse a person? Not that I give a shit what some mangy little kid like you thinks, but..." He scraped the boy's hair again, making Snake smile through the tail end of his tears. "It's nice to know."

"Sometimes, I think I'm the only kid like this. I'll never be like everyone else, will I?"

"No, child. You're not the only one. And thank your stars for that. There's too many 'everybody else's' in the world for us to need one more. We need a few Davids and a few Snakes, to keep everybody else in line, don't you think?"

"What about you? Were you like ... like me when you were a kid?"

David always knew the moment would come when he would have to give the old "When I was your age" speech. He only hoped it would be to some recalcitrant college basketball player and he would be the white-haired dirty old man bribing with candy bars and comic books. No such luck.

"Yeah, I guess I was. Even way back then. Thought I was the only one in the world, too." Funny, he thought, about how they never do a unit in Sex Ed. or Home Ec. about how to grow up and be a real gay person. That would have been more useful than learning about ectopic pregnancies, and listening to the horror stories his female friends told about learning to sew.

"Trust me, though. I learned better later." David opted to leave out another rendition of his torrid affairs with the Northwestern Academy basketball team when he was in high school. "That was just before Edison invented the electric light, as I recall."

Snake laughed and hugged him. The laughter stopped quickly and gasps of crying overtook the boy. He leaned on

David and cried as if his heart would break. David held him close until it passed, feeling the warmth of the boy's tears and spittle soaking through his sweatshirt. Sometimes, a kid just needs to have a good cry; he often wished he could do the same.

"I think you need to find another line of work, young man. Like, maybe school."

"I've got a fake ID. Can you get me in? I really want to go back. I can study at the library and I won't make a mess around your house. I can feed the cat and..." Snake's eyes shone with a fresh batch of energy. The events of the night looked already forgotten, if David didn't know better.

"Hold on, now. Let's not get excited about this. There's plenty of time to discuss this over breakfast, which is in..." He looked at the clock in the kitchen. "...in three and a half hours."

The boy settled down, but the light still shone in his face. David felt doomed to an obligation of parenthood with a street kid flashing ten grand and a fake ID.

"You stretch out here, and we'll deal. In the morning."

Snake did as he was told, stretched out full length on the sofa and said, "Thanks. Daddy." The last part sent him into gales of giggles as he wiped the last of the tears from his cheeks.

"Jesus Christ, a man my age being called 'Daddy.' What will my friends say?" He clicked off the light and went up the stairs in darkness.

David went into the bathroom and sat on the cool wooden seat of the toilet. The room was bright and white under the fluorescent lights. Unreal. A sound stage. He remembered the sight of the kid, and those haunting words, "I don't want to do this any more." He remembered the look of terror as he ripped the t-shirt from the boy's chest, and the cold senseless look as Snake told of driving a nail through a trick's scrotum for three hundred dollars, cash.

He turned on the water in the shower full force to make some noise. Then he was sick in the toilet, tears of rage falling into the water.

✟

Wednesday, 8:00 a.m.

The next morning, the streets were silent, as the early-morning traffic either had not appeared or was hampered by the additional layer of snow that had fallen the night before. David Harriman sat on the edge of his bed, head in his hands, and wondered what was to become of the boy sleeping on the sofa downstairs.

"Snake." He coughed the name out too softly to be heard. David cleared his throat and tried again. "Snake. Could I talk to you for a minute?"

In a few seconds, he could see the boy's head peering up over the top of the stairs as he came up, wrapped in a sheet, the baggy arms of David's lacrosse team sweatshirt balled up around his elbows. "Are you mad at me?" he asked, as he tiptoed across the room and stood at the foot of David's rumpled bed.

David patted his hand on the mattress beside where he sat, inviting the boy to sit down. "I want to ask you something," he said. "Not about last night. This is something else." As Snake sat beside him, David scooted back and curled up against the headboard, covering his shivering legs with the still-warm blankets.

The boy looked at him with the eyes of an innocent, but there was something too rehearsed about the look. David assumed it was one of the expressions that came across the boy's face when he was on the prowl for business – one that earned him extra money above the base rate.

"I want to ask you about a certain man I know, and I want you to tell me if you've ever heard of him before."

"I'll try," Snake said, pushing up one sleeve that had fallen down over his arm. "But a lot of them either don't give a name, or they don't use their real one."

"This man is Richard Parke," David said, watching as no hint of recognition came across the boy's face. "He's an attorney downtown and his home is not far from here on East

Capitol Street. You can see the dome from his front door."

Still nothing from the boy.

David tried to remember the decorating scheme inside of the house and said, "I think there's gold-colored carpet on the floor, and his bedroom is on the third floor." David stifled a gulp as he thought of the bedroom with the bolts sunk into the walls over the bed with the fresh gouges. "He has a golden retriever."

"Rickie!" Snake said, almost jumping on the bed. "I know him, sure!"

"Please, child, let's not get too excited here. We're talking about a man who probably committed some sort of a felony on *your* body." David crossed his arms and tried unsuccessfully to sound adult.

Snake blushed and said, "I was only there once, and that was ... probably three our four weeks ago." After a few moments he added, "It was with him and..." His voice lowered almost to a whisper as he said, "...this other guy."

"Oh Jesus, Lord, child, I *really* don't want to hear this," David said, more to himself than to the boy. *"Two* of them?"

Snake's face blazed red as he explained, "Rickie and the other man did most of the..."

"Never mind," David said, putting his hand over the boy's. "You really don't have to tell me this if you don't want to."

"Oh I don't mind," Snake chirped at him.

"That's what I was afraid of."

"...But most of the ... the stuff happened between Rickie and the man. After a while I went off to play with the dog downstairs. His name was Sloose and he liked to fetch."

"Who was the other man?" David said. "Did he use a name?"

Snake squinted up his eyes. "Not as I remember. He was ugly, I remember that. Kind of fat around the middle, with a teeny little..."

"Yes." David tried to cut him off. "I think I get the picture."

"He was really gross," Snake said. "After he got all his clothes off I didn't want to touch him." The boy looked up at

David, taking his attention away from the nap on the blanket as he said, "There was this big red blotch down the front of his chest and around his fat belly. Made him look like Frankenstein. But that's all I can remember about him, David." Snake looked up at him, his eyes begging for approval for what he'd said. David's shocked expression gave him none back.

"At least that's *something,*" David said, his mind no more at ease than when they'd started. "But can I ask you something else?"

"Sure. Shoot." Snake curled closer on the bed, kicking the sheet away, his golden legs extending below the ragged bottoms of Raymond's old gym trunks.

"I'd like to know where you got that money you showed me." An image flashed in David's mind of the desk in Richard Parke's den, and of the check made out to "Cash" written in a different hand than the others. He wondered in that second if Snake, as young and innocent as he looked, was capable of slitting a man's throat and then forging himself a check for the trouble.

A shadow passed over Snake's eyes. He frowned and said, "I knew you wouldn't believe me about that money. It's mine. All of it. I earned it."

That was just the answer David was afraid of hearing, the one that did nothing to ease his ill feelings toward the boy as he sat and watched Snake pat the mattress, beguiling the cat to join him, watching Andy Frank fall over the boy's hands and kick his paws up into the air as Snake rubbed the cat's throat.

Impossible, David thought, shaking the doubt from his mind as he kicked away the blankets. His legs had started to sweat. Even if Snake had the wherewithal to kill Parke for the money, which seemed too farfetched to him, what could have been the possible connection between Snake and the death of Michael Hudson? Snake, not having a car handy, would have had difficulty getting Michael's corpse up to the school, even if the boy had known where it was. David decided to dismiss the whole scheme, though the newly found money haunted him as sure as did the scene visited upon him at the seminary. There remained only one clear solution to the Snake situation, and the thought of it caught in David's throat as he scowled at the boy and stepped off the bed.

"Let's go get something to eat," David said, leading Snake to the stairs with one hand. And as the boy shuffled down the stairs, cat in tow, David realized that his appetite had suddenly disappeared.

✞

Actually, it had been gnawing at him, probably from the first time the boy came into the apartment. Maybe that first night that they shared ham sandwiches and discreet distrust for how far each of them would go. Maybe it was the second night, with Snake showing up with a week's worth of groceries, being more of a spouse than any David had ever had, only to turn into the child that David probably never was.

"I'm sorry," was all that Snake said over breakfast, as David poked at a sausage with his fork, and repeatedly let his coffee get cold in the mug. "I'm sorry I came here and told you what I'd done." Snake's words reflected up off his plate and at David. Snake coughed once and scratched his neck, looking away.

"You told the truth, boy, and that's nothing to be ashamed of." David went to the sink and dumped his cold coffee down the drain rather than reheat it one more time. He didn't have the stomach for coffee that morning. "If I don't teach you anything else in this life, remember that you should always tell the truth to me, no matter how scary and how awful that truth really is."

Snake looked up at him, a tiny glimmer of light in his eyes.

"You are a worry to me, boy, I want you to know that." David sat down and pulled his bathrobe tight around his knees as he slid his feet up under his chair. "Here you are, running around all over Kingdom Come with all kinds of money in your pocket."

Snake started to speak, but David was quick to cut him off:

"No. That's your money and your business, and I don't want to know any more about it. But I do want to make one thing absolutely clear to you."

"What's that?" A slight curl stretched the corner of Snake's lips as he looked at David, choking back a glimmer of release that passed across his face.

"As long as you are living here with me, there is no reason for you to steal, and there's no reason for you to hustle your butt on the street. If you need money, you ask. Got me?"

A single tear slipped down the side of the boy's face as his smile broke forth in one quick guffaw he then tried to hide.

"Now, I've got company coming over this afternoon, so you need to make yourself scarce..."

"It's that cop again, right? The one who looks at you funny."

"Never mind." David clanked his spoon hard against the rim of his cup as he stirred. "But listen up. I want you to go back to wherever it is you've been hiding out, and get your stuff together. I've got a little business to take care of tonight, and then I want you here where I can keep an eye on you."

"It's going to take some time," Snake said, "a few days, maybe, to round up all my stuff and get it ready."

"You just make sure that's all, then, a few days. And then, you're here with me." He dunked a triangle of dry toast into his tepid coffee as he muttered, "And may God have mercy on my soul."

Snake jumped up, dropping his knife and fork on the floor with loud rattles as he made for David, all arms and hugs. "I guess that means school and everything, right?"

"Get off me, you little fool!" David bit down hard on his upper lip to keep from laughing out loud with the boy. "Of course that means school, and none of this lovey stuff is going to get you out of it, either. And another thing, when was the last time you bathed on a regular basis?"

But, it was too late. The boy was already off, scampering around the apartment, chasing the cat under the furniture and rolling on the floor, giggling as Andy Frank tried to take out the boy's face with a smack of his forepaws.

"I suppose I'll have to try to get you into St. Alban's School," David sighed and tried to push the uncooperative wisps of hair out of his eyes. "Your grandmother will kill me if I don't."

"Grandmother?" The play time suddenly stopped as the boy and the cat both sat up on their haunches and sniffed the air at the mention of Madge Harriman.

"Yes, dear, you have a wonderful old woman with bad taste in clothes who is your grandmother, though I dare say it will be the ruination of her retirement to hear the 'G' word and her name used in the same sentence."

"How about me being a..."

"Fairy in training? Well, I daresay that once she gets over the shock of my presenting her a fourteen-year-old grandson when she didn't even know that I was dating, she will not have much to say about you being a member of the church."

Snake had picked up the cat and was snuggling the animal around his neck like a muffler as David spoke.

"Just do us a favor and please do not let my mother catch you in a dress..."

Snake's eyes became the size of saucers. The thought of dressing up in anything that did not have denim legs and steel grommets on the corners of the pockets had obviously never dawned upon the boy.

"...She can't accessorize for shit."

They both rolled on the floor, laughing and chasing the cat, who was more than ready for everyone to go away and let him get back to the business of sleeping.

As they sat on the floor, David stopped quickly, and, wiping the tears of laughter from his face, had a sudden flash in his mind of what he had just done. For that one fleeting second before he swept the boy up and pushed him off to the shower, David knew how the other side felt. He knew the feeling of the hard-working man who got the girl knocked up and was suddenly saddled with the baby to raise. He knew in that second, as Snake retreated into the bathroom and started tuning the radio to that same jazz station he always listened to, that his life had just changed forever. There was no going back.

David tried to remember the feeling, and hoped that he would live to feel the same way about the kid the following day.

☦

Friday, 9:00 p.m.

Snake was waiting right where he said he would be. Cold January winds whipped around the corner of South Capitol and M as the young boy stood, huddled up against the old church, keeping a protective eye on the four plastic trash bags bundled in frozen wads around his feet. He jumped up from the protective shelter of the building's portico and ran out into the street as the Urban Guerrilla rolled to a stop on a dry spot of pavement.

David stopped the car and bounced out into the cold to open the trunk. The lid popped back against its springs two or three times as Snake stepped quickly toward the car, three garbage bags in tow. He lifted them with ease and dropped them into the trunk, running back for the last one without speaking.

"You lived close by here?" David stepped back into the car as quickly as he could, leaning across the seat to unlock the passenger door.

"Doesn't matter now," Snake said. He pulled the door shut with a heavy slam as David released the parking brake and coasted away from the church. "Looks like I've got a new place over across the other side of town now." Snake pushed the recliner lever and leaned the seat backward until he was almost lying down.

"Don't get used to it." David patted Snake's knees as he winced at the bright light shining in the rearview mirror.

He tried twisting the mirror up out of his sight.

David squeezed the steering wheel and pushed the car faster. "Damn rednecks. Don't they know it's against the law to drive with your high beams on in the city?"

Snake popped the seat upright and turned around to stare out the back window. "Don't look like rednecks to me. Those are some really fly wheels."

David could see the front grille of the car in the mirror on his door. He'd seen it before, assuming there were very few people in town who drove a 560 SEL with a gold-plated grille. "I think we've got company." He tapped the accelerator with a quick staccato, in time with the increasing tempo of his heart. David didn't like what he saw, and he knew in that second that the cataclysm was only beginning. "We might be in a little bit of trouble here."

He tried going faster, but the car behind never fell away from his back bumper.

"This can't be happening to me," he said, swerving the car to the left across South Capitol Street, running interference down M Street, toward the waterfront.

"Who?" Snake plastered his face up against the window glass as he tried to see out into the street and into the speeding sedan that was closing on them. "David, who is that back there?"

As he spoke, they felt the car lurch as the Mercedes butted up against the rear of the Urban Guerrilla.

David pulled down the rearview mirror and shielded his eyes against the glare, as he squinted to see into the car. A short black man drove, his head barely clearing the top of the steering wheel. In the passing glare of street lights, David recognized the driver's grin at once. Vinnie the Popper had finally gotten his wish for the ride of his dreams. He had stolen Granville Hudson's car. Or Granville Hudson had given it to him.

The sedan rammed up against the back of the Guerrilla again as Snake grunted an "Ouch." The sound was more reflex than a signal that he was hurt. "You've got to get us out here fast, David. I think that guy's trying to run us off the road."

"No shit, Sherlock," David mumbled to himself under his breath as he jerked the car around on the ice and headed back out toward South Capitol Street. He figured they would be safer out on the main thoroughfare in the rush of traffic than back on the side streets where most of Washington's murder statistics were written. As he spun the car around into the main street, the sedan slammed into the back corner of David's bumper and pushed the Guerrilla sideways into traffic.

Snake was unusually quiet. He braced his feet against the fire wall as David pushed the gas and stopped their sideways motion. Three cars that were coming toward them swerved into the other lane and sped past, not slowing.

"You know that guy?" Snake eyeballed David without turning his head. His fingers flicked at the dashboard, debating whether to grasp on as David pushed the car closer to sixty over the patches of ice that stuck to the road.

"Yeah. I know him." David swerved into the outside lane, trying to control the tail end of the Guerrilla as it swung wildly across the lanes. The car behind them made the lane change without even crossing over the outside white boundary lines of the street. "He's a little slow, but he's a friend of mine."

"Slow?"

David throttled the car again as they came up on a red light that they did not take. He knew they were heading into the wrong end of town for a car chase with a shoplifting maniac in a hundred thousand dollars' worth of recycled German beer cans. He knew this was going to get ugly. Real fast.

"I think our friend Granville Hudson made a deal with Vinnie to get me out of his hair."

The car rattled loudly as the sedan rammed them again, pushing them off the roadway and up on the sidewalk. David fought the wheel to get back onto the asphalt. He yelled to be heard over the sound of the crashing metal and the front tires bobbing on and off the curbing. David heard the sound of something rubbing on the undercarriage of the car, and he wondered how much longer he had before large chunks of the car started falling away.

"Up there." Snake pointed forward. "Take the Fort Mc-Nair Loop. It'll take you around the back of the Federal Center and the Navy Yard." It was a circuitous maze of little half-deserted streets filled with boarded-up buildings, rusting cars, and abandoned lives.

"Are you nuts, young 'un? If he catches us back there, we're dead. At least out here we have a running chance."

"Get real." Snake was reaching for the steering wheel. "There's no way you can outrun a 560 in this old thing, even if you do drive like a barefoot redneck from the hills."

"Oh." David veered the car across six lanes of late-night traffic, making a left around the back of a deserted souvenir company warehouse. "And *you* are now going to give me driving lessons!"

Before he could finish the last word, the back window of the Urban Guerrilla exploded, sending bits of glass throughout the car.

"Heads up, kid. The man's got a gun." David tried to cram the boy down as far as he would go into the floorboard. With his legs jammed against the fire wall, Snake wasn't moving. "Get *down.*" He pushed on the boy's shoulders. "I don't have time right now to be scraping your brains off the inside of my car."

"Don't you worry about me." Snake spread his knees and slid down until he was wedged up against the dash. "You just lose this guy!"

In the next intersection, Vinnie the Popper tried to pass. They heard the cracks as more bullets dug into the back fender on David's side. David prayed that the gas tank wasn't close to where the bullets were hitting. He had a sudden itch under his arms and found it funny that he would notice something like that, while they were running for their lives through the back streets of southeast Washington.

As he looked up, David saw an old station wagon coming at them head-on. In the second it took him to react, he could see the screaming expressions of a half dozen faces coming directly for him. Snake screamed once and slid further down toward the floor as David pulled the wheel a hard right. Vinnie, who had to go in the opposite direction to avoid cutting the wagon in two, went left.

David took fast advantage of getting away from Vinnie, and pulled the Urban Guerrilla into the parking lot of Commodore Limousine Service. The Honda stopped between two battered and rusting Cadillacs that had been left on the fringe of the lot to die. "I think we'll be safe here." David killed the engine and clicked off the lights.

Even in the dim light of a crackling street lamp, he could see the sharp look of panic on Snake's face. But it was not from the killer prowling impatiently up and down the back alleys looking for them. It was a wide-eyed look of alarm as Snake tried to smear blood off his fingers onto the seat. The kid didn't say anything, he just looked at David and rubbed his hands.

It was too risky to turn on the interior light to see what was the matter, but David had to. He felt a wave of guilt that he had dragged the boy into his personal troubles, and now the kid was hurt. Maybe shot by bullets that Vinnie had meant for David.

"Jesus Christ, boy." David stared back at him, neither of them moving. They sat, unable to turn away from the blood on Snake's hand.

When he could stand it no more, David reached above him to click on the overhead light. As he did, David felt all the air rush out of his lungs as a bolt of pain knocked him into unconsciousness.

He awoke with Snake outside the car, trying to push him across the seat. It hadn't been an itch under his arms. One of the bullets had pierced the door and had gone into David. The driver's seat and door were damp with his blood and made him slide off the seat as Snake worked strenuously to get David out from under the steering wheel.

"Get over there," Snake huffed at him as the boy pushed against David's flanks. "We've got to get out of here before he comes back." Snake stopped and leaned against the open door, panting long white bursts of steam into the cold night air. He mopped at a trickle of sweat on the side of his face with hands warm and sticky with David's blood.

"You can't..." David tried to sit up, but could not. He crawled over the center console, dragging himself with the tight end of the seatbelt. He could feel his teeth digging into his tongue and his mouth filling with blood as he stifled pain-filled screams. "You can't drive us out of here."

"The hell I can't." Snake jumped into the car as soon as David was out of the way. "We can't stay here all night. We'll freeze to death." He twisted the ignition. The Guerrilla grumbled once at him and died. "And you need some help." He scraped the palms of his hands across his jeans as he leaned into the clutch to try again.

On the second try, the motor caught and the car was running. Snake slowly pulled out of the parking lot and into an alley running parallel to South Capitol Street. "Which hospital is closest to here?" He almost let the engine die as they slowed for a stop sign, but he was quick to jump on the clutch and save it.

David's brain was rolling too fast. He was less worried about getting himself to the hospital than about getting the boy away from Vinnie the Popper, before Vinnie had a second chance at them. "Capitol Hill, I guess. It's on Massachusetts and..."

"I *know* where it is." Snake inched out into traffic, looking carefully in each direction for the black Mercedes. He pulled into the stream of late-night commuters and started limping toward the Capitol. They made it two blocks before the car screamed forward from the impact of Vinnie ramming them from behind.

"Shit," Snake mumbled under his breath, looking around for a quick way out of the path of the Popper. There was none. David was sliding down in the seat, looking as if he was napping. He was probably unaware of the problems butting up behind them, and it was just as well.

Snake waited until the lanes coming in both directions were clear, a moment that came as they passed under the access ramps for the Southwest Freeway, which circled around and out of the city toward the open Virginia countryside. It was too late to try for those, to get out of town and lose Vinnie in the suburbs, unless he backed up and tried again.

As Snake passed under the ramps, he hit a light spot of ice and felt the tail of the car begin to spin. He jammed the brakes as hard as he could, throwing David up against the windshield, and driving the back end of the Urban Guerrilla into the front grille of the Mercedes. As they broke free, the Mercedes slammed sideways into a bridge support, throwing the Guerrilla free and popping the trunk on the Mercedes, making it bounce up and down like the jaws of a snapping turtle as the car stopped. Steam boiled up around the car from some broken hose inside.

The cars stopped only for a second before Snake pumped the gas and spun around in the opposite direction. As he came around, one front tire squashed the gold plated three-pointed star that bounced along the ice after being snapped off Vinnie's car.

"I know what you're going to do." David, who was now very much awake, pulled himself back up into the seat. "I have to advise against it."

Snake shifted down and flipped the wheel, trying to gain traction on the slippery road. The smell of something burning came back to them. In the rearview mirror, Snake saw Vinnie the Popper jump out of the sedan to examine the remains of his car. Even though he couldn't hear, Snake could guess the words coming out of the man's mouth, particularly "dead" and "whore."

The Guerrilla was still only inching down the ice as Vinnie jumped up and down in the middle of the street, slipping on the ice as he beat his fists against the broken Mercedes. "Don't do it," David said. "Don't floor it, because if you do..."

Snake pushed the gas pedal as far as it would go to the floor. As soon as he did, the car coughed and died.

"...you'll flood the engine." David began a careful study of his fingernails, realizing they would be the last things in this life he would see. That was it. No memories flashing before his eyes. No making peace with his Maker. No Mantovani music. Just that he had a hangnail on the index finger of his right hand. He coughed once, and the pain resumed.

Snake worked frantically to get the car started again. He jabbed hurriedly at the accelerator while twisting the key back and forth. Nothing.

"Remain calm," David said at last. Behind them, he could see Vinnie kicking the tire on the Mercedes, and then getting back in for one last charge. "There is a way to get it started if you remain calm."

Snake could not speak. His lips fluttered as he stared straight ahead, not believing what he had done. The sweat popped up again on the side of his face and he slapped it away, one hand at a time, as he worked the key. The remains of David's blood smeared across his cheeks from his fingers. He looked like a young fox hunter just back from his first kill.

"Stop." David clamped a hand over the boy's trembling fingers that were locked to the steering wheel. The boy was panting, and David could feel the heat of the panic radiating from Snake's skin.

"Now listen to what I tell you, because you don't have time to do it twice." David's voice got slow and calm as behind them, Vinnie the Popper was rushing the motor in the remains of Granville Hudson's car, about to kill them.

"Press your right foot all the way to the floor, and leave it there."

Snake did as he was told. Vinnie the Popper kicked four thousand pounds of German technology into overdrive. A blanket of white smoke boiled up from behind the car.

"Now." David placed his hand on Snake's knee and held on with a firm grip of command. "Take your foot off the gas."

As Snake's foot came up, they heard Vinnie's back tires find traction, and the sound of the screaming engine barreling toward them. David let up his grip on the boy's leg. "Crank the car, *calmly,* as you normally would."

Snake's eyes glanced to the rearview mirror to see the image of the broken black car looming larger. The motor turned the first time, and he didn't wait to be told to find a forward gear and get in it.

They were heading back out of town again. Snake would have to find a place to hide them in Anacostia, if it was possible to outrun Vinnie while dodging his bullets.

Halfway through the next block, the windshield cracked and pieces of it fell into their laps as a bullet hit the glass. David tried to pull his legs up so he could kick away the glass, or at least enough for Snake to see to drive. The movement caused a scream he could not hide.

"We're not going to make it." Snake was swerving across three lanes of traffic and one sidewalk, trying to avoid another direct hit.

"I know that, damn it!" David was buckled over in his seat, trying to speak calmly through the pain. "How good a swimmer are you?"

"Better than you are with that hole in your side. Why?" The boy glanced at him for a second before his attention returned to the street. Snake's face blanched white as they passed under another light.

"You've got one last chance to get out of here alive." David grabbed the boy's arm, trying to will Snake one final round of moxie. "I won't make it. I can't. Not in this shape, but you..."

"No." Snake pushed the car faster. "I won't leave you, David. You're all I've got."

"Look, kid. Don't give me that romantic bullshit, okay." David squeezed harder on Snake's arm. "Get out of here, and get back to Andy. He'll know what to do with you."

"No." The tears welled up in Snake's eyes and his voice cracked. "I won't. You have to come, too."

"You know what they say in the westerns, babe." David tried to sweep the damp hair out of Snake's face. "I'm hurt too bad. I'll just slow you down. It's me he wants, not you." With his weak smile fading, he looked behind them. Vinnie's car was catching up to them. One of its electric eyeballs had popped out and was dragging the ground, making sparks. "Get the hell out of here and find some other lonely, rich, good-looking chump to take care of you."

Vinnie crashed into the back of the Guerrilla again, breaking away his loose headlight and sending the Guerrilla into a tailspin. David watched through the broken windshield as the spare tire from the Mercedes broke loose, sailed over their heads, and fell out of sight over the bridge railings. The Mercedes slid into an embankment of ice and died. The impact was so strong that the Urban Guerrilla skittered from one side of the lane to the other, finally gliding to a stop in the center of the left lane.

"Now listen up." David clamped his left hand on the steering wheel and his right on the emergency brake, sliding across the seats again, pushing Snake out the door. "You get out of here and don't look back. You got me?"

Snake nodded, wiping the tears from his eyes as he blubbered to himself.

"Don't you worry about me. You've got a whole life ahead of you, kid."

Behind them, the Mercedes was making screaming noises as it dug itself out of the ice with such force that it spun around twice in the middle of the street.

"Quick," David said. "Before he sees you." He slammed the door shut, making Snake dive under a row of plastic barricades that separated the two lanes and kept cars from crashing into each other when the roads were slick. Snake huddled down as low as he could get, gluing himself in among the poles so as not to be seen or hit by oncoming traffic.

He peeked his head out and watched as David tried to get the Urban Guerrilla going again. All David could command was spinning tires and white smoke, as Vinnie's car leapt with a roar toward the crippled Honda. The loud sound of scraping metal came to Snake, a sound of parts rubbing together, but he dared not look behind, for fear that Vinnie would see him. Besides, his eyes were locked on the driver's window as David tried once more to make the little car go.

Their eyes met one last time for a silent good-bye across the cold expanse between them. David winked at him and tried to smile as the sound of an explosion rocked Snake back against the barricades.

Seconds later, the Urban Guerrilla smashed against the opposite wall of the bridge as the Mercedes slid by, missing Snake by inches. Instead of folding into itself, the front of the car tilted into the air, and with a shower of sparks, the entire car flipped up from the roadway, straight into the sky.

After the sound of the impact, there was no noise as the car arced out over the river and descended below Snake's line of sight. Vinnie's car slid to a stop as the Urban Guerrilla hit the Anacostia River water below. Vinnie the Popper ran to the railing as the water gurgled around the car, sucking it to its rest on the muddy river bottom.

The sounds of Vinnie's gun firing hit Snake as hard as the real bullets would have. One or two dug into the top of the sinking car as Vinnie unloaded the rest of his clip into the Urban Guerrilla and whatever was left inside her. Then, there was nothing but the sound of the river moving beneath him, of night traffic, and of far-off sirens rushing toward them. Vinnie threw the empty gun in the river, jumped in the black sedan, and sped away into the bowels of the city.

Snake lay there and cried a long time. He cried until his tears were dry and salty. He cried until he again felt nothing inside himself for anything or anyone. It was back to work for him; he would have to start over, as everything he owned except the $7,900 in his pocket was sinking its way, with David, to the bottom of the Anacostia River.

He lay there until the tears he cried were frozen to his face, and until he heard a gasp from below. It was a familiar voice. Once heard, it was hard to forget. He sat up with a start and shook his head, wondering if he had hallucinated the sound. Then he heard it again.

"Goddammit, boy, this water's cold as hell!"

Snake skittered across the roadway between traffic and leaned over the side to see David sputtering and splashing in the water, holding onto the loose spare tire with one arm as the other floated limp in the freezing river.

"David!" Snake jumped up and down, leaning over the railing as far as he could go. "Hold on. I'll get help!"

"Child, you had better hurry it up. I can't hold onto this thing all night." David's face brushed up against the tread of the tire as he tried for a firmer grasp. "I've got to pee real bad."

As he pulled his free hand up from the water to wipe the falling snow from his face, David stopped, rubbed his fingers across the tire's tread, and said, "And I think I'm going to need a tow truck."

He glanced up to the edge of the bridge to see a white-blond head bobbing down the street, waving down the on-coming wave of D.C. Police cars.

✝

Sunday, 1:00 a.m.

Trying to sleep in that hospital bed was impossible, even without the hole Vinnie the Popper had so graciously blown in his side. If David had leaned one inch farther forward as the bullet hit, it would have been a missing lung, or maybe it would have pierced his heart. At the moment, either alternative was almost comforting as he lay on his back, staring at the ceiling, listening to the incessant beeping of the monitors connected to his arms and chest. He had tried to read a book Andy had dropped off that afternoon, but the story was too slow and his mind kept wandering to images of his hanging there in the water, holding onto that tire, waiting for someone to fish him out of the river. David floated in and out of sleep for a few hours until he heard the sound of his door clicking shut.

"Hello?" he called out into the darkness of the room. The pain in his side held him in place as he inched his hand for his call button. In his sleep he had brushed it off the bed and it now dangled uselessly from his mattress, too far out of reach.

A flashlight came on and shone in his eyes, blinding him.

"Oh. It's you." David said. "I wondered how long it would take for you to show up."

A figure stepped forward, almost to the end of the bed. So close that David could smell the man's cologne, unmistakably sweet and heavy in the warm room. "I didn't want to keep you waiting," Granville Hudson said, giving David's feet a friendly pat. "I hope I didn't wake you."

"Don't worry about it," David said, signaling Granville to step closer. "Now why don't you tell me why you're here. As if I didn't already know."

"Because I'm going to kill you," Hudson said, clicking off the flashlight and standing alone in the light that came from the window.

"Not a good idea."

"It wasn't such a good idea that you killed my brother, either, Harriman."

David pushed himself up in the bed, groaning with the effort as he tried to make his eyes focus on Hudson's face, still shadowed in darkness. "You can think of a better line than that, Granville. You know Michael was alive and well the night I set him out at P Street Beach."

Hudson smiled and said nothing.

"At first you thought it was Parke, didn't you?" David had a sudden flash in his mind of what he had seen the night of Richard Parke's death. The thought did not comfort him as he tried to see whether any weapons were in Hudson's hands.

"No. Parke was too stupid to do anything like that. Even to my little shit brother."

"Now, Granville. Is that any way to speak of the dead?"

"Vinnie took care of Parke for us," Granville said. "Richard panicked. He thought the police were getting too close."

Hudson's fingernails clicked along the iron railing of the bed as he said, "It would have just been a matter of time before they sweated the story out of him."

"Must have made you a lot of money, though," David said.

"What? How would you know about...?"

"Easy," David said. "Parke had connections with people who could make things disappear. Remember his little case with the truck hijackers? He tried to pretend that never happened, but..."

"What do I care about him and his stupid clients?"

"And what do you care about losing a little merchandise from the store? We all know that Vinnie the Popper is one of the biggest shoplifters in town. Or I should say *was*. We are to assume his career gets cut short when he gets pulled in now for attempted murder."

Hudson chuckled. "That's assuming you live long enough to bring those charges. I've got too sweet a deal going here to have some counter jumper like you screw it up for me."

David's nostrils flared. "How much do you get? Ten ... fifteen cents on the dollar for everything Vinnie and his bunch steals?"

"That's just pen money," Hudson said. "Parke's boys could take the goods and sell them off in outlet malls down south for more than we could get from that fence of his in Jersey. Then..." He dug into his coat pocket and pulled out a small length of cord that rolled between his fingers. "...after we sold off the goods, I took the wholesale write-off on the D.C. store's taxes as a loss, *and* a full retail price reimbursement from the insurance claims." He pulled the rope taut between two pudgy fists as he laughed.

"Almost makes me wonder why you bothered to open the store at all." David's eyes lingered at the round fingers and the pink piggish tone of Granville Hudson's skin. This confrontation did not look to be helping Granville's blood pressure, and it certainly wasn't helping David's.

"So how is it that you came to kill Michael?" David asked. "He found out what was going on?"

Another voice came up behind them and startled both men: "Our brother was a conniving little con artist who would stop at nothing to get his way." Francis Xavier Hudson stepped forward, the glint of a gun barrel reflecting the light over David's head.

"What are *you* doing here?" Granville asked his brother as he fumbled to slip the rope down into one of his coat pockets.

"One might ask you as well, but I dare say the reason's the same." Francis shook the gun in the direction of David's face. "To get rid of *him.*"

David tried with no success to reach his hand over the side of the bed for the call bell as he said, "Now just a second, boys. It looks as if I'm the popular one in the room tonight and nobody is willing to tell me why."

"You know well enough," Francis Hudson said. "I think you already have this whole story pegged." He then turned the gun on Granville and said, "Don't you think so, *brother?*"

"Put that damned thing down!" Granville said, almost making a step toward his brother and then stepping back as Francis leveled the gun at his head. "You fire that thing in here and you'll have the whole world down on us. And that's the very reason Michael had to go in the first place. To keep him quiet."

David looked at Francis and said, "You think Parke told Michael about your association?"

"Of course he did. We know he was there that night ... at Parke's house."

"Quiet, you idiot!" Granville Hudson waved a hand across the bed at his brother. "There's no reason to tell him..."

"And there's no reason *not* to, either," Francis said, pointing the gun again at David's face. "The little twink has been so curious about what's going on all this time, there's no reason for him not to know now." He stepped closer, so that David could make out the lines of stress in Hudson's face as he came under the light. Francis leaned closer and said, "Now that he's going to die."

217

Francis Hudson's breath smelled of a very cheap bourbon. "He came to my house that night," Granville said, interrupting, pushing his brother away from David. "He said he knew about the scam and wanted a cut. We scuffled and Michael hit his head against a table."

"I got a call that morning, early from Granville," Francis continued. "He said Michael was hurt and I should get over there fast." Francis rested one hand on the bed and spoke as evenly as if he were speaking of something that had happened that day in the store. "When I got there, Michael was on the floor – he looked dead to me. There was some blood."

Granville broke in and silenced the cold analysis of Francis. "It was an accident. I hit him and he fell and hit his head against a table. Believe me, it was an accident." A slight shaking took up around his fingers as he spoke. "But it was too late."

"We couldn't let him be found in Washington," Francis said, leaning against the bed and crossing his ankles, tapping the resting gun against David's leg. "We had to get him back to the dorm. It was better that he was found at school, as far away from us and scandal as possible." He looked over to his brother, who was wiping away moisture from his face, and said, "We threw him in the trunk of the car."

"Only when we got up to the school, he didn't have the key to his room," Granville said. "And we had to hide the..." A trickle of sweat came down around one brow as he said, "...the corpse."

A sharp pain went through David's side as the two men continued their story. David grunted in discomfort but said nothing more.

"I didn't know what else to do with him," Granville said. "I couldn't leave him rolling around in the car all night..."

"So you hid him in the haunted room," David said, "where he would be out of harm's way, but you could be sure he would be found." He looked at the two men who were growing impatient with this game. "Eventually."

"I figured there may be evidence stuck to his clothes," Francis said, "so I burned them all at Granville's house, except for his underwear. After the police opened Michael's dorm room, I planted them in the bottom of his laundry basket. Eventually, you would identify them and make good our story that he returned to the school and was killed there, rather than in Washington."

"And the matchbook?" David asked.

Francis Hudson looked at him with cold contempt and said, "Somebody had to take the fall."

David slid up as far as he could go in the bed, feeling a sharp pain as something in his dressing broke loose. It probably didn't matter if he bled a little bit just then, as he would be bleeding a lot more in a few seconds.

"Only you forgot one thing," David said as Francis pulled back the firing pin and nudged the gun against David's heart. A fire of terror and stress broke across Granville Hudson's face. David's fingers twitched as he tried to think fast but could not. "You forgot to wrap the body before you stuffed it in the trunk," he said. "That was very sloppy, boys."

A wary look passed between the brothers and then they turned to David, faking nonchalance.

Before David could respond, there was a soft knock at the door and it quickly pushed open. Rod Daniels backed into the room carrying a bouquet of roses and a large box of chocolate doughnuts as he said, "I'm sorry. I know it's late, but getting through hospitals after visiting hours is one of the privileges of..." He stopped when he turned and saw the two Hudsons loitering over David's bed. Daniels's eyes went first to the silver pistol dangling in Francis Hudson's hand, and then to the length of rope his brother dropped to the floor with a soft plop.

"I believe that's the cavalry coming over the hill, boys," David said, waving Daniels into the room. "Come in, Rod. The Hudsons have been entertaining me with the most wonderful story this evening."

Rod Daniels took one tentative step into the room, dropping the flowers and doughnuts into a chair by the door.

"You can't prove a word of what we said." Francis Hudson grinned at David, swiftly putting the gun back in his coat pocket. "You don't have any evidence, and it's our word against yours."

"Not quite," David said, pointing at the table by his bed. "Take a look at the cover of the *Post* this morning."

Francis Hudson pulled the newspaper up and unrolled it to see the front-page story of David's rescue from the freezing waters of the Anacostia River. The photograph was of David reaching from the water with one arm toward rescuers on the shore as he held a firm grip onto Vinnie the Popper's spare tire with the other.

"Rod, darlin'." David peered over at the slack-jawed detective, who hadn't yet caught the full course of the conversation. "Do you still have that tire in evidence?"

"Yes, we do," Daniels said. "And the other four that match it. We caught Vinnie this morning, after he tried to ditch the car and burn it out."

A twinge of pain went over Granville Hudson's face as he thought of his car being left for dead in the nether reaches of the city. It was more concern than he had ever shown for the death of his young brother.

"Careful, Granville," David said. "I wouldn't want you to overtax your heart again."

Granville Hudson made an instinctive grasp for his mid-chest, his face blanched, and he said, "What do you mean by that?"

"How long's it been since the bypass? You think prison is going to be too stressful on the old ticker?"

Granville Hudson's lips moved but no words came out. "I figured it had to be you all along," David said. "Jail's going to be even worse on you when word gets around that you diddle little boys."

Francis Hudson rushed around the bed, grabbed his brother by the neck, and said, "You stupid son of a bitch, I told you to stay away from Parke and his street boys. Do business with him, but that's all. But *no,* you had to..." He was cut off by Rod Daniels dialing the phone and muttering softly to whoever was on the other end. Granville Hudson cried a single tear and fell backward to the empty bed, clasping his chest and saying, "Prison?"

"Thank God," David said, pulling the covers up to his chin. "Maybe now a body can get some rest."

✝

Seven Days Later

After a week in the hospital, David was ready to do anything that did not involve sitting in bed, watching soap operas on a television bolted to the ceiling, or smelling fresh-cut flowers. On his last Sunday before release, he decided to hold court and invited over his small family for a smuggled-in Sunday brunch on the sheets.

Snake was sprawled across the empty bed next to the window, loose pages of the Sunday *Post* scattered all around him. Andy Williamson sat on the edge of David's bed, his feet dangling to the floor, flaking croissant crumbs onto the blanket as he ate.

"So you were wrong," Rod Daniels said, stirring a cup of his faded beige coffee as he spoke. "It *was* possible for Michael Hudson to get it up again after he left you that night."

"Miracles *do,* on occasion, happen," David said, sipping heavily spiked orange juice through a bent paper straw. "It looks as if Michael already knew about the shoplifting scam that night, and when I set him out, he went to Richard Parke with what he knew." David picked the straw from his glass and dropped it in the trash, preferring to take long, warming gulps. "Parke cracked too easily and told Michael the whole story. Then Michael went on to confront his brother Granville, leaving the dorm key with Parke, so they could meet later and discuss the matter in more detail."

Snake looked up from the paper and said, "You don't think it could have been because Michael wanted to do it again with Parke in his dorm?"

"Don't be ridiculous, child." David waved away the idea with an imperious swipe of his hand. "We shouldn't push the realm of physics *too* far, dear."

"But some nights, I can..."

"Never mind." David cut him off. "Eat your breakfast like a good boy and keep your tiny braggartly comments to yourself." A wink and a small private gleam passed between the two.

Rod Daniels took another sip, studied the ceiling and said, "But the Hudson brothers didn't sweat as easily as Parke. You don't believe Granville's tale of Michael falling down and hitting his head, do you? Remember, Michael was suffocated."

"Does it really matter?" David said. "He's gone and nothing we can do now is going to change that." He switched his attention for a second to the window as he bit down hard on his lip.

Daniels brought him back. "The forensic evidence, certain fluid samples aside," he winced at David, "will implicate one of them for the strangulation. And the tire tread matches the bruise on Michael's shoulder, as well as the tracks you saw in front of Richard Parke's house that night." He refilled his cup from the thermos and said, "We've got Vinnie's testimony against them, too. Loyalty is not one of his strong suits, especially when looking down the barrel of a murder charge. Vinnie doesn't want to go to jail alone, and his testimony will be enough to send the Hudsons away."

"I want you to do me a favor, though." David looked at Daniels, who was happily stirring his coffee, slouched down into his overly hard chair. "Can you keep the part about..." David jerked his head toward Snake, "...out of the story?"

"Sorry, kid." Daniels pulled himself up. "It's evidence. He can identify Granville Hudson by the surgery scar and make the association between the two men." His face reddened as he said, "Besides. That's another felony charge." He repeated David's motion toward the boy. "By the way." Daniels squinted one eye as he asked, "How did you know about Granville Hudson's scar?"

"A hunch," David said, picking another croissant off the tray. A vision of the boy's money flashed through his mind again, but David pushed the thought aside as irrelevant. "I was on a road trip and saw something in a drop-a-quarter video booth and made a quick guess." Andy and Rod looked at him with puzzled stares. "And it looks as if I played it correctly. I saw them all together one night – Granville Hudson, Vinnie, and Richard Parke, sharing a booth." Andy shot David a look of extreme distaste as he bit the curly end off his croissant. "When I heard the description of the other man from Snake, I wondered later if it might be Hudson." He gazed directly into Daniels's eyes and said, "The man is just *that* dumb, to carry on with Parke in front of a little kid."

Rod Daniels scraped his chair closer to the bed, which caused the dozing Snake to jump, scattering pages of newspaper onto the floor. "So when did you finally have this whole thing figured out?" he asked David, reaching for the thermos for a refill.

"It didn't come to me until I was floating out there in the river, freezing my *cajones* off," David said. "While I was in the water with nothing to look at but that tire, it came to me where I'd seen it all before." He lifted his glass in a toast to the detective and said, *"That* is why I was so insistent that you keep the tire to match those on the car."

"But what next?" Daniels asked. "What did you plan to do with all that information once you'd figured it out?"

"That part I wasn't quite so sure about," David said. "And then the Hudson boys came calling and took care of it for me." After a few seconds, an idea came to David and he asked, "And speaking of which, what were *you* doing crawling around the dark and lonely hospital corridors at that hour of the morning, bringing sweets for the sweet?"

Daniels's face went bright red and a knowing glance passed between Andy and David. Soft snores from the other bed broke them up into uncontrollable laughter.

⚜

The last day in the hospital was interminably long, as David sat, dressed and ready, waiting for his doctor to come by and sign off on his chart, making David a free man. Rounds had started at 2:00, and now, hours later, he could hear the far-off rattle of dinner carts making their way down the halls as the sun started to sink beyond the view of David's window. Beside him, his chauffeur and escort – Andy and Snake – slept on the other bed, each dangling an arm and leg off opposite sides of the narrow mattress. David tried to entertain himself with back issues of *Boy's Life* that Andy had dug up from God knows where for the entertainment of Snake. In the hours he waited, David learned three new knots and had torn out a recipe for something called "McGoo Stew," a "perennial campfire favorite."

There was a soft knock at the door as it slid open and the white-topped head of an old man peeked in. David saw the priest's collar and silently signaled the monsignor into the room. Dressed in his black suit and bright purple shirt, the priest tiptoed over to a chair next to David and sat, pulling the long ends of his black cape around himself. "I saw yer name on the door," Odell said, "and I wanted to stop in and see how you were getting along." An impish glint came to his eyes as he said, "But it looks as if I'm too late."

"I'm out of here today, Father." David folded the magazines and put them with his suitcase on the floor. "As soon as the warden comes around with my pardon, that is."

"I read about you in the papers." The monsignor pulled at the buttons on his cape, releasing it across the chair and stretching his arms free. "Nasty bit of work, them people. Dumping you in the drink like that. Be glad it warn't the Potomac or you wouldna be in as good a shape today."

"I don't know about that." David reflexively touched his bandaged wound, thinking of how much worse it *would* have been, had he fallen into the heavily polluted river rather than its cleaner tributary. "It would have cut down on my electric bills, what with me being able to glow in the dark."

The monsignor covered a silent laugh with his hand and patted David's knee.

"So what finally happened that night, Father?" A quick flash ran through David's memory of the old man standing at the head of the stairs in that dormitory, ready to do battle and save the young priest. It almost didn't seem to be the same man who sat before him now, quiet and meek, and radiant with happiness.

"The boy's in pretty bad shape," he said. A scowl came across Odell's face for a second and was gone. "You really wouldna recognize him now." He shook his head and clucked his tongue. "Horrible it was. These terrible pox on his face." Odell shivered and pushed the thought away. "And his hair, what's left, went all white."

David could see the pain in the man's eyes as Odell's fingers curled into tight balls and then released.

"But the worst is over for him now. Physical therapy for him starting in a few days, and we hope to get him the use of his arms and legs again before the summer. Doctor says this one's traumatic stress, not neurological."

David felt a sharp pain run through his side at the thought. "I'm sorry," he said. "I'll come back to see him when I'm up and about."

"I can't guarantee he'll know you for a while yet," Odell said, and then changed expressions as he let the last torment of Alexander's condition pass from his face. "But it's all over now." He smiled. "The spirits of two wretched souls in that room can at last rest at peace, and the building is safe."

Odell passed again into memory as he said, "You know, beneath it all, Father Alexander is a good boy, and I'm proud I got to know him." A misty look came to the old priest's eyes that he quickly wiped away. "And how about you now? You're looking fit and ready."

"And busy," David said. "Somewhere between Hell and back, I seem to have picked up a son." He nodded to the sleeping pair on the other bed. "I'm not sure exactly what kind of mother I'm supposed to be."

He looked over to the boy and then back to the monsignor, who said, "You can't be no worse for trying than young Alexander for trying to be a good father." He chuckled softly and brought David away from his concerns.

Odell put his hands on David's and said, "Suffer the little children to come unto me, and forbid them not: for *theirs* is the kingdom of God."

"We're lucky, you and I," David said as Snake rolled over, sleepy eyes opening and blossoming into the same selfless smile the boy always had for David. Snake gave Andy a gentle elbow to shake him awake.

"Count your many blessings," the old priest said. "Count them one by one."

✞

Three Months Later

Washington, D.C., has exactly three days of spring, if the season is running long. This was the second day, and three men – Andy, David, and Tom Brown, the Walking Cliché – were stretched out on a quilt behind the fender of David's new car. The Urban Guerrilla had sunk to the bottom of the Anacostia River, never seen again. As soon as he was out of the hospital, David had signed up for the auction sheet with General Services Administration and bought a new car from a federal drug seizure.

David liked the large BMW sedan because it was white – all white, including the carpets and the steering wheel. Andy liked it because the windows were blacked out and there was a phone in the backseat. Snake liked it because the fifteen speakers inside the car would shake the walls of any federal office building downtown. The Walking Cliché liked the line of bullet holes evenly spaced across the hood.

They had parked in a lineup of conventional middle-class family sedans, as interpreted by the "suburbs" of northwest Washington. Nearby, lines of conventional middle-class families watched their young male progeny chase one another and a soccer ball up and down a field below the National Cathedral. There were Mercedes Benzes of every shade of corporate blue and conservative gray. There were three Rolls Royces, none less than twenty years old, and BMWs, but none like David's with white turbo wheel disks or a license plate frame that looked like a gold-plated cow chain. One Mercury station wagon was thrown in for good measure. David assumed that family was slumming it, or the Rover was in the shop and the Merc was a loaner.

"Jesus." Andy Williamson stretched himself across a good third of the quilt long since passed down from David's grandmother. It was a pattern called Wedding Ring. "So *this* is what life is all about." He reached into the ice cooler, brought out an Iron City Lite, and popped the top off another can of Vienna sausages. "Now which one of those scampering dots over there is our dear little child?"

"The blond one." David clunked another cube of ice into his plastic old-fashion glass. He leaned back against the camphor-smelling fabric, waiting for someone to hand him a peeled grape.

"I don't know if you noticed this or not..." Andy brushed cream horn crumbs out of his lap. "...but more than half the sweating gladiators on the field are blond."

"He's the one with the basket, then." Tom took the beer can away from Andy and began gurgling down the brew. "See. *That* one." He pointed in the direction of the soccer game. "The cute one who's working the ball with his head."

"Cute, indeed." Andy dug his hand into the cooler without looking. He pulled out a short can of Country Club, shrugged, and popped it open. "His looks he gets from me.

The charming personality..." He stroked his fingers around Tom's chest, pondering dessert.

"Now wait a minute." David's voice interrupted further under-the-quilt negotiations. "I know it may have escaped you two vultures' notice, but *I* am the child's mother."

The family sitting next to them, the ones digging caviar out of the back of a Silver Ghost, stopped chatting and looked at the party as if David had just started a session of open-heart surgery on the grass.

"*You?*" Andy sniffed at him as he dug his fingers into the Vienna Sausage can. "Rent. Food. Burberry's. His own VISA card at the most. Everything else..." He chewed on the sausage as he pointed proudly between himself and the Cliché.

"So." Andy wiped his fingers on a fresh paper napkin. "How are the other kids at school dealing with the fact that your son is a...?"

David jumped on the pause: "*Fairy* is the word you're grasping for, Elizabeth."

"Looks more like a hobgoblin to me." Tom crushed his empty beer can and dropped it into the trash.

"Well, let me tell you a secret." David leaned up and dug through the bowl of pickled pigs' feet to find one that was particularly meaty. "See the really big, ugly one down there. The one that's all nose and no neck."

Andy squinted toward the players, trying to make out the one David described. He cupped his hands around his eyes, as if surrounding invisible binoculars. "You *know* what they say about noses and feet."

"That's puppies, dearest." Tom stood up, removed his t-shirt, and wiped his well-chiseled underarms before he dunked the shirt through the open sunroof of the BMW. Tom had a body that came right out of a perfume ad, but lacked the stupidity to go with it: he had his master's from the Duke University forestry school and spent his days swinging around the treetops in the National Arboretum. David assumed this meant lots of grasping of tree trunks with his thighs, as they looked strong enough to bend steel, and were bowed enough to never touch each other again. A gasp rose up from the surrounding diners and caused at least one mother to drop her caviar. "Look at the legs on that kid!"

"If he uses the word 'gams,' I'll scream and scratch my eyes." David picked through the pig bones.

"So this no-neck leviathan isn't harassing the little dear, is he?" Andy, deciding that the sun was too bright, dug out his harlequin sunglasses and spread a copy of *Vogue Uomo* across his lap.

"Depends on your idea of harassment. I was up halfway to dawn last night, driving those two around. First it was dinner at Booeymongers in *George*town, God forbid ... all goo-goo eyes and giggling over fatty corned beef."

"Lord, save us." Andy crossed himself with a pimento cheese–stuffed celery stick. "*You* played chaperon to those two? Which one was G.I. Joe and which one was Ken?"

"And then it was some awful movie up in Tenleytown."

"Guts and chainsaws?" The Walking Cliché looked ready for a recommendation.

"Worse. Nuclear waste zombies."

"Oh yeah." Tom's look of recognition was a bit frightening. He hadn't seemed the type to go in for counts of how many body parts a character could lose in two hours and still walk. "I saw that one last week with..."

Andy handed him a deviled egg. "Thank you, dear, but no thank you. Just sit there and be decorative for a while." He turned to David. "For *this* I work and clean." The pat on Tom's knee belied the ribbing Andy was throwing at the Cliché. "So tell me about young Scott and the Nose out there. Are they a *number?*"

"Not a *real* number. Hardly more than an integer, I'd say. So far, it's not much more than five or six hours a night on the phone together, and the occasional popcorn and hand-holding over a human butcher shop double feature."

"Hmm." Andy leaned back, shielding his eyes with his hands to get a closer look at the object of the conversation.

"And no 'hmm,' either." David popped open a Schlitz can too roughly, making the head spew out across his hands. "No son of mine is going to turn into a little round-heeled tramp like his aunt Andy." He passed what was left of the beer to Tom.

"Now, David, darling, you *know* I didn't mean anything by giving that soccer coach a little pinch. I just wanted to make sure he was in adequate shape to be out there working with these helpless children."

"Excuse me, Miss." David focused his attentions to the sweating hulk sitting on the corner of the blanket, the only one paying any real attention to the game. "Could you tell me, is your husband *married?*"

Andy patted David's hand as he spoke. "Don't pick on him dear, I've only just got him to stop wearing his tree-climbing boots to bed." He then threw David a knowing glance. "So have you been introduced to the boyfriend's parents? Inviting you around for bridge, are they? Swapping Spam recipes?"

"Shhh." David drew their attention to a madras-clad gaggle of Aryans swilling champagne across the hood of a Saab convertible. "They think it's just teammate camaraderie."

The three of them made a soft "Ewe" noise, before breaking up into post-teenage giggling.

On the field, the action had stopped. Snake leaned down against his knees, catching his breath. Tom stood and waved at him, getting his attention. Snake stood, waved, and started jogging toward them. The sweat made his uniform stick to his body as he ran, showing all the picnickers the distinct physical resemblance between the boy and his "uncle," the Walking Cliché. He made it about ten yards before the Nose ran up behind, patted him on the butt, and directed him back toward the game. The Nose waved at David as they ran for the ball.

The opposing team scored a goal that brought up a cheer from the parents on the other side. They were playing against Bishop Carroll, one of the better Catholic schools in town.

David was about to speak when he saw a familiar face in the crowd, passing the bleachers. An old man — a priest with white hair – stopped and spoke to the coach, a thickly built, dark-skinned young man. Then, the old man turned to another man David hadn't noticed before – a younger man in a wheelchair, drawn up into himself, one hand pulled across his chest in an exaggerated claw. The old priest pushed the chair away from the stands and toward the shade of the trees.

David squinted his eyes against the sun and tried to get a better look as the priest toddled the chair down into the grass, facing away from the game. David strained to see, until Tom's words pulled him away.

"He did what he did to survive out there," Tom said. "Just like the rest of us. Every day."

David had forgotten what it was like to deal with the Walking Cliché on anything other than a physical basis. It had been years since that one time he and Tom fell into bed together. It was after David lost Raymond, and before Andy found Tom.

Beyond the ecstatic physicality of the man, the way he always had to touch, to cuddle, to go out in the woods and climb a tree, there was his forthright sense of getting directly to the point. He didn't edit what he said to match the likes and dislikes of the listener. As far as David knew, Andy never heard about that one night, so many years ago, even though David thought of it still, and smiled.

"That *is* what we all do," David Harriman said. "We survive."

Other books of interest from
ALYSON
PUBLICATIONS

GOLDENBOY, by Michael Nava, $9.00. When a young man is accused of committing murder to keep his gayness a secret, Henry Rios agrees to defend him. Will new murders, suicide, and a love affair keep Rios from proving his client's innocence?

THE LITTLE DEATH, by Michael Nava, $8.00. When a friend dies under suspicious circumstances, gay lawyer Henry Rios is determined to find out why.

COWBOY BLUES, by Stephen Lewis, $7.00. Detective Jake Lieberman is called upon to investigate the disappearance of a young gay cowboy, and discovers that the case is only one part of a much wider scheme.

THE CARAVAGGIO SHAWL, by Samuel M. Steward, $9.00. Gertrude Stein and Alice B. Toklas step out of the literary haut monde and into the Parisian underworld to track down a murderer and art thief. The two women, along with gay American writer Johnny McAndrews, rely on their wits to bring the murderer to justice.

MURDER IS MURDER IS MURDER, by Samuel M. Steward, $7.00. Gertrude Stein and Alice B. Toklas try to solve the mystery of the disappearance of their gardener's father.

FINALE, edited by Michael Nava, $9.00. Murder and the macabre are explored in these carefully crafted stories by some of today's most gifted mystery and suspense writers. Michael Nava, author of the Henry Rios mysteries, has selected well-known authors like Samuel M. Steward and Katherine Forrest as well as newfound talent.

BETTER ANGEL, by Richard Meeker, $7.00. Fifty years ago, *Better Angel* provided one of the few positive images available of gay life. Today, it remains a touching story of a young man's discovery of his sexuality in the years between the World Wars.

BI ANY OTHER NAME, edited by Loraine Hutchins and Lani Kaahumanu, $12.00. In this ground-breaking anthology, hear the voices of over seventy women and men from all walks of life describe their lives as bisexuals in prose, poetry, art, and essays.

BROTHER TO BROTHER, edited by Essex Hemphill, $9.00. Black activist and poet Essex Hemphill has carried on in the footsteps of the late Joseph Beam (editor of *In the Life*) with this new anthology of fiction, essays, and poetry by black gay men.

IN THE LIFE, edited by Joseph Beam, $9.00. In black slang, the expression "in the life" often means "gay." In this anthology, black gay men from many backgrounds describe their lives and their hopes through essays, short fiction, poetry, and artwork.

UNNATURAL QUOTATIONS, by Leigh Rutledge, $9.00. Do you wonder what Frank Zappa thinks of lesbians and gay men? How about Anne Rice? This collection of quotations by or about gay men and lesbians reveals the positive and negative thoughts of hundreds of celebrities and historical personalities.

THE GAY BOOK OF LISTS, by Leigh Rutledge, $9.00. A fascinating and informative collection of lists, ranging from history (6 gay popes) to politics (9 perfectly disgusting reactions to AIDS) to useless (9 Victorian "cures" for masturbation).

THE GAY FIRESIDE COMPANION, by Leigh Rutledge, $9.00. A rich compendium of unusual and interesting information by the master of gay trivia. Short articles cover a wide range of topics. A favorite gift item.

GAY MEN AND WOMEN WHO ENRICHED THE WORLD, by Thomas Cowan, $9.00. Gay history springs to life in these forty brief biographies, illustrated with the lively caricatures of Michael Willhoite. Cowan's subjects offered outstanding contributions in fields ranging from mathematics and military strategy to art, philosophy, and economics.

THE MEN WITH THE PINK TRIANGLE, by Heinz Heger, $8.00. Thousands of gay people suffered persecution at the hands of the Nazi regime. Of the few who survived the concentration camps, only one ever came forward to tell his story. This is his riveting account of those nightmarish years.

REFLECTIONS OF A ROCK LOBSTER, by Aaron Fricke, $7.00. Aaron Fricke made national news when he sued his school for the right to take a male date to the prom. Here is his story of growing up gay in America.

THE HUSTLER, by John Henry Mackay, $8.00. First published in German in 1926, this story of a young hustler provides a rare look at Berlin's sexual underworld in the 1920s.

QUATREFOIL, by James Barr, $9.00. First published in 1950, this novel presented two of the first nonstereotyped gay characters in American fiction.

THE ALYSON ALMANAC, by Alyson Publications, $9.00. Gay and lesbian history and biographies, scores of useful addresses and phone numbers, and much more are all gathered in this useful yet entertaining reference.

STEAM, by Jay B. Laws, $10.00. A vaporous presence is slowly invading San Francisco. One by one, selected gay men are seduced by it – then they disappear, leaving only a ghoulish reminder of their existence. Can anyone stop this shapeless terror?

MASTERS' COUNTERPOINTS, by Larry Townsend, $10.00. A handsome actor is kidnapped, tortured, and raped. As his therapist helps him investigate, they find adventure, S/M sex ... and a father-son partnership that's gone too far.

THE COLOR OF TREES, by Canaan Parker , $9.00. What is it like to be gay in a boys' boarding school? What's it like to be black, and from Harlem, when you're surrounded by privileged white boys? A story of young love that crosses racial and class boundaries, this hauntingly erotic first novel explores the limits of freedom and loyalty.

THE BUCCANEER, by M.S. Hunter, $10.00. In this well-researched historical novel, M.S. Hunter presents the exploits of Tommy the Cutlass and his shipload of randy homosexual pirates.

CHANGING PITCHES, by Steve Kluger, $8.00. Pitcher Scotty Mackay gets teamed up with Jason Cornell, a catcher he hates. By August, Scotty's fallen in love with Jason, and he's got a major-league problem on his hands.

THE ADVOCATE ADVISER, by Pat Califia, $9.00. Whether she's discussing the etiquette of a holy union ceremony or the ethics of zoophilia, Califia's advice is always useful, often unorthodox, and sometimes quite funny.

THE ALEXANDROS EXPEDITION, by Patricia Sitkin, $6.00. When an old schoolmate is taken hostage by fanatics in the Middle East, Evan Talbot sets off on a rescue mission. What he doesn't know at the time is that the trip will also lead to his own coming out and to the realization of who it is that he really loves.

B.B. AND THE DIVA, by Rupert Kinnard, $7.00. Meet the Brown Bomber – a fearless superhero with a bedsheet pinned to his shoulders – and his best friend, Diva Touché Flambé, as they take on Jesse Helms, the right wing, and badmindedness in general. Kinnard's work delivers incisive wit and a long-needed black gay sensibility to the world of comics.

THE CRYSTAL CAGE, by Sandy Bayer, $9.00. Stephanie Nowland used her psychic powers to put an escaped murderer behind bars in Bayer's first book, *The Crystal Curtain*. Now, she feels she must use those same powers against another lesbian.

THE CRYSTAL CURTAIN, by Sandy Bayer, $8.00. Stephanie Nowland has always used her psychic powers for constructive purposes. Now, a sadistic killer seeks revenge on her for putting him in prison. Visions of her death and her lover's death fill his thoughts. Stephanie can see them too.

EIGHT DAYS A WEEK, by Larry Duplechan, $7.00. Can a black gay pop singer whose day starts at 11 p.m. find happiness with a white banker who's in bed by ten? This love story is one of the funniest you'll ever read.

EMBRACING THE DARK, edited by Eric Garber, $9.00. Eleven chilling horror stories depict worlds of gay werewolves and lesbian vampires, and sexual fantasies that take on lives of their own. Contributors include Jeffrey N. McMahan, Jewelle Gomez, Jay B. Laws, Jess Wells ... and nineteenth-century gay rights pioneer Karl Heinrich Ulrichs.

I ONCE HAD A MASTER, by John Preston, $9.00. In this collection of erotic stories, John Preston outlines the development of an S/M hero.

ENTERTAINMENT FOR A MASTER, by John Preston, $9.00. John Preston continues the exploration of S/M sexuality that he began in *I Once Had a Master*. This time, the Master hosts an elegant and exclusive S/M party.

SOMEWHERE IN THE NIGHT, by Jeffrey N. McMahan, $8.00. The realms of nightmare and reality converge in eight tales of suspense and the supernatural. Jeffrey N. McMahan weaves eerie stories with just the right amount of horror, humor, and eroticism.

VAMPIRES ANONYMOUS, by Jeffrey McMahan, $9.00. Andrew, the wry vampire, was introduced in *Somewhere in the Night*, which won the author a Lambda Literary Award. Now Andrew is back, as he confronts an organization that has already lured many of his kin from their favorite recreation, and that is determined to deprive him of the nourishment he needs for survival.

CHINA HOUSE, by Vincent Lardo, $7.00. A gay gothic novel with all the suspense, intrigue, and romance you'd expect from this accomplished author.

THE TROUBLE WITH HARRY HAY, by Stuart Timmons, $13.00. Harry Hay has led a colorful and original American life: a childhood of pampered wealth, a Hollywood acting career, a stint in the Communist Party, and the founding of the Mattachine Society – forerunner of today's gay movement.

Alyson Wonderland
books for kids

THE DUKE WHO OUTLAWED JELLY BEANS AND OTHER STORIES, by Johnny Valentine; illustrations by Lynette Schmidt, cloth, $13.00. Five original fairy tales, colorfully illustrated, about the adventures of kids who happen to have gay or lesbian parents. Ages 5 to 10.

DADDY'S ROOMMATE, by Michael Willhoite, $9.00. In this first book for the children of gay men, a young boy, his father, and the father's lover take part in activities familiar to all kinds of families: cleaning the house, shopping, playing games, fighting, and making up. Ages 2 to 6.

FAMILIES, by Michael Willhoite, $3.00. Many kinds of families, representing a diversity of races, generations, and cultural backgrounds, as well as gay and lesbian parents, are depicted in this coloring book. Ages 2 to 6.

THE ENTERTAINER, by Michael Willhoite, $4.00. In a story told through pictures, the award-winning author of *Daddy's Roommate* tells about Alex, a talented boy who discovers what's really important in life. Ages 3 to 7.

BELINDA'S BOUQUET, by Lesléa Newman; illustrated by Michael Willhoite, $7.00. Upon hearing a cruel comment about her weight, young Belinda decides she wants to go on a diet. But then her friend Daniel's lesbian mom tells her, "Your body belongs to you," and that just as every flower has its own special kind of beauty, so does every person. Belinda quickly realizes she's fine just the way she is. Ages 4 to 8.

SUPPORT YOUR LOCAL BOOKSTORE

Most of the books described above are available at your nearest gay or feminist bookstore, and many of them will be available at other bookstores. If you can't get these books locally, order by mail using this form.

Enclosed is $_____ for the following books. (Add $1.00 postage when ordering just one book. If you order two or more, we'll pay the postage.)

1. _____

2. _____

3. _____

4. _____

name: _____

address: _____

city: _____ state: _____ zip: _____

ALYSON PUBLICATIONS
Dept. I-0, 40 Plympton St., Boston, MA 02118

After June 30, 1994, please write for current catalog.